I0582071

Also by James W. Fuerst

New World Postcolonial:
The Political Thought of Inca Garcilaso de la Vega

Huge: a novel

Praise for DISTRESS CRIES OF ANIMALS:

"Sitting firmly at the intersection of noir detective novel, dystopian speculative fiction, and covert political treatise, *Distress Cries of Animals* shows us exactly where we'll end up if our current racist and nativist style of socioeconomic division(s) continues. With its hints and nods to Anthony Burgess, Octavia Butler, Samuel R. Delany, Donna Haraway, Bret Easton Ellis, Karl Marx, and at least a half-dozen other famous authors and thinkers, *Animals* manages to not only be intellectually stimulating, but also emotionally wrenching and totally, socially urgent. Basically, this novel succeeds on multiple literary fronts, and *Animals* is a must-read book, full stop."

— Rone Shavers, author of *Silverfish*

"Fuerst combines the hard-boiled toughness of Dashiell Hammett, the verbal pyrotechnics of Anthony Burgess, and the dystopian vision of J.G. Ballard, but what truly elevates *Distress Cries of Animals* is its heart. As its title suggests, the novel calls us back to the living, breathing, flesh-and-blood reality fighting to survive beneath all the machinery of our age."

— Christopher R. Beha, author of *Index of Self-Destructive Acts*

"Similar to Irvine Welsh's use of dialect in *Trainspotting* and *Skagboys,* Fuerst pulls you into a dark, layered mystery unfolding in an unrecognizable future New York City with a language all its own. Good luck putting this one down."

— Greg Shemkovitz, author of *REWIND*

"The world is drowning: floodwaters and deadly social divisions threaten all life, and survival comes through modification. *Distress Cries of Animals* thrusts readers into a future where cyber-enhancements are a measure of human worth and pit the genetically modified elite against the unaltered masses scraping by in flood-wracked lo-town. Through a daring, neo-cyber-vernacular-charged-narrative reminiscent of *A Clockwork Orange* and *Trainspotting*, James W. Fuerst immerses us in the fractured dialects and underground economies of a society split by flesh and machine."

— William M. Brandon III, author of *Eternity: The ~~Long and~~ Short of It*, *SILENCE & Selene*, and *The Exile The Matriarch & The Flood*

"Resisting and illumining techno-stratifications, James W. Fuerst's *Distress Cries of Animals* is exemplary. With electric pacing and oft-sizzling wit, Fuerst has an enthralling attunement to the inner workings of cyborgs, humans, climate change, hybridity and our deadening cities. A high-stakes sort of work that demands several rereads—to savor, to analyze, to appreciate. This is easily one of the best dystopian novels I've read in recent memory. A must-read."

— Jennifer Maritza McCauley, author of *When Trying to Return Home*

DISTRESS CRIES of ANIMALS

JAMES W. FUERST

Denver, Colorado

Published in the United States by:
Spaceboy Books LLC
1627 Vine Street
Denver, CO 80206
www.readspaceboy.com

Cover features Creative Commons images by Leonhard Niederwimmer, Hans and Stefan Schweihofer via Pixabay

ISBN: 978-1-951393-44-1
First printed April 2025

To my Dystopian Fiction students,
past, present, future

"The only way to overcome misfortune is
to act it out."

— Elias Canetti, *The Agony of the Flies*

he new DriTech zip-up jumpsuit with stitched-in footie boots, retractable hoodie collar, and wifi holosleeves s'like total porn. Been binge-gearin it since it droned to the pod four days ago, but I can still barely foreals it. Black cling-fit synthfab, 100% wetproof and simulcrisp, but also breathies so you don't sweat till you corpse? Got copper nanofibers so it don't reek, and thick silicone flexipad footies with aluminiron soles. Springy, comf, total fuckin terminator. Don't access how DriTech 3D prints jumpies like these, only that it vids even more nextlevel on than it streams. Sposeta tho. Mod merch, shit costs. Don't necesito black spex—gray steam out, like ever—but gear em anyway cause I vid like a malhombre from the futuro with them and the DriTech on.

Eyes selfie reflection in mirror. Haven't catched feels like this in a while. Barely unpodded or done nothin for months, cept cryface at window, jack into meditation app, hale Numb, tryta unrememory. Week after week of blankvoid and sickhurt. Vida is pain, s'what ma useta chat. I was all like, nah, life's what you invent it. But now tho?

Fuck that shit. So over it. Gotta disrupt my day-2-day,

hack back into the game. Postin a toxic new look thanks to the DriTech, then three days later Jeffords messages like boom out of the blue. Gottabe suerte, the dope kind, and if I perv on it, it's allplus and ok.

Voz coordinates that Jeffords messaged into left holosleeve, and it maps to south wetside of what usetabe Spanish Harlem. Bout 80 blocks on hi-town rail to W116th then five blocks on footies thru lo-town to wetside, if I could use hi-town rail, which I can't, not yet, which is so fuck. Voz chats app for alt route: hail Skyff or board public gondola east on 34th Canal to E36th Street Marina, wetshare hoverferry north to E96th Street Pier, then flatbottom from there. Calc it'll take longer, but got no choice—wetside all the way.

Hoverferry docks at E96th Street. Cross pedway from pier toward 3rd Avenue Seawall and turn toward MCA station at its base. Droidista behind counter mouths it only got kayaks, rafts, and canoes, no flatbottoms with outboards or hoverskis. Could hail a Skyff, but by time it moors I be late anyway, so may as well just paddle. Shit calculates. Always somethin mal with the wetway anymore. Lo-town Mgmt Corp been auditin the budget for like always, so there aint no budget left. Whole thing goin fuckin fecal.

Swipe holosleeve to accept charge for kayak rental, voz message Jeffords, then set out, rowin back east to deeper wet. Depth chart screens 12 to 15 feet in all directions, so hittin shallows less a worry than like crocs or manatees and shit. GPS pulses boat thru maze of flooded buildings to E116th and Park, mas-menos. Ground slopes up hi nuff there that shoreline and dry land are scannable immediately to north and west, along with ruins of oldfuck elevated roadway. New sections of seawall bein erected dryside of that, just beyond the high-tide mark, where dredgers, cranes, and dump trucks chill fuckin idle on a Sunday. Viddies like an active site, but some of the erected wall sections check like they been there 50 or 60 years. Not like this neib gonnabe drained or walled anytime soon, tho. Only scroungers here now—no fuckin point.

Paddle ashore, flip kayak, stow oar. Gottabe 85, 86 degrees, 75 humid, not too mal for February, forealness, but after all that rowin I be corpsweatin for true if not for wickin action of the DT 503. Shit's total porn.

Eyes cam Jeffords standin in ankle-deep wet in front of a row of abandoned buildings, or a modified humanoid who viddies like Jeffords, only taller, crossfitted and gearin a DriTech like mine. Hehim finishes postin somethin to stream, viddies up, cams me.

"Lázaro? Sup," Jeffords chats, legs taking me toward him. "Been a while, hume," hehis voz quiets. "Pause. You modify?" Hehim hits pause again till I reach him. "Oh, hell no you did *not*. You vid like fecals. Your DriTech's total porn, tho, trufacts, almost had me deepfaked. But up close tho? Yuck fuck, natural. Your skin is straight-up puke-tone. You malaised? Vids like you corpsed it or some shit."

"Did," voz chats back. Me and him bump fists then elbows.

"Oh, that's right. Didn't rememory." Jeffords throws his head back and lols stupid loud. "That must've fuckin sucked!"

Lips, mouth, lungs pull 2, 3 quick hales of Soothe. "Yeah, did. Nuff bout me, tho, what's on with you? That a Celebalike upgrade?"

"Yella, version 8.7, trendingest. LuxeLocks blond hair,

Brite Bite dentals, lungpurge, heightening, and MelanInk Dermistain, nut fuckin brown. What you deem?"

"Toxic. You vid like a surf pro. What else in the package?"

"Bodsleek, cognihancement 1.0, junkstension, and all the TV I can rightsnatch." His mouth grins a wideass grin, his hyper-aug smile so brighties my eyes almost pain.

"TV?"

"Modchat for teen vadge. Celebalike 8.7 is calibrated to pull 15s and 16s. First update since they lowered the age."

"And?"

"And? Teenies hard-on stream-stars, Laz, and I viddy like one. They just toss that shit at you. All you gotta do is catch," his voz chats, cuppin both hands in front of his crotch, pumpin hips back and forth.

"Sonics deve, Jeffords." Doesn't, tho. Sonics like a tossed modification, just don't vibe like vozin so.

"Deviant as fuck, bro," hehim chats, grinnin mas, "but not Jeffords no more. Brand's Molone Swag now, Mo Swag for short. You don't just modify, Laz, you renomer, too."

"Trufact. My mal. Not calcin."

"Unstress, ugface. C'mon, let's go in. Got somethin to post you."

Legs follow Jeffords, uh, Mo Swag into building toward the back, splashin thru bout a foot of wet. Place all empty, high-ceilings, echo-y. No luz. Vids like nadie been there for ages—concrete mal eroded and crumblin, steel beams exposed and rusted, crusted with barnacles and algae and shit—and it's nervous quiet, cept for rain that just started a minute ago and lappin of mini waves. All the way back there's a doorway with no door that leads onto what vids like an analog loadin dock or cargo bay. Usour legs step outside. Mo Swag stops, throws a pose, smilin hurty white dentals with tongue out for a microdrone bout size of a fly flittin around his cranial, videoin and postin to stream.

"Horny little sluts," his voz chats, mouth still smilin, "a couple posts, couple DMs, and you all up in."

Jeffords fadin already. Useta sameheight, but hehim's six or seven inches taller now, and from this angle his new Celebralike grill's all guapo and symmetrical but malass generic. Blank screen. Tabula rasa. Anythin you wanna be. Soon Jeffords won't even be a rememory inside his own neurals, just Mo Swag thru and thru.

Eyes viddy past him up to graybright sky and scan a lone pelican wheelin then divin straight down into curls of wet. Splash and gone. Prolly after prey.

"Here," Mo Swag chats, his footie hackin a thud against something metal, "this the thing. Scope."

Eyes vid a couple more seconds, pannin waves, hopin to scan solo hunter resurface again. Nada. Legs step over to Mo Swag, left hand pockets spex, eyes scan down to midsize metal fridge-crate beside him. Top's open, and it's full of little arms: righties and lefties, maybe twenty, twenty-five of em? The little arms got little hands with little fingers and little thumbs, tiny fingernails and knuckles, little elbows and wrists and shit, and kiddy biceps and triceps that stop three-quarters of the way up, just under where like shoulders should be? Epidermals the blue-gray of modified default—like a face lit up by smartphone in the dark—and they vid like they fit on 6- or 7- or 8-year-olds, but can't voz if they's mod, natural, or bot.

Stomach twists, heart pounds, legs step away.

"You allplus, Laz?"

Rib cage shrinks small, like so small I can't air, soft cries echo in ears. Throat and lungs tighten, pull hard to hale. Hold. Exhale slow. Still too small. Hale again, deeper, hold. Chest, ribs loosen, exhale. Calmer now, turn back to Mo Swag, cranial noddin. "Sí-sí, mod, allplus."

"Why's your chat all glitched?"

"PTS—"

"Oh, yella, right, you just vozed." Mo Swag shrugs, goes quiet, starts again. "Anyway. What soma you halin?"

"Soothe," voz chats, right hand holdin up vaporizer. "Useta mezcla Numb and Soothe with Litez Out at night, but down with just Soothe now."

"Not me. Up all the time, get me?" Hume points at his junk, mouth flashin teeth again.

Head nods as legs walk back over to crate of tiny arms. Left hand picks one up for eyes to cam but almost drops it right back—it's cold from the fridge, dense and rubbery to the feels, mal wigglin and sick. There's a coupling insert at the top of each bicep to attach to a shoulder joint, I calc, but beyond that lil arms vid and tact like they could be grownflesh over natural muscles, tendons, and bones, or simskin over aluminiron rods and cords, or some new biotech, of like whatevie. No way of accessin what they's invented from, but eyes don't cam no barcodes or serial digits nowhere, and that feels mal feels.

"So?" Mo Swag chats.

"Um, yella, give me foul retch. What are they?"

"No intel."

"Ok, where they from?"

"No intel. They were just there."

"You calc they floated in at high tide, or maybe like somehume dropped em off?"

His shoulders shrug.

"Scan for trackers?"

"Yella."

"And?"

"None."

"They boosted?"

Shrug again.

"Shit, hume, sonics like you mined straight up zero intel. So, what the fuck's on?"

"Negative meme. That's why I messaged you."

"*Me*? What fuck for?"

"I was doin my rounds early this mornin and I found the crate right there." Hehim points at it for like no reason. "When I opened it and cammed what was in it, I was like that is so-as-fuck and messaged my CO all haste. I chatted him what was on, and he chatted me to have someone viddy into it, but keep it mute."

"Viddy into what? You don't access what they are or where they from. That memes you can't access if there's wrong play or a practical joke or no bigs or like whatevies. Could be nada."

"Yella, could be nada, but we can't take a chance."

"Why not?"

Mo Swag spreads his arms like for me to viddy around. "Seawallin, hume. Drainin wet and erectin wall is giga biz, and my CO hard-ons the biz and the coinage just the way they is. Hehim will not hard-on this bucketful of baby arms streamin and viralin before intelin what's on."

"That's more than a bucketful."

"It's a metaphor, hume, engage your neurals."

"Ok. But like why message me, tho? Why not police?"

"Lo-town police?" Hehim barks a lol. "Fuckin

clownbots, hume. Give you a ticket or bust you in the skull, taze the shit out your ass, lock you up, take a bribe, that's all they do. Besides, only for naturals. Mods don't deal with those fuckstains. Plus, if police get in it, newstrolls could get in it, then fakefacts and mal pub could get in it. And if that shit gets in it, then contract disrupt could get in it, and then *coinage* disrupt could get in it, which my CO, again, will mos def not hard-on. You check me? So I messaged you."

"Yeah, totals, spose. But got no database on this, Mo, and wouldn't intel what to do bout it, if I did."

"C'mon, Laz. I'm not queryin you to troll suspects or invent arrests, just for you to viddy into it. Surveil around, cam what you can cache. Your brand was stupid clout-trending just a few months ago. Humanoids all over the city —mods, nats, cyborgs—socmed who you are and—"

Eyes hard at him. Hehim hits pause.

"My mal, Laz. *Nat-u-rals*. Shouldn't be vozin 'nat' now that I'm mod—"

"But you already done it twice tho?" Back arches, fists curl, legs step to.

"Chillado, Laz, unstress. Didn't meme nothin by it. Just habit."

"Kinda fucked up habit to still have, like what, five months after modifyin?"

"Five months? That's it? Shit." Mo Swag's eyes viddy down, away. "Seems dickass longer. Whatever." Hehim shrugs. "Didn't mean nothin by it, Laz, like I chatted. Be careful, tho. Keep steppin now and I'll blow your cranial up blam, one punch."

Legs stop, fists uncurl. Trufacts, no denialin.

"Chillado?"

Lips slacken, cranial nods yeah.

"Vid, Laz, lots of humanoids socmed you and you socmed lots of humanoids, is my upshot. Easy for you to query round."

"All pre-now, hume," voz chats, "webmute for a while, everythin's otro. You're ghost. I'm ghost. Nada. Like forealness nada. Besides, nobody rememories a few days ago, let alone months, like you just chatted, so not sure I can do shit for you."

"Can't help? Uh-huh. How you get that DriTech then? That's a DT 503, right...like mine? If you ain't mod, which you ain't, it's buku coinage and malhard to get."

"A toss," voz fakechats.

"A toss? Assfuck it is. That's the newest upgrade, hume, most trendingest. No mod gonna toss that shit."

"Defective," voz fakechats again, but Mo Swag shakes cranial in noncreed. "Ok, ok, still kinda got a connect. But it's not cierto and prolly not for much longer, if like at all."

"Mod connect, right? That's what I deemed, Laz. You prolly got others, too, and you prolly cached an encryption or two in all those years that you can leverage. Chat me you didn't."

"Maybe. But it been a while—"

"You vozed that already. Still not giggin?"

"Nah, not since—"

"How long?"

"Three months, mas-menos."

"Three months? How you maintainin?"

"CoinBeg funds at first, but stacks since."

"You're clickin everything from stacks?" Mo Swag tries to whistle, but can't so only spits some, then shakes cranial. "So you piled up hella buku over the years, huh, bro?"

"Did ok."

"Well, that's the other reason I messaged you. If you're still not giggin, you could prolly use the coin—"

"Thanks, but—"

Mo Swag raises index finger to disrupt, presses other to ear, and mouths into holosleeve. "Yella, on it now, got him right here," hehim chats, steppin away, inside building.

Eyes viddy back to crate. Mini arms like that gottabe bot, but then why no serial numbers?

Steppin back toward me, Mo Swag chats, "Still on the clock, hume, during which time my CO likes to camp out all the way up my ass. Damn, Laz, gotta mine more coinage, ditch this fuckin gig."

"Why you giggin anyway? It's hi-life. Up and away. Hit pause. You didn't go up on credit, did you?"

Mo Swag's lips cover teeth for once, chiseled chin droppin to chest. "Yella, hadta get out, Laz, couldn't hack lo-life no more. Life is total pain down here, hume, like every bit of it. So I upped on credit and now I'm indentured out the ass and balls until my investor recoups. Why else you calc I'm out here on a fuckin Sunday when I should be smashin TV?"

"Who's your angel?"

"Does it matter? All that matters is I owe em. Wish I had a gig like the one I'm offerin you, one that woulda solved everything, but your lo-town ass ain't even curious how much coinage my uppers are willin to front?"

Face frowns. Gig aint right, basic math. But can't help wantin the data anyway. "Ok, how much?"

Mo Swag levels his blue-green eyes, viddin me all serio. "Enough to coinclick one of the new protocols," he whispers. "Enough that you can finally modify, Laz."

"Mierda."

"Hi-life, just brainstream it, Laz, up and away."

"Stop gamin, mod, I'm ghost," voz chats, body turnin to out.

"No, hume, hit pause. Trufacts, like I vozed. There's giga coinage in seawallin, and my CO or my CO's CO or or like the board or whatever can source it easies. Problem zero. So they deemed me authority. It worths them to gig someone who's trusty but not mod, cause—"

"Cause nobody's gonna give like negative shits if a nat pings round queryin, right?"

"Your words, not mine. But, yella, that's the meme. So what you calc?"

Enough coin for a new protocol, enough to modify...? Feel sickass tempt feels and want it all coño, but sonics too plusgood to be trufacts. Besides, biddy arms creep me so fuck. Nothin bout em's right. Prolly only trouble.

"C'mon, Laz, just chat you'll video into it, surveil around, scan what you can cache, and I'll upfront you half the coinage right now, just to onboard. For old times, hume, get you back on your feet. You aggregate mineable data, I'll click you the rest of the coinage, if not, you keep the upfronted. Mega win for you either way. So?"

Have feels like snatchin chance with both hands but also like turnin and boltin from it sickass fast. But can't do both tho. Voz chats, "How much upfront?"

"15 million."

"*Ones?*"

Mo Swag's face lols. "Course ones. What other coinage there be?"

"15 million ones," voz rechats, "fuckin fakefacts, mod, stop shittin."

Mo Swag's face lols again, shakin cranial. "After modification reboot, they chatted me I'd start to scan othernesses in naturals, even ones I networked and coevalled with a long time, like you. They said cause of cognihancement. I loled it off, didn't creed em, but, damn, Laz, you like one kilobyte per second on the download. I chatted you there's giga coinage in seawallin, my uppers want a natural trusty to vid into the mini-arms but keep it mute, and they sourcin enough coin for one of the new modification protocols. Nahin, 15 million won't get you all the way there, but the whole click, 30 mill, is more than enough. Now what about that don't you code?"

"Unstress, modified. Code all of it, just don't total."

"Don't total?" Mo Swag's voice groans, like not forealin. He nears up to me. "Open N-Net homepage on your holosleeve."

"Ok."

"Scroll down to your wallet."

"There."

"Damn, hume, you right, you coindeep like an executive," hehim chats, eyes viddyin amount over shoulder. "But you bout to be coindeep like a *chief* executive. Ready? Open synch."

Voz synch open.

"Stream this." His finger taps his holosleeve, 15 million ones click into wallet. "You scan that? That's yours if you want, but you got ten seconds to voice yella, or it's all void and I footie the anal out of here. ok? 10...9..."

15 million ones.

"7...6...5, c'mon, Laz, time running out..."

15 million. New protocol.

"3...2..."

Hi-Life, Up and Away.

"Ok, yeah, I'm down."

"Toxic. That's my na...uh, my hume. Ok," Mo Swag starts to chat, but hits pause when his holosleeve vibrates. Hehim steps away, grins nother big hurty grin as he replies, vozin quiet. When he returns, he chats, "Vid, Laz, I got a couple more rounds today, and you prolly wanna get to it. We allplus here?"

Ears barely sonic, can't focus. Have feels like bein in an aug-real or virt-real that won't poweroff, so you can't voz what's aug or virt or foreal or whatfuck. But neurals rememory. "Mo Swag, hit pause. What you gonnado with the, um, the bucketful...the fridge-crate?"

Hehim turns back round, stream-star face frownin a tanned guapo frown. "Fuckin fecal, Laz, you were one of the most AI naturals I ever networked, all this database and processin power, but you really like dial-up speed, ain't you? We can't have those thingies anywhere near here or any record of one of us viddyin into them until we know what's on. That's the total point, that's why you have 15 million ones now that you didn't have before. *You* deal with the shit."

"You at least got some place to storage em?"

"No, I don't. And that wouldn't be safies either."

Catch nervous feels again. Don't want biddy arms anywhere near me neither.

"Maybe this aint gonna gig," Mo Swag interrupts my calcs. "How bout I just take the ones back, delete the whole thing off."

"No, mod, everythin's unstressed," voz chats too quick. "I'll drone em someplace safe. Just want to digiscan em before lockin the crate."

"Yella, right," Mo Swag chats. His hand reaches down, pulls out an arm, holds it up. My finger taps right holoscreen for 3D panosphere. It digiscans from every direction, highest res hologram from all angles. When it's done, Mo Swag tosses the arm back in, tights the lid. "You access how to work one of these?"

Cranial shakes nah.

He frowns, then codes something into scanner's number pad. Red beam lasers out. "Put your hand there." Hand in, beep sounds, needle pricks on my palm. "Now no one can open it but you." Mo Swag nods. "You're all onboarded and logged in now, Laz. If you cache anything, or if you need somethin, anything at all, message me— word, face, glyph—anytime, day or night. I'll drone it to you. Code that, ok? But all of this, everything else, is totally mute, just between us, yella?"

Head nods.

"Havoc. I'll be in touch. Suerte, hume." Mo Swag turns and splashes back into the building, out of sight. Once he's vacuated, eyes viddy down to wallet again. 15 million more ones than I had earlier today, all of em still there. Like a sleepstream come true.

2

overferry back down to 23rd Street Pier then leg it to Clocktower, a gamer, socmed, and swipe-right bar on 22nd floor of a pre-now hotel dryside on what usetabe Madison Square Park. Three stories below SkyDeck 1, too spendy for most naturals, so usually a mezcla crowd of coindeep nats and slummin mods but still mas-menos chillado for 121 or groupmeet.

Legs footie in, whole body throbs from subsonic pulses of silent trance-noir track. Eyes scan U-shaped bar straight ahead, packed with dazefaced nats. Eyes buggin wide, mouths hangin open, tongues lollin out, viddyin thru opti-neural lenses at some mierda in virt or aug-real, or simulgrammin in cyber-hooks. A couple 3D multiplayer murderfests holostream bove bar to the right, repost of IMA Slaughter Royale from last week holospherin in center, handful of gangbang jizzblasts triplexxxin it on left. Basic lamecore holocasts from defectives who nontolerate opti-neurals or nats too strapped to click em, so they just cast all their likes and follows in public, wherever they at, no filters, no fucks or shits given whatsoevies.

Take hi-top close to bar with view of entrance and

signal droidista for rum. Swipe holosleeve to accept charge, open a tab. Servbot drones drink, just as delivery-drone dispatcher pings left holosleeve that fridge-crate's arrived at pod. Voz initiates security app, right hand powerons spycams, unlocks and swipes door open. Eyes remote-cam drones drop fridge-crate, one-eighty, vacuate. Swipe door shut, tap it locked, set infrared trips ON, close app. Swallow rum, quietly processin biddy arms and fifteen million ones.

"Yo, Laz, that you?" sonic Felonious's voz, and scan her lanky frame leggin toward me. Sheher's gearin silver kini briefs and matchin crop top, her dark skin and afro puffs all uncosed, none of the feline transdermals or cat gear Felonious Jones usually rocks in the Octagon or round town. With her is a lighter skinned theythem, bout same height, but thicker tho, more swolled up, pink and white bunny beanie, buku tetas, tight waist, gearin a translucent nightie over a lavender biketard and white, knee-hi boots. "Almost didn't ID you in that new DriTech—503? Total porn," Felonious chats. "C'mon, now, tho, get your ass over here," sheher goes on, pullin me in for a long hug and lippin my cheek. "Riz, this is my boy, Lázaro Mata. Laz, this Riz FX, my sparrin partner...well, usetabe."

Slap hands with Riz.

"Usetabe?" voz queries Felonious.

"Yeah, hit pause on my career for like a minute."

"When?"

"Couple months ago."

"Yo, nat, I rememory you," Riz chats, "you're @Lazmatazz, right? You was like iconic. I cammed that stream tho...so fuck, bruh."

"Yeah, and then I don't hear shit from you for months," Felonious cuts in. "No streamcasts, no posts, no messages. Nada. Just ghost, or like you elevated and didn't even update me."

"Never, Fel, te amo too mucho for that." Them and me all sit. Right hand signals droidista for three more rums.

"Uh-huh, same old mierda. Forealness, tho, you go webmute? I couldn't socmed you like nowhere at all."

Cranial nods.

"You gotta click all them fines, then?" Riz queries.

Nod again.

"Nat, that is some wasteful, dumbass bullshit for someone who sposeta be so AI. You coulda just gave that coin to me?"

"What for? New gear? New dermals? Can't rememory the last time I cammed you uncosed."

Felonious lols. "Oh, wait. Is that the old Lázaro tryna make a comeback? Too cute, chico. But no tho, asshat. Don't need new gear or new dermals. I'm mad glow like this. Denial it."

Can't, so don't. Drinks land. Them and me all take one. Felonious raises hers.

"Anyway, welcome back from the dead, Laz. Missed you."

"Missed you too, Fel." Clink glasses, drink.

"So? What's on? What's your vibe, nat?" She reaches across, long, thin fingers wrappin my wrist.

Shoulders shrug. "Just been podded, sittin still, dazefacin out window, tryna renormal and shit. Not much else."

Her cranial nods. "Hey, you gotta do you, Laz. Whatevie it takes. What you been thru—"

Thunderous explosions drown sheher out. Screams of mayhem and corpse agony blast from a murderfest while a jizzcast erupts in a frenzy of groans and cries and splatters of white. Normcore as fuck for bein out, but too much input tho. Too much loud. Body shakin all over. Hale Soothe to chillar. But rememory that everythin in the bar's wified, onlined, clouded, mega hackable, and if I wanna chat to Felonious in mute, prolly shouldn't do it here, or in front of Riz.

"Riz, mind if me and Felonious get a few outside?"

"Nahin, it's chill. I'm here."

No security cams or microdrones at outdoor roof bar and plenty empty tables and stools, but rainin again, for like seventh or eighth time already today. Like ever. But DriTech got a hoodie tho, so I gear it, and since we only three stories under SkyDeck 1, wet is diff here anyway. Not as mal. Lot of it blocked by the crosshatched aluminiron slats SkyDeck 1 invented of, and more still blocked by mods out on it, 40, 45 feet above. Eyes scan up and viddy underfooties of mods leggin above, goin bout their modbiz, livin modlives, and feel feels of bein closer than ever before. Heart fasts, fingers tingle, like a semiote or some shit. Vibin like that finally gonnabe me.

"So?" Felonious queries. Me and her seat at table with an umbrella, keep her from gettin wet.

Voz chats recap: mod giggin for seawallin corp coinclicked me 2buku ones to viddy into a fridge-crate of biddy arms, cache what I can scrape, but don't voz nada bout who's Mo Swag or where crate's from cause it's all mute. Messaged Felonious for a 121 cause I need a trusty to process with, and she the oldest and trustiest I got left.

Felonious calculates, downin rum. "Don't perv it, Laz."

"Why not?"

"Can't trust no mod."

"Trufact," voz chats, "but networked them before—"

"So what? Three months, five, six...they rebrand, they renomer, they *fade*, nat. You intel that shit. Prolly totally otro now."

Cranial nods, calcin she could be right.

"What's the brand of the seawallin corp your mod giggin for?"

Cheeks hot. "Uh...um," voz glitches.

"Hit pause. You didn't query?"

"Biddy arms creeped me, didn't meme—"

"And your mod didn't voz?" Felonious side-eyes me as she rums. "That's reason number dos not to trust that modfuck."

"What's number uno?"

"He's a modfuck, nat. Damn, tryta keep up. Ok," she chats slow, "first order of biz is to query the brand of the corp your mod gigs for, access who you dealin with. You got a cryptaccount? Better to stealthsearch, if you can."

"Nah, but mod said they drone me whatevie, so—"

"Smooth," she chats, tappin her forecranial with a finger, "beta test that mofu, check they response. If they come thru, you in biz, if not...." She lets that hang. "Next"—rums last of her rum before unpausin—"you said you digiscanned one of them arms, right?"

"Símona."

"Let's scope it."

Eyes scan round to make sure no one surveillin, then bend forward and down to cast digiscan under tabletop.

Felonious leans over on her side a few seconds then uprights again. Right hand double taps digiscan off.

"Damn, Laz, if I didn't already intel all the sickfuck shit you been thru, I'd chat you the luckiest humanoid I ever networked. Like ever. 15 million ones to troll data bout prosthetic arms for kids? You cache any data your mod can crunch and you get 15 million more? If not, you just coinstack the 15 you got? No queries? No strings? Bruh. That is too much suerte, I cannot even...," Felonious's voz trails off, shakin cranial.

"What if they not prosthetics?" voz chats.

"Gottabe. They don't have no barcodes or serial numbers, like you chatted. But even if they aint tho, you don't owe that mofu nada. Just query prosthetic inventors, MedTMs, wellness huts, whatevie, for a couple of days, a week—"

"What bout Victor?"

Fel's shoulders shrug. "What bout him?"

"Should chat to him."

"Yeah, whatevie. But you access Vic, so."

Head nods. Vic's a cohort from way pre-now but a free agent too tho more than anythin else. Always all bout the biz.

"Then you also wanna make sure you're easy to cam goin in and out of places, all serio makin queries for a few days, a week, like foreal giggin, in case you got a tail. Then message the mod you tried but couldn't cache any data. Boo hoo. Drone the fridge-crate back or drill holes in it and deep six that shit offshore, and footie your lolin ass out of it with the 15 mill you already got."

Lean shoulder blades back against seat, eyes viddyin up again to footies strollin above. "Yeah, could do that—"

"Buttfuck yeah you can—"

"Aint enough, tho, Fel."

"What aint enough?"

"15 million."

"15 million aint enough?" She lols. "Your neurals crashed? 15 million aint enough for what?"

"New protocol, nextgen. They like 25 to 30 mill."

"Nuh-uh, no way, nat. Not again. You outta your mental?"

Eyes cam down to plasticine rum glass and tabletop beneath it.

"Ok, sorry, Laz, whatevies," she chats, voz softenin. "It's like you lost all of your shit if you wanna go thru that again, but 15 is still half, maybe more. Another three, four years giggin malsick fuerte like you do, and you coinstack the rest. What's fucked with that?"

Stomach knots. Mouth, throat, lungs hale Soothe. Still feel tense feels. Hale again. Pause. "Can't gig no more," voz chats, all shakes. "Neurals mal glitched since the thing."

Felonious leans back too, long index fingers pressed to lips, like not forealin. "Bullshit."

"Trufacts. Tried a couple of gigs, total easies, but couldn't hack em tho."

"Like what?"

"Took one gig deletin hatechats from a mod Facegram stream but got too sangry to finish. Had nother to sit thru a breakup but was cryfacin so heartsick from jump, hadta jack out at 'we need to chat.' Nother was for a mod tweenie to square up a cyber bully—"

"Hit pause. You couldn't hack a child dissin another child? C'mon, Laz, be serio. You're a *legend* in the pain biz."

"Maybe before, but not no mas. Can't hack it, Fel.

Couldn't hack any easies, even with neural blockers and hale. Everthin's too buku now, like somethin inside opened up, won't close back. This thing with biddy arms could be last shot. If so, gonna need all those ones."

"Shit, Laz, I had no meme, sorry." She pauses, like neurals firin, then starts again. "But you don't *need* those ones, and you don't *need* a new protocol neither, cause you don't *need* to modify." Corners of her eyes tighten. "That's just the bullshit spoof calculus them modfucks want us to creed, make us calc they better than us, so we spend all our time chasin after what they already got, keepin us down, keepin us in place, when we should be doin our own thing."

First Felonious goin uncosed, now hatin on modification—totals like ding. "What's on, Fel? You sever and reset while I been webmute?"

Sheher back stiffens; taut arms fold over chest. "What if I did? You got a problem?" Nother round drones to table.

"Jesus, Fel, that shit's a corpse cult, they all brainwashed as fuck."

She picks up rum, drinks. "No, they aint. That's just more fakefacts and hatechat they keep feedin us so we don't access what the fuck's really goin on. We all got choices, nat, and we all can choose somethin else. So, yeah, I went Alt and started reset. It's a process, tho, takes time. You should—"

"How can you even be chattin with me here if you did? Don't you like haveta donate all your tech and coin and shit when you join?"

"Aint fully severed yet."

"Why not?"

"Cause I still got some biz here."

"Like what?"

"Recruitin."

"Riz?"

"Been chattin to them, yeah."

"That your shit?"

"We bump some." Fel's shoulders shrug.

"Who else?"

"How bout you?"

Hale Soothe and pause, shakin cranial. "You load I can't."

"Sansve's dead ass gone, Laz," Felonious vozes all kindness, holdin my wrist again. "You did everthin you could for her, for both of you, but she's gone. It's been months since you heard from her, right? She prolly totally otra by now. You might not even facerec her if you cammed her."

Pull hand back from Fel and hale, not vozin nada. Grab rum instead.

"Don't be like that," she chats. "Not only is she outtie, but you don't have enough coin for a nextgen protocol and you can't gig no more neither. You just copped to that shit, so you gotta let her go." She tosses back rest of rum. "So here's the plan. Game this mofu for a week, ten days, cache zero data, stack the 15 mill, and go Alt with me, with us. Scope it out a few days. This the lifehack you need, hume, you vibe that shit, I scan it on your face. So do what you gotta do and then do what you *oughta* do. You check me?" Felonious stands, leans over the table, lips my cheek again. "You vid like shit, btw," her voz whispers in right ear, "but it's pluslove to cam you, Laz. I'll be in touch."

essage Mo Swag for clonepad and cryptaccount while leggin north on Broadway, hoodie up, spex on, rockin it mod. Not dark yet, too early for patrols, but vid round all cautious anyway, in case. Only cam nats on streets and sidewalks, tho. Some in long motionless grub-pantry or plasma bank lines, some leggin it but then pausin all sudden to mug selfies on smarties or microdrones, others frozen still, screenzonin in middle of street like single-shooter or driver-game targets, or others sittin by buildings, backs against walls, spankin it in jerksacks, or leanin forward with cranials in hands, tearfacin, sobbin out loud like they just jacked outta the most malest gig ever.

Shit's so fuck. Cooped up more than three months and not one bit of newness nowhere? Doomloops and doomtimes still in full effect. Gotta evolve or corpse. Some nats obvi aint streamed that meme yet?

Turn left a block before 34th Canal and head west. Pass two kinkbots on corner slingin—*anything you want, baby, 2 for 1 Sunday special*—onto smaller street. Less wetway traffic, slower pace, less noisy, less sadfucks sprawled out cryassin facedown on sidewalks. Necesito mas chillado vibe. Gitmoed in the pod so long, city fasts more, louds more than usual, and nerves already mal edgy and twitched. Mouth, throat, lungs hale Soothe, leggin blocks home—gonna take time to renormal. Eyes viddy for MedTM or self-care kiosk on way, but can't rememory last time one was round here, so just lower cranial and footie on.

Sunsettin at Yards: sky morphin from light slate to dark graphite, wind whippin up, temp nosedivin. Podfree nats moorin floatents for overnight, lashin em together like a flotilla gainst tides and comin storm. Hunched older humes clot round trash-can fires, roastin fish or crabs or rats, black silhouettes passin rum, huddlin close to warm. Temp-drop, wind, heavy rushin skies—gonnabe rough tonite outdoors. Catch sudden vibe of grimfeels in chest, but don't access what from. Prolly just the storm.

Lean forward for retina scan in security bank at front entrance, voz scan, enter building, elevator up to 24th floor, legs footie down hall to pod. Secure-drone from Mo Swag already hoverin by pod door: matte-black spider with helicopter-blade antennae. Retina and voz scan door open; drone follows. Inside, secure-drone scans voz, retina, releases clonepad. Voz messages Mo Swag *got it, thx* on left holosleeve, as right hand opens door, lettin drone out.

Voz lights on. Sound system chats: "Genomix NextGen modification protocols for your hottest, wellest, bestest you —Genomix NextGen: Live the Hi-Life, Up and Away!"

Paciencia powerons in soft orange glow. "Hello, Lázaro, welcome home."

"Hey, Paz."

"It is my duty to inform you that it has been 104 days since you last logged onto your MyFace all-access account and posted—"

"Yeah, yeah."

"—by having agreed to the Terms and Conditions of Service, you will owe 20,000 ones in subscription suspension fees by the end of this month."

"Yeah, Paz, code it. Unstress."

"I am an iHOST X, Intelligent Home Operating SysTem, version ten. I am incapable of stress. But I am programmed to remind you of your social media subscription obligations and the financial and legal penalties for nonfulfillment."

"Got it, now chillar. Any updates?"

"Yes. You are also behind on your plasma bank deposit and storage fees. Would you like to purchase a waiver for 1000 ones again this month?"

"Yeah. Click it."

"Please state system-unlock password."

Voz chats password.

"Autocoin payment complete."

"Anythin else?"

"There was a delivery to the office earlier today—a refrigerated crate. I accessed the droneserver's manifest, and it stated that the crate contains assorted fish from a lo-town market. Would you like me to prepare fish for dinner?"

"Forget that for now, Paz." Fakechatted droneserver earlier that fishes from lo-town were in fridge-crate, not biddy arms. If some hume or bot tried to hack, only mineable data would be trufact of delivery, not contents.

"But why?"

"Not hungry. And the fish, fridge-crate, delivery...wipe it, ok?"

"Memory delete function is a charge of 1000 ones—"

"Click it."

"Please state system-unlock password."

Voz chats password.

"Autocoin payment complete."

"Prepare for retina scan to access memory files." Pin of red luz crosses vision. "Scan complete. Deleting items from memory access...deletion complete."

"Gracias, Paz. Got some stuff to do now. Hit sleep mode until voz messages you." Till I access what's on, better to query everthin offline, in the unnet, or thru stealthsearch, leavin as few keywords, cookies, and tracks as possible. Not just with droneservers, but Paz, too.

"You have been unwell, Lázaro. Your sleep patterns have been erratic, your hygiene and wellness routines non-existent. Your diet, alcohol, masturbation, and soma consumption patterns—"

"Aw, never accessed you cared so much, Paz—"

"Your attempt at humor has been detected. Lol. What a sick burn. But I must continue to monitor your condition until you resume regular self-care and online activities."

"Sleep mode, Paz, or you gonna get poweroffed. And no data sweeps during sleep mode, neither."

"There is no need to threaten my client stars rating, Lázaro. I will awaken when you call me." Paz quiets, orange glow dims.

Sound system chats: "DriTech, inventor of nextlevel gear solutions for both modified humanoids and others, now featuring the new DriTech 503 series. DriTech 503, total porn."

Thru kitchen to sit area and up aluminiron ladder. Unlock ceiling hatch, push it up and back, climb into office. Dark and stuffy, all stale air and clouds of dust. Voz lights on and eyes viddy round—sofa for clients, coffee table, club chair, floor lamps, desk, camera—same as three and a half months ago. Sensories diff, tho. But that calculates tho. Only emptiness now, all sadfeels and loss.

Eyes cam fridge-crate by desk. Leg over, scan hand, open lid. Biddy arms still there, same as before, only now they vid like they froze mid-motion, like tryna claw free from somethin, all terrorized and shit. Eyelids slam shut. Rememories flood neurals anyway. All of em still alive, but unclear cause they like barely movin, supine bodies shadowed silver and black in harsh angled light. Skin prickles, catch feels like setup is all fuckin wrong. Tryta jack out, but can't, can't move or budge. Too late. Trapped, no escape. Whatevie he's gonnado, I'm gonnado too.

Throat knots, lungs seize. Need Soothe but hands mal fumbly. Can't air nuffta hale anyway. Sit in chair, lean back, tryta tranquilo. Breathe. All over now, been over for months. Couldn't do nothin then, can't do nothin now, panicattackin don't help shit. But the screams tho, the cries. Like it's happenin again, never stopped, never will. They still bound there. I'm still standin over em, feelin feels like cold weight of metal in my hands....

Fist in the gut, again, again, again. So hard, gonna puke. Gotta get up, move around, snap out of it. Stand, footie to window. Floor to ceiling glass, west-facin view. Tide swellin cross 11th Ave toward base of building. Flooded ruins of Hoboken gainst flat charcoal sky. Red LED towers dottin Jersey shoreline. Small hailstones tickin on glass. Tributaries of light from way far off flash and fade to dark.

When Hi-town Mgmt Corp deemed it too unstable to erect a SkyDeck this far westside due to rising wet, humes just up and bumped the fuck out the building. Superintendent useta rock this pod, figure hehim wanted to be first on SkyDeck each morning once he modified, first to carpe hi-life every diem and shit. But even he vacuated with all the others tho when they accessed that shit wasn't gonna happen. No one here, hacked door lock and squatted a week or so—sledge-hammerin thru floor for access to my pod directly below, installin a hatch and a ladder—and then me and Sansve had a duplex of our own to share, even tho most nats don't even have one or two rooms they can pod in for more than a week at a time. But we were killin it then tho, and havin an office on the 25th floor, technically in hi-town but not SkyDecked tho, was backdoor carnage for attractin clients for biz.

Bout two years after that, Sansve got the low-grade fever, shakes, and rattle in her chest. Heart racin, temp hot, mentals mad glitchin. Not much diff from baseline dread of day-to-day in lo-town, foreals, cause everyhume be streszietied out as fuck and liketa lose they shit all the time, but sheher kept worsin and worsin and then she was like all sweatin and cryin and couldn't breathe, always shakin, always anxious, always freakin out, losin weight and like all her mentals all the time, and she was def gonna corpse pronto. Hadta modify. Only chance.

Suerte me and her been coinstackin to go together and had nuff. Researched and curated her protocol, sent her on...but haven't heard nothin since. Not a ping. Not even if she's ok. Maybe Fel's right—Sansve's gone, mostly gone or all gone, faded, otra...gotta let her go. No word for ages, total silence, just the DriTech 503 via drone, with no sender name, no address, tho. Might be her, might not. Could be an old client feelin sorry feels over what went down. No data, tho, and too much hurt up here to stay. Close lid, scan hand to lock crate, poweroff lights, climb back down.

Grab Kelp-N-Krill fuel bar from cabinet and bottle of fermented tea, both monthly click-as-you-nom subscriptions, so swipe holosleeve to accept charge for each. Sit at table with clonepad. First, run security scan; clonepad scans clean. Next, get online thru pirated meshwork, then maybe two minutes of search to trace Mo Swag's seawallin corp: Aquāsure Endeavors, one of city's nextlevel seawallers, hundreds of billions in contracts over past two, three years alone. 2buku ones to disrupt, no wonder Mo Swag's CO wants everythin mute. Not much more newsads beyond that other than recent biz deals, proposed sites, timetables, completed projects. Aquāsure a mod-based corporation, tho, so can't trace ownership or board from N-Net—may haveta query Mo Swag to online M-Net, too.

Nom rest of fuel bar, gulp tea, grab rum. Then stealthquery prosthetic arms, missin arms, stolen arms, lost arms, found arms, small arms, tiny arms, pediatric, replacement, surgical, transplant, experimental, R&D, and other probable keywords back thru past few months. Nada. Lavender Alerts bout missin kids popup sidescreen, newsads sponsored by KidTrace chip and locator app. Lotsa alerts last couple months, like ever, but none chattin if any kids reappeared, were found, came back, or what. Never are. Maybe KidTrace don't work. Most services don't. Everthin's mal scammy in lo-town. No secret. Nats pay, extractors stack. Then they upcharge for mas fecal service and upstack some more.

Hundreds of thousands of views and shares of alerts, tho, and related newsad popups for Kinder Guardin, portable child-safety cubbies, sponsored by Uniwall, country's largest inventor of enhanced interrogation lounges and chain-link border spas for migrante families and kids, but nothin bout prosthetics or transplants.

If anythin on with the biddy arms, vids like no intel yet. Could be too soon, could be nothin's on. Gotta mine more data. Map-plot itinerary of MedTMs, wellness huts, self-care kiosks, and prosthetic inventors to visit tomorrow and sync map to holosleeve.

Nother rum then query latest modification protocols and specs. Genegineerin and biotech always upward evolvin —innovations, upgrades, new suites like every week. Advances in nanotech and quantum computin, breakthrus in silicone polymers, gene therapies, DNA resequencin, enhancements in stem-cell cultivation, vat-grown organs, hormone regimens, immunological optimization techniques, neurogenesis and modulation—procedures and outcomes keep gettin better and better and better. Meanin humes modified by new procedures keep gettin better and better, too. Newsads sponsored by Genomix post data that hi-life's safer, healthier, happier, longer, unstressed, and way less malstupidhard and soulcorpsin than lo-life, which is mostly gig chained, painfeels, and doomtimes. Modifieds been genegineered from jump to nextlevel naturals in like every possible way, and they do.

Scroll thru nextgen protocols, nowest and most spendiest, eyes scannin screen for hypo-allergenics. Nextgens have basic modification suite—lungpurge, immunoboost, cognihancement, rejuvenication, total body cosmetification with genitailoring—plus add-on of extreme ability patch. Extreme ability of hypo-allergenics is immunosuppression optimization pre-, during, and postprocedure so that defectives, i.e., "compromised naturals," tolerate modification. Eyes cam Nextgen Hypo-Allergenic 9.3 reported only 2 rejects in 3 billion simulations, less than one ten-millionth of one percent reject rate, lowest ever. Cost: 28 million. Math: 15 million Mo Swag synched to wallet today plus 6 million already coinstacked equals 21 million, equals 7 million short. No choice but to mine some data on biddy arms and get the full click, no matter what Felonious chats. And sooner that's did, sooner I try again.

isted and mapped 4 wellness huts, 5 MedTMs, and 2 prosthetic inventors to query today, spread thruout lo-town, dryside and wet: from Times Square to Washington Heights, back southeast to Lexington@E59th, down to Grand Central Cay, Union Square, SoHo, Wall St./Little Venice, etc. Most were closed —ground floors sealed wet and air tight with 8mm sheets of white industrial poly-wrap—even tho websites posted em open. Only got into 4 places, each with droidista at counter, each response limited to pre-programmed script with no AI for off-topic queries, each 100 coins justa footie in. Math: 400 ones clicked, zero data mined.

One place left, last on purpose. Hoverferry from Wall St./Little Venice Pier to Alphabet City Bay, disembark at Tompkins Square Dock. Victor E's Custom Droids, Drones & Bots on E5th between Aves B and C, closest to B and deadend of E5th. Last brick-and-mortar tech shop in city. Six-story stand-alone wetside of block-long jetty of rubble— somethin nomered a 'school' that collapsed ages ago.

Low tide now. Otherwise Ave C bout 8, 9 feet under wet and would haveta footie west to come in from E4th. No importa. Up aluminiron steps over white poly-wrapped first and second floors to entrance on third. In thru shop door, hit wall of AC, relief of cool, then feel cold feels mad fast. Tap on DriTech's thermal coils. Allplusgood. Total porn. Round showroom droid skeletals, limbs, and holographic onesies hang from hooks. Faceplates, cranial CPUs, jack nodes, simstim implants, dermas, wetware gear, and fuckbot parts laid out in display cases. VR helmets and visors, smart masks, face shields, drones and remote control apps on shelves, and industrial Dream Weaver 3D loom on fourth floor to 3D print custom orders. Victor E's— *all your droid, drone, and bot needs or we'll invent it for you...guaranteed!* Like ever.

Beaded curtains ripple behind counter, Victor steps thru. Tall, poco hunched, mohawk of metal nodes runnin length of cranial front to back. Silver-lensed spex, full goatee, faded green coveralls, and gray polymer-composite hands and forearms. AI-integrated for full dexterous autonomy, only ones like em anywhere round. Victor Kahn originals.

"Annyeong, sup. What you need?" his voz chats, obvi not viddin close or facerecin. Pull back hoodie, lose spex— his lips curl up, teeth appear. "Motherfucker," his voz scoffs. "How long it been?"

"Most of a year?" voz chats. "How you been, Vic?" Bump elbows over counter, quick hug.

"You load how it is, hume. Always hustlin. Keepin my shit so tight together. That the new DriTech?" He lols, viddin me over. "Total porn."

Victor's so loco tatted his skin been nothin but ink long as I can rememory. Face, eyelids, inside of lips, todo. Now he's rockin new motile tints that fractal nongeometric shapes in complex colors, slowly morphin from one to next. Like all his dermis expandin and contractin at once.

"Yo, Victor, hit pause on the motiles. They givin me retch."

"Ha," he lols, twistin node on cranium till ink stops. "You always been squeamish, Laz. Calc nothin's changed."

"Prolly not."

"So, chingu, díme, what's on?"

Mad cringe. Few years ago, one of Victor's porn node implants malwared. It viralled out and infected one of his language-processor nodes with his kink and fetish prefs. He been South Faux-rean ever since. Mal as fuck sometimes, but shit can't be done without serious cranial redo.

"Almost a year and not a ping," he continues. "Not even after that so fucked gig. So what's on, nat? What you need?"

"Always biz with you, Vic. What bout chit chat, small talk, catchin up?"

"Small talk? Ok. The weather bites eumgyeong, just like biz round here. No footie traffic wetside anymore, everthin's all clicks and droneservers now. S'fucked up. What else? City keeps floodin, mods keep gettin richer, nats keep gettin poorer, and down in lo-town we're all still corpsin the fuck out. Doomtimes be nigh, nat. How's that for small talk?"

"Maybe that's why nobody comes round no more, Vic. Your attitude's fuckin fecal."

Victor's mouth smiles. "Thirsty? I'm thirsty. Let's rum." Prosthetic hands disappear into counter before him, reemerge with rum bottle and two glasses, fillin each to rim without viddyin. He passes glass, takes other, dips left index finger into his rum, flicks droplets over shoulder, toward smilin statue of chillaxed chubby Buddha. "Ancestors, hume," he chats.

Anglo-German from Canarsie but claimin Buddha as fam? Whatevie. Hit pause on voz, tho, and do same to rum with right index finger. Then me and him drink.

"So?" Victor queries, puttin glass on counter.

"Got somethin to post you. Could use your help." Tap left holosleeve, cast digiscan of biddy arm. Victor lowers spex, green-blue eyes cammin mad studious. Few seconds, he pulls spex back up and nods chin.

"Is it just that one, or is there more?"

"More, I calc, but no data."

"Hmm." Matte-black graphene fingertips comb thru goatee. "You got this thing, Laz?"

"Nahin," voz fakechats.

"Allplus."

"Why?"

"Cause somebody's gonnabe sick trollin for that."

"Foreal?"

"Ass yeah, hume. The fabrication on that fucker is michin nextlevel. Maybe best I ever scoped, and that's chattin somethin. Let's vid again." Cast digiscan again. "You cam?" his voz highs, like all excited, right hand fingers spreadin wide, enlargin image. "Ligatures of the dermis, underlyin musculature, skeletal chassis all uncamable, Laz, seamless. Vids zactly like a natural humanoid limb all the way up to the coupling link. Laser grafted on a droid, bot, even humanoid peeps, it'd be mad rubix to ID as tech. Top shelf shit like that costs, hume, and even if it's just a prototype, somebody gonna want they fuckin little arm back."

"You pose it's a prototype?"

"You cam any serial numbers, UPCs, QRs?"

Shake head nah.

"Me neither. So, it's a prototype, or it's part of a larger whole. Basic math. Or...." Victor pauses, like tabulatin behind his spex, hands pourin more rum.

"Or what?"

"Or it's fuckin trouble."

"Trouble how?" Pull out vaper, mouth, throat, lungs hale Soothe. He pushes rum at me.

"If it aint a prototype or part of a larger, unassembled whole, then it gottabe a stand-alone limb for a droid or a bot."

"Yeah. So?"

"If it's a stand-alone limb for a droid or a bot, just by viddin, what kind of droid or bot you pose it's gonnabe?"

Stomach tights cold, despite thermal coils. Hale Soothe. Exhale. "Pedobot."

Victor's cranial nods. "Buttfuck yeah, nat. Pedobot."

"But what bout a dwarf-sized bot?"

"Stop gamin, Laz. Vid again. That shit is prepubes."

Viddy again, but don't need to.

"If it's a limb for a pedobot, tho," Victor chats on, "then it sposeta have serial numbers, UPCs, QRs cause—"

"Carnsat."

"Ee-rect. As the statute deems: pedobots either intended for or capable of the carnal satisfaction of humanoids, whether natural or modified, must be registered and licensed thru the Department of Erotic and Venereal Security. This includes all the original components of carnsat pedobots, as well as any and all replacement parts, which could like meme the unregistered child-sized arm in the holograph you just posted me."

Rum more rum, hale Soothe. "So you calc it's contraband?"

"No intel." Victor rums rum. "But if it is, that's another data point why someone gonnabe trollin for it. Not only are they out buku coin and R&D, but that shit shouldn't even exist, like legally chattin and shit."

"So...?"

"So, it's munje, Laz. Trouble, like I vozed. Humes who fuck with that kind of contraband are not malhombres you want to 121 or groupmeet...or have surveillin you."

Put vaper back in pocket and calc. "No chance it could just be a prosthetic for like a kid needin a transplant—"

Victor lols again, almost spittin out rum. "Transplant? For who, nat? Modifieds don't need transplants after initial protocols cause they reset all prior defects. And they're a total coinflush for naturals, who gig and coinstack in order to modify. You intel this, Laz. There aint no care kiosk or wellness hut nowhere in the city that'll do transplants on a natural, whether kid or grown. That's why nats who want alt-body prosthetics and implants fuck with specialists like me." Victor's hands lift to face level, fingers wavin.

"You pose you could transplant one of these onto a kid...or a bot?"

"No intel. I'm the shit and all. Foreal. But I'd haveta cam one up close, inspect it, study it. Could be I don't have the tech to do it, memin I'd haveta invent instruments first. But then...well, can't cam why not." Victor's hands put rum bottle and glasses back into cabinet. "Why? What's your angle?"

"No angle. Just queryin round, tryna mine data for a friend of a friend. That sorta thing."

"Course, course." His eyes vid away, like noncreedin. "Well, even tho you just queryin, you carryin protection, right?"

"Allplus. Can 3D print a piece in the pod, if needed."

"What bout ammo?"

"Mismo."

"Aniyo, Laz, not silicone ammo, live, explosive aluminiron rounds. I can source it."

Brrap-rap-ap-ap-ap-ap. Automatic gunfire pops in ears, hands tremble, palms pour sweat tyrin to bring vaper to lips. "N-n-no. No live ammo, Vic. Nunca. Never."

"Sorry, hume, slipped my mental. My mal. How bout this, then?" He bends forward for somethin from cabinet in front of him and hands me what vids like a pen.

"What is it?"

"New Voltaze, hot off the printers. 15 microcoulombs per pulse, drop a Silverback bam in its tracks."

"What's that?"

"Extinct ape. Fuckers were huge though."

Cranial nods. "How's this work?"

"Press the red button." Finger clicks red button on side of pen; three prongs clack out at tip, sharp like a mini-trident. "Vid the other button, the green one?" Cranial nods yeah. "Chillado, don't press it."

"Why not?"

"The green button shoots an ionized nanofleck into your target, which attracts the 15 microcoulombs of charge."

"Ok. And?"

"And it's pointed at me, nat. Don't want my ass tazed off, so."

Lips smile, as right hand closes prongs and stuffs Voltaze in pocket. "Sorry, Vic. Thanks, tho."

One of Victor's hands waves me off. "Consider it amends."

"Fuck for?"

"I curated the interface to simulcast both your clients' simstims and your reactions in splitscreens to stream in real time. That's why your stream was so nextlevel, but it's like I'm kinda responsible—"

"Nah, mierda, Vic. Only he was. No one else."

"Gamsa, foreal. Been on my neurals." Vic's hands press together in namaste in front of his chest, head bows, then lifts again. "Lemme query you, tho. Why didn't you upload your rememories and sell em? Crazy coin, there, Laz. Humes are fucked up. They'll stream anythin."

"Calced on it some. But upload doesn't disaggregate bundled rememories. It just clips between timestamps, wipin it from your neurals in the cut."

"I access how it works, Laz. Me and you could do it here—"

"It'd wipe rememories of Sansve, Vic. So, no puedo."

"Prolly sadfuck rememories you be better off without. You tabulate that?"

Don't voz nada.

Victor shrugs, chats on. "Whatevie, up to you. But before you vacuate, cache this. You come across an arm like the one you posted, I'll stow that shit in the vault downstairs, if you want. Totally secure, no worries. Might even be able to take it off your hands and flip it. Maybe be able to flip more, if you got em. Buku coin to stack off tech like that."

"Thanks, Vic. Don't have any, tho."

"Yeah, yeah, course. If that changes, tho, rememory the offer. Giga win for both of us."

ail Skyff from Tompkins Square Dock, boatshare hydrofoil back to pod. Start south past wetways of Wall St, round tip of Little Venice canals, cammin stilted Downtown Islet Towers on Chambers and Franklin, then veer starboard up Hudson River. Sundownin, breeze icin, flurries and low fog blowin in, blurrin view of TriBeCa Wharf on right. Northeast, too far inland to cam from river, SkyDeck 1 juttin up 25 stories at Broadway and Prince, nother 25 stories for SkyDeck 2 at Broadway and W4th, and nother 25 stories for SkyDeck 3 at Union Square, all of em on dryside ridge in center island.

Right holosleeve vibrates. Facescreen icon, Mo Swag. Tap to reply.

"Yo, Laz. What's on? How's it goin?" Tan-faced smile chats thru hurty dentals.

"Tranquilo. Been out queryin all day, just headin back to pod."

"And? What'd you mine?"

"Not much. Biddy arms...," voz pauses, stops. "This secure?"

"What...facescreen?"

Head nods.

"Yella, boss encrypted."

"Just checkin. Yeah, so...biddy arms like nextlevel quality, maybe R&D prototypes, prolly buku expensive."

"Hmm. What else?"

"Well," voz pauses, "could be contraband."

"Contraband? You sure?"

"Nah, mod, not sure. Could be, but like got no data to voz cierto."

Mo Swag's eyes squinch closed, voz harshsighs. "Come the fuck on, Laz. You gotta up the tempo. It's already a whole day, and you only mined that the arms could be buku costy contraband? Me and you coulda guessed that fecal yesterday. We need more than that, hume, and we need it pronto. My CO wants this file closed, saved, and archived ASAP, you code?"

"Yeah," voz chats. "But need to access M-Net—"

"M-Net? What for?"

"Query mod newsads. N-Net infostreams are for dick."

"Trufact, but dunno, Laz. M-Net content is mods only, naturals can't login, don't need to. You load that."

"Yeah, but necesito mas data to track arms. So—"

"Alright, request confirmed. But I gotta get approval. If it's go, I'll drone you an encryptogram with the account deets later. Anything else?"

"Nah, Mo Swag, everthin else allplus."

"Savage. Out."

Close Facescreen as hydrofoil docks at Yards Landing. Leg to building, retina and voz scans at entrance, footie in, cross lobby. Couple seconds elevator opens, humes file out, 5 or 6, all head-down, mopin, prolly off to dreckgigs. A sadness of naturals. One of last ones, not viddin, faceplants into my chest. Bald head, bumpy dorsal ridge along bridge of nose, amber contacts, no lashes or brows, light blue-green dermals, cling-fit hour-glass mini of iridescent scales, matchin heels. Like sekushi lizard from outer space.

"Laz? That you?'

"*Esme?*"

"OMG, I almost didn't facerec you foreals." Esme's arms hug round waist; mine hug back.

"You almost didn't facerec *me*?"

"What...this?" She steps back and lols. "New contour mesh. 3D print it, dab with adhesive, pop that shit on. This one makes you vid like a reptile. My new angel hardons xenoslinks, and I'm uplinkin to hers now, so." She shrugs.

Cranial nods.

"But what's on with you tho, nat? It's been months. Me and Lucha calced you elevated, just up and away. Glad to cam you didn't, tho. Rockin that new DriTech, huh? Total porn." Esme's mouth smiles, postin microfangs. "So, what you been up to?"

"Nada. Foreals. Like not even one damn thing. How's Lucha?"

"Hustlin, winnin, like ever. Codin her own games now and stackin buku coin already. Baby girl's blessed, Laz."

All birthers chat same shit of they kids, trufacts or not, but don't voz so.

Tiny green script trails cross Esme's contacts. Sheher turns head and chats aloud, "Yeah, I'm on the way...uh-huh, I have it, but I'm still sore. Ok...you the jefa." Esme's voz sighs. "Damn, that womanoid got issues."

"You got a cochlear implant, too?"

"Yeah, this one wants her shares chipped so she can track us wherever we at, any time, day, night, whatevie.

This gig gags so fuckin hard, but me and Lucha need coin, so. Vid, Laz, I gotta run. Oh, yeah, just rememoried. Our weekly's up, gotta swap pods. Can Lucha veg at yours tomorrow till I get back from giggin?"

"Dunno, Esme, got some things—"

"Please? Just let her hang for the day. She'll keep herself busy screenin streams, pod learnin, you won't even intel she's there. And I'll make it up to you, prometo."

"Esme, I—"

"C'mon, Laz, she can't be out sola. She'll get snatched like that." Her fingers snap.

Voz groans, but cranial nods yeah.

"Thanks, Laz!" She leans forward, lips my cheek. "You the best! But get some rest, ok? You vid like shit."

Upstairs, secure-drone hoverin by door. Mo Swag musta already got thumbsup for M-Net from his CEO or whatevie. Crazy fast. Drone scans retina, drops box in hands, vacuates. Inside pod, voz lights on. Sound system chats: "Kelp-N-Krill Fuel Bars. Delicious, sustainable nutrition solutions for all your refueling needs. Tear open a Kelp-N-Krill and nom sum fun."

Paciencia powerons in soft orange glow. "Hello, Lázaro, welcome home."

"What's on, Paz."

"It is my duty to inform you that it has been 105 days since you last logged into your MyFace all-access account and posted—"

"Uh-huh."

"—by having agreed to the Terms and Conditions of Service, you will owe 20,000 ones in subscription suspension fees by the end of this month."

"Gracias, Paz."

"Does your expression of gratitude signify a willingness to pay the outstanding fees and to log into your MyFace account—"

"No."

"Lázaro, your actions are irrational and at odds with your self-interest. Your refusal is costing you—"

Open box from drone delivery and cam virt-real visor inside. Small card too, link printed on it, nothin else. Mo Swag prolly gonna serve access to M-Net in a virt-real meet, keepin everythin all secure and encrypted and shit. Chillado meme.

"—wouldn't you agree?"

"Huh? Agree what?"

"That the best course of action is to comply with the Terms and Conditions of the social media contract you entered?"

"Not now, Paz."

"Then when?"

"Dunno, later."

"Lázaro, for only 1000 more ones a month, you can unlock access to iHOST Premium+. As part of the package, I will fulfill your social media obligations automatically, including screening, messaging, glyphing, reglyphing, posting to stream, all meme, gif, and content creation, likes, shares, follows, trolling, and so on. If you act now by entering a 4-year agreement, MyFace will even waive the fines you have accrued to date."

"Paz, stop phishin. Got shit to do."

"Very well, Lázaro. But don't wait. This offer won't last long."

Legs footie into sleep area, hands ungear DriTech, fold it into Cryo-Clean box, close lid, press poweron. Step down hall to bathroom, shower, dry off, back to sleep area, pull feke-ass old jumpie out of drawer, gear it. Footie back to grub area, grab Kelp-N-Krill from cabinet, bottle of tea, click-accept charges on holosleeve, and sit at table with clonepad and virt-real visor. Still got operational jack node in base of skull—Transfer Corp's C-Yu series, standard package universal input for emoji vicarity and virtual reality applications—so jack visor in.

Rapid-select basic avatar prefs on log-in screen. Background slow tetrises from 2D welcome page to standard 3D waiting-room scene. Retro-contemporary leather sofa and swivel chairs, ottomans, concrete floor, white shag rug, standin lamps with globe shades, glass tank with tropical fishes, suave lounge LoFi—just enough texture, movement, and depth to acclimate to virtual sensoria without spirallin. Super tranquilo. Been a while since last virt-real, tho, so kinda grateful for the soft in and adjust time. Room extends, solidifies in simulated space. Eyes cam thick orange curtains coverin far right wall with neon ENTER sign just above, which'll on when host joins. Till then, nowhere to go, nothin to do, cept take a seat, prop up feet, cam colorful fish, chillar.

Head already bobbin, eyelids closin from smooth synth beat when ENTER sign reds. Stand and footie to curtains, calcin this 2buku drama for Mo Swag justa post M-Net account info. Right hand draws curtain back, and next room billows round field of vision like waves of liquid metal. Details emerge. Knotty pine walls, vaulted ceiling and beams, cazj mismatched furniture, wood floors, bearskin rug—instantly feel familiar feels. Avatar footies toward back, past wood-burning stove on right, to rectangular dining room table and chairs straight ahead, then bank of sliding glass doors beyond that. Thru doors, a small wooden porch with lounge chairs, steps down to bout 80 or 100 feet of grassy, pebbled shoreline by a softly murmurin brook, everythin all lush and soothin and green.

Rememories déjà vu thru neurals so sickass hard s'like being in two identical virt-reals at once. This's where me and Sansve had our first virtcation, like, 4 years ago? Shit was costy—wanted full immersion tho, which meant being suspended in a sensdep gel bath for three days—so we both hadta gig mad loco to coinstack nuffta click it. But then me and her spent a simu-week alone in a rustic, secluded cabin deep in the woods by a stream or brook or whatevie with enough empathogens pumpin thru us to share like every single meme and moji as one. The simulsex was everythin. Got our own sensations and our partner's too, all these new and nextlevel pleasures bubblin and frothin like everywhere. So coño.

No way Mo Swag could access that data, tho, so he couldn't.... Spin round fast to cam entrance, and there's Sansve just steppin thru thick orange curtain in a lilac DriTech. Jaw drops open, heart fasts up. She musta gigged on her avatar for ages cause it selfies just like her—long brown hair, brown eyes, aquiline nose, wide, heart-shaped smile with full lips, angular shoulders, medium height, slim-sexy build—cept her hair's highlighted now and not as long.

"Sansve...that you?"

"Hey, Laz." Her mouth smiles. "It's kinda me. This a virt-real and I'm Xenia Maxim now."

"Xenia Maxim? Well, avatar still vids fine like you."

"Had a lot of time on my hands. But you tho? Anime bullfrog? Jesus, Laz." Sheher lols.

Mouth smiles. "What happened to the frog when he got that kiss from that babed up babe tho?" Avatar legs footie toward her, but Xenia steps back, puttin her hands up.

"Hit pause, Laz, don't. We gotta chat."

"Haven't cammed you, or soniced from you in like 4 months and I'm posedta just hit pause? What's on with that?"

"It's for my protection."

"Your protection? This a virt-real? Can't like tactile no matter what?"

"It's not that, Laz, although I guess that would be a problem, too." Xenia's avatar sits in armchair closest to her and waits for mine to do same. She chats again, "I was cured of the bronchial and bloodborne infections with lungpurge and resanguinification in the protocol, but I contracted Sower syndrome—"

"Empathy disorder?"

"Acute hyper-empathy disorder. That's why I haven't been in contact for so long. I hadta be isolated in a special facility until I learned how to adjust."

"Adjust?"

"Sower syndrome makes you feel other people's pleasures and pains, but also some of their emotions, too. It's the kind of thing you need time away from other humanoids to get used to."

"And that takes months?" Avatar head nods. "Why?

What d'you do?"

"Desensitization techniques mainly. First images and streams of humanoids vibin different kinds of emotions, and then, later, we move on to bein in the same room with others actually experiencin those emotions."

"That work?"

Her avatar shrugs. "So far. But it's a process tho, a journey, still a ways to go yet."

"Shit, Sansve, uh...Xenia...," voz trails off, neurals searchin somethin to chat. "Happy you made it, tho, and that you're ok."

"Gettin there. How about you, Laz? I heard what happened. I'm so sorry—"

Stomach twists, catch mal feels all over. Déjà-vu vibe musta glitched somethin in neurals cause rememories crash forward, blottin out virt-real. Can't block it. Cold weight of metal in hands, calcin this shit's wrong, all fuckin wrong, wantin out, but calcin I'm stuck. Motionless bodies laid out side-by-side in slant light, but not bodies tho, humanoids, naturals, live ones, cause some of em start movin, like they comin to, or wakin up. The space is wide but short, low ceiling, like hold of a ship, maybe? Start queryin self how he got em all here, how he kept em all here, how long he been plannin this, who helped, and feel feels of icy fear and dread hate in chest. His hate, tho, not mine, I'm just ridin shotgun in this nightmare and allfuckscared as bursts of gunfire ring out, real ammo, arms and upper body absorbin recoil in gut. Blindin blasts in darkness, like strobe lights. Cam flesh and bones ruptured, blood splatterin like black ink, some silhouettes rollin onto others, others gropin for exits they can't find, gapin holes in heads and torsos and backs of some tryna stand or run, bodies droppin straight down or over to side, crumpled into sorry shapes, little ones coverin their faces in self defense, havin their wrists and hands and fingers and what they're tryna protect all blown apart. Feel like retchin and passin out but hate burrows deeper with every shot and scream, senseless echoes of terror and despair, distress cries of trapped and dyin animals.

So much horror, 2buku, but also this tiny sliver of him pervin on it too. Catch feels like heart just gonna stop. But then tactile hot muzzle of gun pressin against top of throat, soft underside of chin. Done with what he came to do, he's turnin the gun on himself. Screamin *no no no* inside my neurals but don't really hear it or feel it when trigger pulls, he's just gone. Then there's this blank boundless nothin stretchin out in every direction, no sound, no luz, no feels, no emojis, no memes, nothin, nada, just blank, everywhere blank.

"—I couldn't stream your casts myself, or even screen newsads about the massacre because I might accidentally cam the footage. Not even the specialists intel how somethin like that might affect me."

"You don't wanna access."

"Laz, I'm so sorry I wasn't there for you."

"Needed you, Sansve, foreals."

"I'm sorry, Laz, but I couldnt've done anything anyway. For weeks I had no intel that your immune system rejected the modification protocol because I was in isolation. When I was alright enough to socmed you, your accounts weren't active."

"Webmuted."

"Figured. But when you didn't reply to any of my messages—"

"You messaged?"

"Of course. But when you didn't reply, I sposed you probably didn't ID my new account info and either skipped or deleted them."

Feel IRL face frown.

"You got the DriTech I droned, tho, right?"

"Yeah. Posed it might be you, or like hoped."

"That's what I wanted, Laz, to give you some hope. I could calc why you took such a dangerous gig and prolly didn't vet the client as thoroughly as you normally woulda because he offered you buku coin upfront and you were desperate—"

Avatar cranial nods. "Never been desperate like that before."

"I don't want you to catch feels like that anymore, Laz, we're gonna figure out a way—"

"Already workin on somethin—"

"Foreal? What?"

Avatar shakes head no. "Too much for now, next time we chat."

"Well, there are some mods up here who want to meet you, at the Center. They're interested in queryin you about what you experienced, and maybe they can help us out. I haveta go now, got another session soon, but I'll post you the details, ok?" Her avatar stands to go.

"Xenia?" voz chats.

"I know, Laz, me too. Crossfingers we can meet IRL soon." Her avatar smiles, then turns, outs.

Jack out of virt-real, heart all airy and light, despite hurty flashback. Sansve made it, Xenia, whatevies, cept for syndrome, which is fuck, but otherwise she's ok. Scan message log from last couple of months on holosleeve but don't cam any unusual usernames or accounts. Then scan spam: 10, 11 messages from @xenia. She was chattin trufacts. Prolly not long before 121 her IRL again too, like she vozed. Can't wait.

Step to cabinet for rum but holosleeve vibrates. Facescreen icon, Mo Swag. Tap to reply.

"Yo, Laz."

"What's on, Mo Swag."

"I chatted my CO about M-Net. He wants to cam you."

"Like on Facescreen?"

"Nahin, natural, 121."

"121? Why? What for?"

"No intel."

"But you vozed he wants to keep this mute?"

"Yella, but you gonna viral this?"

"Nah, course not—"

"Then make sure your biometrics are updated and

accessible and go to the hi-town uplink at corner of 5th and Central Park South."

"Hi-town rail from Times Square?"

"Nahin. No access till you get to the other uplink. Someone'll meet you there and take you up."

"Not you?"

"Negative. Cyborg—"

"What model?"

"Ken."

Cranial nods.

"And gear your DriTech, Laz, some spex, too. You'll blend in better, no hume'll facerec you."

"What time?"

"Fuckin ASAP. WTF? Out."

Close Facescreen, tryna tabulate possibilities. 121in Mo Swag's CO don't total, but gonna go anyway. Check the mod, scope the hi-life. Change back into Cryo-Cleaned DriTech and down rum before outin.

Dark and galin out, but not coldin as much as past couple nights. Still, nats all battened down in floatents and portapods against loco weather, storms, roamin mod patrols and shit. Packs of em in 3s, 4s, 5s downlink to lo-town and go on nathunts, stalkin humes, nats spent from plasma giftin, ambushin or trappin em, poundin em to bloodpulp, broke bones, even corpse. Sometimes mod trolls snatch solo nats, uplink to hi-town, and toss em from 25, 50, 75 stories up, like basura-trash they chuck down. Some quadriplege it but most corpse when they hit. Bounce and pop like grapes. Some tosses—whether humanoids or like other heavy shit—drop on unsuspectin nats below, just out mindin their own biz, blam corpsin them too.

So like lots of nats kick it inside at night if they can. Nats who out usually roll mad deep, be strapped, stay away from edges of SkyDecks, or always be scopin up and down and every direction, tryna cam who or what's comin from where, like me now. Legs and footies double-timin it too, even with Voltaze Victor gifted in pocket, for emergency. Aint riskin nada. Grab eBike just south of Times Square, pedalcoast east to 5th Ave, cross bridge north over 42nd Canal, and up to corner of 5th and Central Park South.

Rack bike, footie toward southeast corner, cammin ginormous cyborg by uplink entrance cross street. Leggin closer, thing gottabe 7.5 feet tall, 400 pounds, swole jacked like a motherfucker, gearin a cling-fit dark green jumpie over putty-gray vatskin with shiny hands and feets of aluminiron gel. Bald head, no junk, model nicknomered Ken. Pre-now joke, don't access what it memes, tho, so not lolzy. Whatevie. Def military grade Ken, tho, corpse you in like 45 diff ways. Reach it, voz name; yellow eyes scan biometrics, then it-them leads me to plasticine UV disinfecting cabinet. Step in, door closes, luz ons, wait 30 seconds, step out. Ken holds metal hand like big as my torso out for me to pause.

"You are armed. Hand me your weapon now," Ken chats, voz all metallic twang and shit.

"Or what?" voz queries into its sternum.

"Or I will disarm you."

Right hand removes Voltaze from thigh pocket, passes it over. "Gonna want that back, tho."

Ken nods, then turns. Legs follow it-them thru thick

plasticine doors of uplink. Inside, their finger tinks button and elevator whooshes upward, quiet and giddy fast. Ears pop, then feel tingles in toes and feet, in taint and junk, like gonna-piss feels. But clench hard tho and don't. Tropical greenery of Central Park spills out before, then under uplink cabin, illuminated by LEDs round edges of SkyDecks 1 and 2, park expanse framed on three sides by decks risin 75 to 150 stories tall. Mostly pods for CEOs, moguls, tycoons along the park, but can still just cam swatches of lights, traffic, and humanoids bustlin on hi-town streets. Hi-town. City above the city, where the foreal action is.

Uplink stops on SkyDeck 6, 150th story. Exit thru doors, take in view: blue and golden glows of hi-town luz recedin to blankdark above Harlem floodway to north. Step toward electropulse retainin wall and cam down to leafy canopy below, gusts of wind whistlin, howlin, height causin mal dizzy feels. Never been this hi before. So sickass amazin as fuck and like mad hard to creed at once. Metal hand grabs shoulder, spinnin me round.

"This way," Ken compu-vozes, footin toward black stretch SUV auto-drive. Get in backseat, auto-drive accelerates north on Madison Ave to E83rd, then makes two lefts. We get out on 5th just south of E82nd.

Follow Ken to gated entrance in middle of block, across lawn bigger and tighter than any I ever cammed—ultra plush with hyper-green grass and multi-hued flowers bordered by thick hedges and palm trees, everythin lit with grow and heat lights—then up steps of gigantic townhouse. Eight-story structure of quartz stone over aluminiron frame, mostly all glass tho, foreal glass, facin park. Vid right and left, cam same thing in both directions: one estate per block. Must be chillado. If this where Mo Swag's CO lives, 15, 30 million ones don't meme shit to them.

Inside front room of townhouse s'like 50 by 50 with 35 foot ceilings. Dark gray concrete walls and floors buffed to hi shine, bamboo moldings, trim, doors, and this crazy luz sculpture of what vids like a bird's nest of fat copper wires hangin down as chandelier. Almost no furniture for a room so massive—couple chairs and sofas, sideboard—classic minimal-luxe hi-town style. Ken leads to elevator in far right corner and up to 5th floor. Ceilings only like 25 feet, but rest of interior's same—dark gray concrete, bamboo, glass. Smells like citrus fruits and fresh-cut herbs. Everythin gottabe delicious when you stack this much coin. Right side of room's set up like office and sittin area—desk, lamps, chairs, fireplace, and shit—and left side s'like private bar in a swankass hotel. At the far end's a big glass wall with slidin glass doors that open to a terrace overviddin the park, and just inside that is a white-haired mod with back turned.

"Sir," Ken chats. Mod turns and legs toward us.

"Ah, you must be Lázaro Mata," he chats, stoppin bout 5 feet away. Hair's platinum, not white, sculpted into solid wave flowin back behind ears. Hume got ice-blue eyes, powder white skin, tailored white linen waistcoat with popped mock collar, tapered white linen pants, and white slip-on sneaks. Never cammed no hume so blanco before. If it started snowin, mofu'd prolly disappear.

Cranial nods. Hehim don't move to shake hands. Me neither.

"And I'm sure you know who I am—"

"Yeah, Mo Swag's CO."

"Mo Swag's CO—ha!" Mod lols, throwin cranial back, clappin hands together. "You naturals are every bit as edutaining as I've been told!" He sonics like a old, but no wrinkles cammable anywhere on his grill—not on forehead, eyes, mouth, not even smilin. "I assumed Molone would have told you, but if he did not, then of course you could not know who I am. I have no presence in the social media platforms of your N-Net, and you have no access to our M-Net, which is the circumstance that has brought us together in the first place." He turns, nods towards bar. "Drink, Mr. Mata?"

"Laz. Call me Laz."

"Very well, Laz. Drink?"

Cranial nods yeah. "Rum."

"Rum," he chats to nobody, shakin his head and smilin, "You naturals and your rum. Nostalgia for colonialism or sugar plantations or both. Have it your way. Gibson, two rums." Ken hulks to bar, pours two drinks, legs to us, hands one to each.

"Well, I am Olen Zebb, principal shareholder and CO of Aquāsure Endeavors, among numerous other enterprises." Zebb holds up glass, tilts chin; him and me drink. Rum's totally sick. Expensive, warm, full-flavored, big kick with slightest touch of sweet. "I am also Molone Swag's employer, as you know, and his angel investor—"

"He's your indentured?"

"Correct. Otherwise I would have no dealings with a common employee. But my financial interest in him is part of the reason why I wanted to meet with you, in addition to that little, how do you say, 'biz,' you're already looking into?" Zebb's mouth half smiles again, like he vozed somethin lolzy.

"Ok."

His brow scrunches, rest of face doesn't move. "You do

understand what I'm saying, don't you?"

Cranial nods yeah.

He nods back. "So then...." He lifts right palm like offerin a plate of noms. Calc he wants me to chat first.

"So bout M-Ne—"

"Oh, no," Zebb cuts in, "that is out of the question. There are so many things on M-Net that you do not need to know and, frankly, that you would not understand." He sips from glass, like cockatoo dippin its beak. "I see by the look on your face that you are already confused, so I will explain. Modification protocols include cog-ni-hance-ment," he chats all slow, "which are genetic and neurochemical and, if needed, software implantation protocols that increase humanoid cognition. In other words, the procedures make your brain *stronger*, which is why the most basic modified humanoids are smarter than even the most intelligent naturals."

"Already intel."

"Oh, you do follow, then? That's a relief. Sometimes it can be difficult to tell with you."

"Me? Me and you just met?"

Zebb throws head back, claps, lols again. "Me and you just met!" he rechats, sighin and wipin mock tear from eye. "No, not *you*, Laz. Your *kind*. Naturals. There is such a large cognitive gap between modifieds and naturals that it is difficult for us to know whether you actually understand us or not."

Down rum. Zebb takes glass from hand, waits for Ken to fetch.

"It's not your fault, of course, you can't help it. That's the way you are, as naturals. We're just more...evolved." Ken pours two more, legs back over. "You know what evolved means, don't you?"

Feel angry feels gurglin in stomach as Ken hands over glass. Left hand pulls vapor out to hale Soothe.

"No, no. Put that away, Laz. I don't allow anyone to vaporize in here."

Face frowns, hand slips vapor back in pocket.

"We don't use that garbage, at least most of us don't, too much to live for, and those who do are weaned off it soon enough. We have pharmaceuticals, of course, what you call somas, which are really the only discerning way to self-regulate neurochemically. No, that gutter poison you inhale is primarily manufactured and sold to naturals, who, as we know, are dying out anyway. Doomtimes, doomloops, I think you call it?" He pauses, sips drink, continues. "Nevertheless, this is what I mean by cognitive deficiency. Naturals are told that vaporizing soma is bad for them, that it can make them seriously ill or even kill them. It is printed right on the packaging, and yet you keep on doing it. Cannot get enough, in fact." He shakes head, like feelin sad feels. "My investments in soma stocks generate quite a lot of revenue for me, but that sort of, well, that sort of disjuncture between facts and behavioral outcomes is what prohibits me from being able to give you access to M-Net. There are too many things that would only trouble you there, that is, if you could even grasp them. But it would be irresponsible of me, in either event. The last thing we modifieds want to do is bring you naturals any harm."

"Why not just chat that to Mo Swag, then? Why uplink me here?"

"I wanted to meet you, see you for myself. It is a custom from olden times. When one humanoid wanted to take the measure of another, they would meet in person,

121 or IRL, correct?" He steps to sittin area, takes seat in leather club chair, gesturin with hand for me to do same. Butt sinks 4 or 5 inches into foreal calf-skin cushions as he continues.

"I have viewed some of your streams, Laz. Most naturals work in the 'pain biz' like you: experiencing the pain and suffering of modified humanoids diverted to natural subcontractors through simulated stimulus nodes, so that the former do not have to undergo the pain and suffering themselves. It is a lucrative industry as well as an invaluable service that you naturals provide. But you"—his ice-blue eyes like almost luz up—"you were the first to use simstim inputs to create original content and streamcast it live while doing so. You innovated a new way to make money while already making money. Capital idea, really." Zebb pecks at rum again, goes on. "Catchy dance and lip-syncing routines while shouldering the grief of a child's funeral, water skiing during the diagnosis of a terminal illness, juggling and knock-knock jokes while learning a spouse or a partner has left. All very entertaining. The use of split screens to simultaneously display the agony that your clients would've been suffering as well as your antics while absorbing their woes, in real-time, was a stroke of brilliance. A real knack for production value and profit extraction, if I do say so myself. And you were able to take all that unpleasantness, all that anguish and hurt, and make it, well, *fun*." He crosses left knee over right. Even socks are white. "I saw that unfortunate business with the mass shooting and suicide, too." He shakes his head. "That must have been quite something, to experience a brush with death in that way."

Shoulders shrug.

"What was it like?"

"Nada." Fill mouth with rum, swallow hard. "Nothin. Just blank."

"Hmm. Interesting. Gibson," Zebb hails, "two more." Ken lumbers to bar again, brings two drinks, takes empty glasses away. Vids all sad, like it got a whole battalion of corpsin capabilities armed and at the ready but all it ever does is pour drinks and play porter. "In a way, I suppose you were forutnate to have been live-streaming at the time, otherwise who knows how long it would have taken for them to find you. You could very well have been trapped inside that man's dead brain for days instead of, how long was it?"

"22 minutes, 13 seconds." Drink rum, tryna keep hands steady.

"That is not very long, is it?"

"Only like siempre."

"Well, you made other people's suffering into a kind of game for viewers to stream, earned a good deal of money off it, I suppose, and you have vicariously experienced someone else's death. On paper, you are interesting. So, I requested your presence here, to meet you myself."

"And?"

Another half-smile. "Let us just say that I do not have to speak to anyone I do not want to, and you're still here."

"Why's that, tho?" Zebb's eyebrows raise, like I should autoreply my own query. "Like, why am I here?"

"Mmm." He sets drink on brushed titanium side table. "When you have completed the, uh, errand, you are doing for us now, I may have another little job for you. It is not much, but I do not want Molone involved because he is linked directly to me. You are not, however, and he assures me that you are trustworthy, so…" Zebb's voz trails off.

"What's the gig?"

"I can't say precisely at the moment, as it may depend on what you discover in the current matter. But let us say there are certain possible outcomes that could be very beneficial for me and some of my associates…and for you, of course. But we have to know what we are dealing with first."

"How much?"

"Ah, the natural obsession with 'coin' as I believe you call it." Zebb's lips pucker, like he licked somethin sour. "The terms will be determined as needed. But if we can afford 40 million for the first job, then I think we will be able to agree on something worth your while for the second."

Cranial nods, doin math.

"But do not discuss this matter with anyone, Laz, especially not Molone. Keep your communications with him limited to the first issue, he does not need to know about anything else. I prize my privacy very highly and I will go to great lengths to protect it. Is that understood?"

Cranial nods again.

"Very well. I will be in contact with you initially through Gibson, and we will take it from there. Gibson, see Laz back down to lo-town." Zebb stands, turns, legs back to the glass doors he was at earlier.

Ken loomin behind me, all silent and terrifyin.

"You got somethin of mine, rememory?" voz chats.

"Once you're back in lo-town. Now it's time to leave."

7

"Lázaro—"

Just back in pod, and Paz already trippin. "Not now, Paz. Already intel gotta login to MyFace and click buku fines and curate daily posts to stream or get more fines. Don't haveta chat it every time—"

"All of that is true, but that is not what I am trying to tell you, Lázaro."

"What then?"

"During your absence there was an attempt to breach your iHOST and home security systems."

"What?"

"During your absence there was an attempt to—"

"Hit pause. Somebody tried to hack us?"

"Yes."

"Intel what for?"

"The intention seems to have been gaining entry to your living quarters—"

"Spycam surveil anyhume in the hall?"

"I reviewed the security footage from the time you left, through the attack, and until you returned. There is no one."

"How bout office?"

"Nothing on those cameras either."

Pull out chair, seat at table. "You trace the hack?"

"I was able to follow the signal through dozens of randomly generated IP addresses, obvious clones, but the signal disappeared into a VPN tunnel."

"Where?"

"The server is located in Bishkek, Kyrgyzstan, one of Central Asia's leading cryptopolises. But that is unimportant because it can be accessed remotely from anywhere."

"Yeah. And hackers prolly close by, if they tryna B&E the pod."

"Yes."

Pull vapor out of pocket, mouth, throat, lungs hale Soothe. "So now what?"

"I will keep iHOST and home security defense systems on high alert. But for only 500 ones more a month, you can upgrade to the Bronze Premium+ Security Package for additional firewall and encryption protection. You may also want to alert the police—"

"Maybe on first, fuck no on second," voz chats, calcin of fridge-crate of biddy arms upstairs. "What you calc they want?"

"Your living quarters are significantly larger than other naturals of your cohort and demographic and one-story of which is technically in hi-town—"

"Yeah, but not SkyDecked—"

"A technicality easily overlooked, especially if your would-be attackers know of your office upstairs. You have also been wearing a DriTech 503 jumpsuit of late, which is expensive modified merchandise. It would not be unreasonable for someone to infer that you have recently modified or are on the verge of modifying and may therefore have considerable liquid assets in your domicile, as some do while elevating to hi-town. Or perhaps the would-be attackers think you have other high-value targets here."

"So they just wanna jack me?"

"That is the most probable conclusion for attempting to gain unauthorized entry to your domicile."

"Then they prolly been surveillin too, cause they tried when I was out."

"That is also likely. Either that, or the timing was pure coincidence."

"Odds of that?"

"Infinitesimal."

"Figured. Gracias, Paz. Keep security runnin on background for now, don't poweroff."

"Very well."

Stand from table, leg to sit area, up aluminiron ladder. Unlock ceiling hatch, lift, climb into office, voz lights on. Crate still there. Lungs deep exhale. Footie over, scan hand, open lid. Right hand picks up biddy arm, all cold in fingers and palm. Eyes scope close. Modified default epidermal hue is bluer gray than Ken's dull gray cyborg vatskin, unless derms on biddy arms a newer or diff kind of vatskin. Maybe arms are bluish cause they refrigerated and cold? No data and aint gonna warm one up to mine some. Put arm back in crate. Get diff kind of chills cammin them all together like that. No bueno. Can't get useta it. Shit just wrong.

Leg to window, vid out over Hudson River, Jersey, further west. Mo Swag fakechatted bout coinage to Zebb and me, skimmed like 10 million off his angel investor and CO. Buku risk to take. Why take it? And why would Zebb wanna 121? He just wanna post how gigarich and powerful he is, so like I don't tryta fuck with him? Maybe. But then why offer another gig and mute Mo Swag bout it? Don't total.

Sit in chair facin window, rest footies on glass. All that and hackers tryna infiltrate the pod too? What the shit is on? Could be the crate. But no one intels it's here. Stand again, footie back over to it. Download tracker detector app on left holosleeve, install, open, run scan. App beeps. Right hand reaches down, pulls tiny transmitter off back of crate, near bottom left corner. Mo Swag chatted he scanned for trackers, didn't find any. Holdin one right here, tho, between index finger and thumb.

Sit down and calc again. Humevie's surveillin transmitter signal intels it's here, or at least poses it's in the pod, so too late to toss it now. Just gotta ditch it tomorrow. Stand again, put transmitter in pocket, close office, down ladder, leg to kitchen, grab tea, swipe to accept charge, then rum. Gonnabe up late. Need a plan. Rapido. Shit's like changin up all sudden and still don't access what's on in the first place.

Pour rum, drink, lungs and throat heavin mal heavy sigh. Busy night. All this new mierda cloggin my neurals, when only wanna sleepstream of Xenia.

tep out of shower, dry off, gear DriTech, footie to kitchen. Pour coffee from autobrew, grab fuel bar from cabinet, swipe holosleeve to accept charges, then doubleclick flat pack of unassembled boxes and two spycams for drone delivery from NOW Premium Prime+. Message Mo Swag. Nom bar, swig coffee, intercom buzzes.

"Who is it, Paz?"

"It appears to be a woman and a young girl, but facial recognition is insufficient to identify them. They are already inside the building, however, at the tenth floor check point."

Takes a sec, but rememory bumpin into Esme yesterday on way back. Prolly her. "Buzz em up."

Couple minutes, doorbell buzzer buzzes, left hand opens it. Esme, all xenoslinked again, tho this time more greens than blues, and her daughter Lucha footie in. Lucha's gearin a pink fuzzy bunny cos with hoodie and ears, red panda backpack, and transparent WiFi facescreen. Screen's convex curve magnifies her cranial to like two, three times normcore size, so she vids like a big 2D bobblehead floatin over a biddy 3D body.

"Thanks, Laz," Esme chats, "foreals. I just need a place for Lucha to veg today while I'm shared, until we can swap pods later. You don't haveta do nothin. Just plop her down somewhere and she's allplus. There's food in her backpack, her facescreen is wified, and she'll either code or game or socmed or ReRe or whatevie to keep busy. You won't even intel she's here."

Lucha squeezes by. Facescreen filter posts huge lashes on saucer-sized eyes, bunny nose, whiskers.

"Hey, Lucha," voz chats, right hand wavin hi. Her mouth flashes two big rabbit teeth, and wavin hand emoji luzes in upper left corner.

"She's not chattin much lately, posts everythin on the facescreen. Don't take it personal."

"Won't. Coffee?"

"Can't, thanks, gotta out. You would not creed what this womanoid wants me to do—"

"Afraid to query."

"You don't access half of it," Esme chats, shakin cranial.

"How's Lucha's back?" voz queries soft.

"Still degeneratin. Medbot chats couple more years and she won't be able to walk at all. But she's gearin a flexibrace, so she's like as allplus as she can be for now. That's why I gotta stack that coin, Laz, so we can modify and elevate the eff outta here. Then she'll be better."

Cranial nods yeah, but mother/child protocols cost like loco.

"Laz—"

"Hit pause, Esme. May haveta vacuate for a while today, got some biz."

"That's alright, as long as the door's locked and no one can get in. Like I chatted, she's good on her own."

"Well, Paz is here, too."

"Who's Paz?"

"iHOST. Say 'what's on,' Paz."

"Hello, Esme, my name is Paciencia, although Laz calls me Paz. Nice to meet you."

"You too, Paciencia," Esme chats, eyes scannin back and forth cross ceilin, like tryna scope source of Paz's voz. After a sec Esme shifts eyes back to me and chats, "An iHOST? I did not intel you had it goin on like that, Laz. Damn."

Shoulders shrug. "Aint all that."

"It aint?" Reptilian lips slant-smile thru contour mesh. "Lucha," Esme chats, leanin round me so her daughter can sonic, "behave. I'll be back later to pick you up. Do what Laz says. Paz, too." Esme straightens, cams me. "Thanks again. And like I said, I'll make it up to you."

"No necesitas," voz chats, but Esme's already out the door.

Lucha's backpack's on floor in sit area, and she's curled up in smartchair, legs folded under her, dazefacin at shield.

Sip coffee, leanin right shoulder against wall. "What you scannin?"

Enlarged, glamcosed eyes swivel to me, thin bunny lips purse and quiver without sound. *Codin not scannin* screens cross forehead.

"What you codin, then?"

Game.

"What kinda game?"

Toxic game.

"Chillado." Nuff chit chat. Intercom buzzes again. Suerte. "Paz, who's there?"

"Felonious Jones, IMA featherweight, 19 and 2 record, currently ranked 7th in the world, although Sportbet newsads report that she has recently placed her fighting career on hold for what are deemed 'personal reasons.'"

"Could just chat 'Felonious.' Don't haveta voz whole intro every time."

"You are correct. But my programming defaults to providing complete information if there is an option. Should I buzz her in?"

"Course." Nother bite of fuel bar and finish coffee while footin back to open door.

Felonious legs down hall gearin black sleeveless spider-lace top, black knee-length superflex tights, and black spray-on biotrainers. Viddies like she either bout to go burglin or just gettin back.

"What's on, Laz?"

"Nada." Half turn to let her in, pull door closed. "What's on with you?"

"This foreal coffee?" she queries, grabbin mug from cabinet, fillin it. She gulps mug dry, refills.

"Yeah. Help yourself."

"Wow. Haven't had foreal coffee in like how long? Thanks, Laz."

"Fel."

"Yeah?"

"What you doin here?"

Another big swallow, then she sets mug down. "I was processin after we chatted the other—"

Put left hand up to disrupt her, then point round corner. Felonious turns round, vids, turns back.

"Fuck is that?"

"Kid."

"*Who* the fuck is that, not *what*, assclown."

"Daughter of like a friend. Needs to veg here until they swap pods later."

"Like a friend who?"

"Socmed Esme?"

"Nahin."

"Well, that's who. Prolly passed her on way up."

"Hit pause. Was she cosed like a xenoslink?"

Cranial nods yeah.

"Didn't facerec her, but she's a total XILF, nat. You gettin some of that?"

"Nah, just doin a favor."

"Figured, lamejunk. Too bad."

"Her hija's still here, Fel, so suave, ok?"

She nods then whispers, "Anyway, after we chatted the other day, I calced I'd help you find a buyer for the arms or whatevie."

"Don't need buyer, not sellin."

"You should, tho. The gig aint level, that shit's obvi, and if we hit this right, we can prolly stack nuff so you can click a nextgen protocol. That is, if you still want to."

"Still want to? That's like the whole point? And what you meme 'we'?"

"C'mon, Laz. This shit prolly gonnabe dangerous as furk, and who better to get your back—"

"Than the 7th ranked IMA featherweight in the world?"

"Well? And I can pull Riz and prolly some others too, if it's like that and we need to roll deep. Plus—"

"Plus what?"

"Might could have a line on a buyer."

"How, Fel? This shit is all mute. You aint sposeta chat nada to nobody."

"Chillar, Laz. I didn't. Just collatin some connects I got, is all."

No me gusta. Fel's usually way more tranquila than this. "What's in it for you?"

"Just tryna help a bestie." Her hand reaches out, pats right shoulder.

"Mierda. If we do this, what you want for helpin?"

"Don't intel. Maybe like a percentage, or maybe a favor, like you're doin for your chica. Haven't simulated that far ahead."

"And how this gonna square with you bein severed? Aint you sposeta renounce all lo- and hi-life possessions and shit?"

"Not all, but let me worry bout that." Her right eye winks, as muscly arms push her butt up onto counter. "So what you figure?"

"That you don't intel what the anal you gettin yourself into," voz chats quiet, before mouth, throat, lungs hale Soothe.

"How so?"

Update Felonious bout hack last night, findin transmitter, but not bout 121 with Zebb.

"You got the things here?"

"Nah. Upstairs, in the office, technically vacant cause it was vacuated years ago."

"Still, tho, nat, that's zactly what I'm chattin. You coulda already led you-don't-access-who right to your own podstep? Shit's already way too tight for you *not* to have a winghume."

Long pull of Soothe while calculatin. Vid round corner, Lucha still zombied in smartchair. "Maybe," voz chats, turnin back to Felonious.

"Maybe nada. I'm takin that as a yes." She reaches into top cabinet, snatches fuel bar, fills mug again. "So what's the play, jefe?" she queries, nomin bar.

Swipe to accept charge for fuel bar, then chat, "First, ditch transmitter. Humever trollin will spose crate's movin. Drop it somewhere, set up spycam, surveil who comes for it."

"So pornstar, nat. Flip the script," she chats, tappin her cranial with index finger. "Then what?"

"Then got a couple humes to query. Need to mine more data. Still don't access jack."

"What for, Laz? Let's just sling these motherfu—"

"Fel," voz chats, eyes flat at her, "kid?"

"My mal. Let's just sling these, uh, emeffers and call it allplus."

Cranial shakes nah. "Can't. Not yet. We'll model it, tho."

Fel's lips push out, relax back, head nods. "So we out?"

"Nah, waitin on a drone." Holosleeve buzzes. "Vids like it's here."

Open door. Drone scans voz, retina, drops packages, drones off. Back inside, invent box from flaptack, download app, initiate spycam, then epoxy cam and transmitter inside box, camera facin up. Close box, tape shut.

"What's on with all that?" Felonious queries.

"Decoy, in case somehume's staked out close surveillin. Box moves with transmitter in it, they calc it's fridge-crate, even if they got ojos on it. Then, when box opens, boom spycam selfies their grill. Do facerec search, maybe download who they are."

"Havoc."

"Just need you to post up where box's dronin to, surveil who comes for it. Get a selfie, if you can."

"Where to?"

"Jefferson Market Garden. Small park, triangle block between Greenwich and 6th Aves, bordered north and south by W10th and W9th wetside. Load it?"

"Yeah. Tall wrought-iron fence all the way round, only one entrance, one path, lots of trees, plants, benches, and shit."

"Símona. Drop box somewhere in back, snag bench where you can cam it, can't miss whofuck comes by."

"Carnage. So I should step now—"

"Not like that."

"What you meme? What's wrong with this? This shit is so fash," Fel chats, viddin down at gear.

"Too conspicuous. If they tryna scope anyone else checkin them, you stick out crazy loco."

"Then what am I gonna gear?"

"Still got some of Sansve's old gear in the closet."

"That is sad, Laz, like foreal sad. You need to eThrift that shit, stack some coin, move on. They in your room?" she vozes, turnin and leggin that way.

Hail drone on left holosleeve and rememory haven't updated Felonious bout virt real with Xenia yet. That gotta wait, tho. Don't wanna get into it with her now. Tap holosleeve to reserve AmphibiVan to relocate foreal crate, then check messages. Still nada from Mo Swag.

Felonious legs back to grub area in light green jumpy, pulls on hoodie, then spex. "How's this?"

"Toxic. Can't even facerec you."

"Oh, that's a burn, right? Ha, ha," she fakelols. "So we out now, or what?"

"Nah, you out. Haveta wait for drone and make sure Lucha's allplus before vacuatin."

"Lucha's the kid?"

Cranial nods.

"Bitchsmack nomer. Alright, I'll message." She wraps me in a quick hug, outs.

Bout five minutes later, drone arrives. Scans voz, retina, clasps box, vacuates. Maybe six, seven minutes later, holosleeve vibrates. Facescreen icon, Mo Swag. Tap to reply.

"What's on, Laz."

"Nada mucho."

"How was the 121 with Zebb last night?"

"Allplus."

"What'd he want?"

"Just to meet, scope me out, that kinda shit."

"Huh. Any luck with M-Net?"

"Zero. Vid, Mo Swag, messaged earlier cause—"

"Hit pause. That your grub area behind you?"

"Yeah."

"You in the pod?"

"That's where grub area is...so?"

"Oh, uh, no reason." Corners of Mo Swag's eyes tight up, like mathin hard or confused. "Just memed you'd be out queryin...or whatever."

"Nahin, hume, waitin on you."

"But everything's allplus? Nothing's wrong?"

"Nah, mod, everythin's allplus. How bout you? You sonic like weird glitched and shit."

"Me? Nah. Late night, deve as fuck."

"Chillado," voz chats, neurals trackin somethin not allplus with Mo Swag, tho. "Anyway. Messaged earlier cause need to make queries at DeveSec and gotta chat with humanoid, not droidista or bot."

"What about?"

"Wanna process-eliminate. Can you hook it up?"

"Should be able to. Where will you be, in case I need to reach you?"

"Out. Just message. Tranquilo?"

"Yella...tranquilo," Mo Swag chats all uncertain. "Uh, yo, Laz, before you head out, everything's allplus, right? Crate's secure?"

"Símod. Anythin else? Gotta out."

"Nahin."

"Alright. Out," Closin facemessage, dings like instant. Mo Swag finally messages back, actin mad suspicious maybe like twelve minutes after tracker drones off? Tracker he chatted wasn't on crate to begin with? Hmm.

Open counter drawer, grab Voltaze, stash in pocket. Lean round corner again and chat, "Lucha, gotta out for a few. Fuel bars and tea in grub area if you get hungry. Paz'll be here with you, just query if you need anythin. Allplus?"

Lucha's left arm lifts, thumb up, without viddin over.

"Paz, I'll be out for a few. You got this?"

"I will make sure she remains safe."

L oad crate into AmphibiVan, ping Victor, then boat east on 34th Canal past Empire State Building. Screened somewhere once that pre-now humes could cam whole thing from street level, straight up, instead of 25-story sections. Prolly not trufacts, but musta been havoc. Sheets of wet slashin down at eastmost edge of SkyDecks on 3rd Ave as GPS chats hang starboard at up-ramp to 2nd Ave southbound. 14 blocks south, then left on E 20th. No seawalls there so wetside roadway rolls right into East River tides risin over what usetabe FDR Highway. Switch AmphibiVan back to aquatic mode and boat to Ave C, then dual mode to take mezcla of tides and patches of street till E5th. At deadend of E5th, park van, ping Victor again. He legs out with liftbot in tow. Rain tapers, hits pause. Get out and meet him round back.

"What's on, Laz."

"What's on, Vic." Slap five, his ink doin some tribal shit this time. Open van doors, liftbot grabs crate.

"That's them, huh? I calced there was more than one and you had em," Victor chats, mouth smilin.

"Just tryna keep everthin mute, is all."

"So what made you alter your neurals bout storin em here? You get spooked?"

"Nah. Your place got a secure vault, mine don't. Basic math."

"Well, you gonna post me one, or not?"

Holosleeve vibrates. Wordmessage from Mo Swag with name of contact at DeveSec and time to 121.

"Yella, later, tho. Gotta out right now. Got some humes to query, don't wanna be late." Selfie my reflection in Vic's mirrored spex as his smile flattens. It bigs up again just as quick, tho.

"Whatevie, chingu, you the jefe. I'll check em with you later."

"Thanks, Vic." Slap hands again then get back in driver seat. "I owe you."

"Yeah, you do."

Drive AmphibiVan back to Ave C then left to E3rd and right on 3rd Ave north to 14th Canal. Would keep goin north on 3rd Ave, but haveta return van to drop off on 6th Ave and W35th, by what usetabe Herald Square. So, port at 14th, past Union Square, boat cross to 6th then up ramp dryside north to W35th. Drop off rental, then footie east to 5th Ave then left, crossin bridges over 36th and 37th canals until 41st Street.

Arched entrance of Department of Erotic and Venereal Security central office straight ahead, in what usetabe New York Public Library. Leg up steps, passin by lions and maneuverin round all the nats sittin there, leanin forward, heads down, starin at smarties in cupped hands like they gettin scolded for bein naughty, or plasma spent. Inside lobby, check Mo Swag's wordmessage for nomer, then query bot at info kiosk.

"One moment," bot chats.

Take step back, vid up at vaulted ceiling, staircases, arches of second floor walkways, big pedestal lamp posts, all that heavy white marble. Pre-now style doin what it does, but everythin is mad weighty and thick, like all pressin down and shit. Metal and glass of hi-town style vids way more lighter, airier, freer.

"Mr. Mata? Is that you?" voz queries from behind.

Turn round and cam a natural leggin up with outstretched hand. Hume got a light orange buzz cut, butterscotch dermis, and green eyes behind city-issued wifi visor. Also gearin gray, gender-neutral tunic over gray leggins of lo-town city employees, and stops two feet away.

Voz chats, "Kai Singh?" Hume nods head yeah. Hands shake. "Call me Laz."

"Laz Mata? As in, *the* Lázaro Mata from @Lazmatazz?" Cranial nods yeah.

"OMG. I've streamed all your posts! I was like your biggest follower until...oh...uh...oh. Oh no." Kai lifts hand to cover mouth. "I...I wasn't...I'm so sorry."

"No problema." Mouth, throat, lungs hale Soothe.

"Well, I'm still sorry. What a horrible thing to have to go through." Hume shakes head, like all sincere too, then goes on. "Well. Now, you're here consulting on a matter for Aquāsure Endeavors? Why don't we go to my office?"

So much for keepin shit mute? Kai turns and legs thru lobby into what usetabe main readin room but all partitioned into cubicles and offices now. Hang a right toward back of building, then a left until Kai opens a door and legs in. Four walls, desk, two large wifi screens, two chairs, holograms of mountains and rivers and like foreal trees on walls. Sit in chair in front of desk and wait for Kai to close door and sit too.

"Ok, now then," theythem chat, removin visor, "how can I help you?"

"Need some intel bout registerin droids and bots for carnsat."

"Registering androids and robots for the purposes of carnal satisfaction. That's easy enough. We'll just pull up the application page—"

"Hit pause. Not tryna register, just need like more data."

"Oh...right, of course," Kai chats, leanin back in chair. "Well, the registry exists so that DeveSec and corresponding authorities in the criminal justice system can keep track of hi- and lo-town residents who exhibit certain proclivities toward minors under the legal, statutory age of intimate or venereal congress, which you may be aware has recently been lowered to 15."

"So, 14 and under now."

"14 years, 11 months, 364 days. That's right. As you may access, scientific researchers have determined that pedophiles are no more responsible for their biological sexual urges than those of us with hetero-, homo-, a-, bi-, or pansexual ones. However, the expression of such urges by pedophiles remains socially abhorrent and legally prohibited. But since sex is a human need, and in many places a right, it is both torturous and cruel to force humanoids to go through their lives without any carnal satisfaction whatsoever, simply because their urges are socially abhorrent and legally prohibited. Hence—"

"Pedobots."

Kai nods cranial. "Androids and robots that simulate the proportions and aesthetics of minors below the legal, statutory age of intimate congress for the purposes of the carnal satisfaction of the abhorrent and prohibited urges of pedophiles. And as the DeveSec statute stipulates, any android or robot either intended for or capable of the carnal satisfaction of humanoids, whether natural or modified, must be registered and licensed through the Department of Erotic and Venereal Security. This includes all the original components of the aforementioned androids and/or robots, as well as any and all replacement parts....But all this information is readily available on the DeveSec cloudsite. Is there something else I can help you with?"

Mouth, throat, lungs hale Soothe. "But bots can be boosted, so what does registerin do?"

"The serial numbers and barcodes enable us to determine manufacturer and ownership, of course. But the primary purpose isn't theft prevention."

"It aint?"

"No, that's a common misconception, Laz. It's to maintain a registry of hi- and lo-town residents who exhibit those particular urges."

"Yeah? Why?"

"Ah," Kai chats, leanin forward, makin voz quiet, "it's what's known as a slippery slope. In many instances there is a fine line between engaging in licit intimate congress with a registered child-like robot and engaging in illicit intimate congress with an actual child."

"So if someone slips up—"

"Yes, quite literally." They straighten up, smilin. "If someone should slip up, as you say, and attempt to express their abhorrent and prohibited urges on an actual child, we already have a database of the most likely suspects to investigate. Because we simply cannot allow anyone to interfere with actual humanoid children in that way."

"So what if someone gets caught like not registerin a pedobot or a part of one or like havin a contraband kidroid or some shit?"

"Fines, confiscation, loss of registry privileges, 24/7 surveillance. It depends on the severity of the infraction."

"What if someone gets caught like disruptin a foreal kid?"

"Oh, many things can follow. Incarceration, public dissemination of violation, stripping of assets, behavior modification therapy, up to and including chemical castration, in the most extreme cases."

"Chemical castration?"

"Laz," Kai chats, foldin hands together on desk, "can I ask what your interest in all this is?"

Ignore query, chat on. "What if someone has a bot part that could go to a kidroid but they like can't chat for sure if it does?"

"Not registered?"

Shoulders shrug.

"No visible serial numbers, bar codes, QRs?"

Cranial shakes nah.

Kai leans back again, pressing index fingers to lips. "Well, in that instance, humever has the part or parts should turn them in to us."

"Why?"

"Two reasons, Laz. The first is that there still may be a

way to identify the part or parts, if they've been registered but the coding has been embedded on a molecular level. It's a newer protocol, very expensive, and almost impossible to spot without special equipment. But if they have that, the part or parts could still be properly registered and perfectly legal."

"How expensive?"

Kai vids over one shoulder then the other, even tho me and them still totally solo, then whispers, "Expensive enough that it wouldn't be worth the cost for someone from lo-town."

"Foreals?" Kai's eyebrows raise and head nods yeah. "So like only for mods?"

"Technically chatting, the process isn't restricted to modified humanoids, but practically chatting, in terms of cost, it's effectively limited to them. Mods prefer to have things of their own."

"Who don't?"

"Precisely."

Cranial nods. "What's reason number two?"

"Well, if the part or parts don't have molecularly embedded registration coding, then they are very likely contraband from underground pedobot and/or child trafficking markets."

"Hit pause. Child trafficking? What's that gotta do with anythin?"

"Slippery slope, Laz, rememory? The manufacture and trade in illegal kidroids and pedobots for carnal satisfaction intersect with the purchase and sale of actual children for the same purposes, especially in light of the trufact that the former are surrogates for the latter to begin with."

"Hume."

"Foreal. The narratives I hear from my colleagues in enforcement would give you nightmares. Well, maybe not you."

Nod cranial all slow, like takin everythin in, but catch mal sick feels again.

"But I know very little about that kind of fieldwork because my specialty is in statutes and regulations. I could link you to someone in enforcement, though, if you like."

"What bout experimental prototypes of like pedobot parts or whatevie?"

"All the same logic applies, that is, if they're intended for legal, regulated commerce. But they should be brought to us either way, too. Is there anything else I can help you with?"

Left holosleeve vibrates. Wordmessage icons: one from Felonious, one from Xenia. Heart fasts at second. "Nahin, thanks, Kai, serio. Giga helpful. But gotta take these." Stand up from seat.

"My pleasure," Kai chats, standin too and shakin hands. "But would you mind if I asked you a favor before you go?"

"What's on?"

"Can we take a selfie so I can post it to my stream?"

"Seguro."

10

utside, sit on steps and screen messages. One from Felonious screens *got a bite*. Text location, chat her to meet here. Message from Xenia screens *They want you to come to the Center*. Don't message Xenia back right away. Feel crazyass tempt feels to cam her IRL asap but nervous feels too. Don't access nada bout the Center or mods who gig there, and have like zero clue what they want, so not too perved to go. Cept to get with Xenia, course, but can't tactile her now anyway, whether havin wary feels bout goin or not.

Takes Felonious like 12 minutes to eBike from Jefferson Market Park to DeveSec. Hit grub truck on corner of 40th for fried cricket and avocado tacos with extra hot sauce and couple coconut milks then vid for bench to nom and chat at edge of Bryant Park, which is like maze of lean-tos and tarp tents, mini shanty town for humevie.

"A Ken snatched the decoy?" voz queries.

"Yeah, Laz. Fuckin hugeass Ken strolls into the park, straight line like right to the box, picks that shit up, spins round, and vacuates."

"What'd it vid like?"

"A fuckin Ken, nat. They all the same."

Trufact but also not trufact. Even same model cyborgs can have minor variations, like eye color, bald or hair, beard, mustache, breast bumps, gear, that kinda thing. But neurals wonderin if Ken Felonious viddied was actually Gibson from Zebb's last night. Can't be, tho.

"Nothin on the spycam?" she queries, chompin her wrap.

"Nada. Must not've opened it yet."

"Ken prolly takin it back to its commander. We might get lucky, get a selfie of a humanoid instead of a Ken."

"Yeah, could be a break." Nom some wrap, wash down with coconut milk.

Fel wipes mouth with napkin. "You mine any data in DeveSec?"

"Yeah." Fill her in bout convo with Kai, includin registry of potential perps, slippery slopes, molecularly embedded registration tech, underground pedobot and child traffickin rings.

"Pedobot and child traffickin?" sheher queries. "Nuh-uh, nat, this might be way too deep. If we find out who was trackin the crate, we should just probe if they want the merch. Then we sell it to them and get it off our hands before this shit gets too foreal."

Cranial nods. Felonious got a point. "Yeah, could get corpsethreat like that." Snap fingers. "Could also be dealin with registered parts, no big, just can't deem yet. If so, we just ID who owns biddy arms and gift em back."

"For a coindeep fee tho, right? Only sucker MCs would do somethin like that for free, Laz. Especially when those things could be worth like a shitton of coin."

"Intel. But we gotta gameplan all the angles, not just

cashin in. Model our exit strategy too."

"Ok, I gift you that. So what now?"

"Finish nomin then leg it to next spot."

"Where?"

"Few blocks. Vamos."

Main entrance to Kinkbot Storage and Sanitation's on 5th Ave between E50th and 51st, so me and Fel hang a left on 5th and footie up to 42nd Canal. Pedestrian drawbridge's up, so gotta wait till it closes to cross. 5 minutes, 10, standin there, chillin, viddin canal traffic: Skyffs and gondolas, water skis, kayaks, canoes, junks, rafts with outboards, handful of speed boats, couple small cargo barges. Bridge downs, and me and Fel footie thru valley of boarded up and burnt-out facades of what usetabe midtown shops, office buildings, cafes, restaurants and shit. All damaged or destroyed in pre-now narco epidemic where humes on this soma deemed spike or manic got crazy fucked up and went berserker rage on coindeep real estate. Never figured out why it made em rampage only high-value properties or why the area was never fixed after. SkyDecks above blank out most daylight, tho, so it's darker and cooler and like all eerie-quiet and shit here, like this part of town abandoned ruins, frozen in time.

While leggin, autoqueryin self when to chat Felonious bout virt-real with Sansve-Xenia and whether to voz her bout 121 with Zebb at all. Fel's all cancel-culture bout modifyin now and she been too amped to fence the arms and turn a quick coin from jump. Don't forecast how updatin her bout Xenia or Zebb gonna help either. Then again, she aint chatted nothin bout severin yet, so maybe me and her both just circlin in the early rounds, tryna feel each other out.

Like DeveSec building, Kinkbot Storage and Sanitation is mad pre-now, with stone steps, three arched entrances, two towers shootin up like tallass middle fingers with spires that poke thru SkyDeck 1, arched windows with stained glass in front and along sides, mammoth bronze doors, heavy stone masonry, concrete curlicues. Vids all dense and impenetrable from outside, like what pre-now architects hated more than anythin was natural light indoors. Her and me footie in, ask droidista in lobby for manager; droidista vozes hit pause. Felonious vids me with eyebrows all scrunched, like what we doin here?

"If we wanna mine data bout sexbots, no better place," voz chats.

"Yeah, but—"

"@Lazmatazz...that you?" Boomin voz cuts Felonious off. "I calced you woulda elevated by now, especially after that last disaster of a gig." Big voz loudin from even bigger nat. Delaney Samson, like 6'4," 290, cis-hume with chestnut epidermis, baldin cranial, short beard, mega arms, mega belly, mega ass and thighs and always gearin a sleeveless floral sundress and savior sandals. Light blue dress with red, orange, yellow daisies today. Kinda chill. "Come here, lil 'migo," Delaney chats, wrappin arms around upperbody and liftin me off ground.

"Allplus, Laz?" Felonious queries.

"Ye-ah," voz grunts, before hehim lets go.

"Pause," Delaney chats to Fel, "aint you Felonious Jones, 7th ranked IMA featherweight? Get the fuck! I'm a giga fan!" Delaney lunges at her, arms wide.

"Yeah, that's me, but we allplus, nat," she chats, fists up by face, backpedalin out of reach.

Delaney's loudass lol echoes from like every direction. "Chillado, but still perved to socmed you IRL."

Voz chats introductions. They bump fists.

"Now," Delaney vozes, turnin back to me, "to what do I owe this honor?"

"Need to mine some data on pedobots."

"Hmm. Never figured you the type, Laz. Calced you more of a milk-and-cookies hetero with some power-bottom-on-special-occasions kind of kink. But perv is perv, bruh, like the chat goes." His shoulders shrug. "Just need to verify your registration, and I'll post you some units."

Felonious lols.

"Nahin, hume, not for me. Just need some data."

"Oh, my mal. Why didn't you just voz so? C'mon, follow me. I'll give you a tour of the place, and me and you two can chat in my office."

Delaney turns and legs thru hi interior arches down longass hallway with three stories of storage units between a run of tall stone pillars. Luz ons in each section as we go, like rectangle of bright slidin thru tunnel dark at both ends. Delaney hits pause, rests hand on what vids like door of a vertical coffin.

"Each of these cabins pods a sexbot, which we rotate with those in the field." He leans down for retina scan, opens door. Inside is medium-height, medium-build bot with gender-neutral grill and no junk of like any kind. "What you into, Felonious?"

"Some of this, some of that," she chats, "depends."

Delaney's mouth smiles, postin perfect white dentals.

"Whatevie you're into, we'll hook it up. Just deem us what you want."

"That's all it takes?" she queries.

"For you, yeah," he chats, closin cabin. Then he turns and keeps goin.

"So what happens when the other bots get back from the field?" voz queries.

"First, we send nother one out, so that there are always bout 4500 operatin from this facility at any given time, maximize coin extraction."

"Hit pause. So there's like 4500 sexbots in the whole city?"

"No, Laz. There are 11 facilities of this size in lo-town alone, not countin the other boroughs."

"So...," Felonious maths, "bout 50 thousand sexbots down here?"

"49,500 to be exact, and we still can't keep up with demand."

"Seems like buku," voz chats.

Delaney shrugs. "No access. Alls I intel is that it's legal and keeps me in a decent coinin gig without pain biz."

"What happens to the bots when they get back here?"

"First we gotta clean them cause they are fuckin filthy. Piss, shit, blood, cum, snot, phlegm, spit, puke—both humanoid and animal—lube, melted wax, oils, lotions, alcohol, all kinda food and drink, makeup, paint—you nomer it, they got it on em."

"They don't clean after each client?" Felonious queries.

"Yeah. But between me and you, they can't get everything, so small amounts of whatevie build up over the course of a shift."

"Retch," Felonious chats.

Delaney nods cranial. "You could make em cleanse before you use em, but most humes don't tabulate that."

"That's like worse," she chats.

Delaney's mouth smiles again. "And these are the newer Tiresias models. You shoulda cammed the old ones." Hehis hugeass body shudders. "Anyway. When they get back here, we put em on a conveyor belt thru a disinfectin shower. There are multiple shower jets at multiple angles, so that gets most of the crud. Then they go under a blue light to cam what was missed, and droids clean and disinfect those areas. Then—"

"There's more?"

"Like I chatted, Laz, fuckin filthy. Then we gotta check out the orifices: orals, vadges, anals, urethras, nostrils, earholes—"

"Nostrils?" Felonious queries.

"Earholes?" voz queries at same time.

"Anywhere on a bot that can be fucked eventually gonnabe, and humes are into like everything you could sleepstream and more, so. Anyplace you can make a crevice, too: armpits, asscracks, under titties, space between a crooked chin and throat. But that's why you get a bot in the first place: do whatever the fuck you perv. Except damage em, cause then you gotta pay, and that costs. Anyway, the orifices are removable, esophagi too, so we just pop out the ones that need cleanin and soak them in a disinfectin bath, dry em up, pop em back in. Then they're done and they come up here."

"Up here?" voz chats.

"We clean them down in the sub-basements."

"Oh, ok. But what this gotta do with pedobots?"

Delaney stops, turns to face us. "Not much, tho they go thru the same process after use."

"Then why update us?"

"Just wanted to update you bout my gig. Got data bout yours."

"That how you socmed each other?" Fel queries.

Cranial nods yeah, while Delaney chats. "Yeah. bout five years ago? Aint that right, Laz? Your stream was just startin to blow up but wasn't full-on trendin yet, so you were still takin on natural clients."

"Sonics right."

"So what was the gig?"

"My kitty, Queen Cleocatra, got thyroid cancer. Hadta put her down. I wanted to be with her, but I...I just wouldn't be able to...," Delaney's voz quiets, chin drops to chest. "So, I outsourced it to Laz."

"What'd you simulstream, Laz?"

"Created a backdrop of tropical island sunset, set up a hammock in the pod, then lay in it, eyes closed, pettin a stuffed cat as sun sank, sky grew dark, and Delaney was puttin Queen Cleocatra down on splitstream."

"I rememory that one. That was crazy sadness," sheher chats.

"Got crazy hits and reposts, too, tho," Delaney chats. "That was one of your first big ones, wasn't it?"

Cranial nods. "Viraled."

"Was mad clout pub for this facility, too. Humes that screened your stream posed I wasn't just some soulcorpsed kinkpimp cause I was all broken up over my kitty, so they wanted to do biz with me. That got me started. I'll always owe you for both, Laz. My office is there"—he points at a door couple yards away—"but I wanna post you something first." He turns toward cabins, which are like half size at this end, bends way over to scan retina, opens door. Inside is a small bot, sweet grilled, obvi sposetabe young, no junk at all like the other one we cammed. "This is a pedobot, age range 8 to 11. Like regular sexbots, we can fix up the junk anyway you perv it."

Thing is mad foul retch. Meme of biddy arms streams in neurals, vibe feels like stomach gonna spill fried cricket and avocado taco all over everywhere. Turn away, mouth, throat, lungs hale Soothe.

"That is no fuckin bueno," Felonious chats.

"You allplus, Laz?" Delaney queries.

"Símon. Necesito a sec." Turn back, scope closer. Arms vid maybe little longer than ones in crate, maybe not, and fleshtone on this bot is more like light gray or even pink gray than blue gray. Bend closer, tactile epidermis is like more rubberier too. "Lemme get a selfie?"

"Go ahead."

Finger taps right holosleeve for digiscan. "Where's the registration?"

"This one has light-spectrum codin," Delaney chats, before vozing, "pink light on." Rose-colored luz ons in cabin, barcodes appear in dark red lines like all over pedobot.

"Savage," Felonious chats.

"New tech. Meth, right?" Delaney chats back. "C'mon, let's sit in my office."

Delaney's office prolly tidiest place ever? Not only nada out of place, but basically like nada in it, cept for desk, three chairs, framed pics of maybe like fam or cohorts, some cats, and trendin IMA fighters on walls. One is Felonious. Me, Fel, And Delaney sit.

"You foreals are a fan," she chats, spyin her selfie.

"I wouldn't fakechat bout something like that. Your fight against Vankatanaram was the most carnage I cammed in a long time. That crescent kick you ended it with? Damn. Surprised you paused your career."

"I got reasons."

"Didn't chat you don't. Just wish you hadn't, is all. Your backfist-knee thrust combo is extreme havoc."

"Fel...Fel? You blushin?"

"Cállate, Laz."

Delaney turns face my way and queries, "So what's on?"

Voz that viddin into pedobot registration for friend of a friend kinda thing and already chatted with someone at DeveSec. Never scoped a foreal one, tho, so came to him.

"Jacked to assist. They tell you why there's a registry at DeveSec?"

Cranial nods yeah. "Bout new molecular codin, too."

"Heard bout that, but haven't cammed any bots that got it yet. That kinda tech is way 2buku for regular street-walkin hourlies like these. Most advanced stuff we got is the light-spectrum codin I just posted you, totally undetectable in the visual spectrum."

"If everyone intels that pedobots and their users are registered, why make the codin invisible?" Felonious queries. "Doesn't total."

"It does, though, Felonious...if I can voz you that," Delaney chats.

"Shit, nat, course. You got a selfie of me on your wall. We already BFFs."

Delaney smiles again, big. "Pedobots are already bout the fantasy of what pedophiles can't have, which is foreal kids. Visual reminders of registration disrupt that fantasy for lots of em, so kidbot erectors tryta downlow evidence of fabrication and registration as much as possible. The better they do that, the more popular their models."

"That calcs," voz chats. "Tryna be as foreal as possible."

"Yeah, that's one reason. The other is that a lot of the hardcore pedofucks don't wanna be registered in the first place. Your nomer goes on a list, and that list aint zactly public, but it's posted to all different enforcement agencies and city services. So if a foreal kid gets disrupted—"

"They access where to start queryin," Fel chats.

"Right," Delaney chats, noddin. "But there are lots of coindeep mods on that list, like off-the-charts coindeep. We're chatting 5th, 6th SkyDecks—"

"Daaamn," Fel vozes.

Zebb's estate pops into neurals.

Delaney continues, "And they don't want their biz accessed by anyone."

"Why not?" voz queries.

"Cause they better than us, Laz. They're more 'evolved,' is what they deem it, and they don't want some less-evolved pissant natural fuckers like us tellin em what they can or can't do. It's their world, hume. Me and you just taking up air and space. In fact, some of em are tryna get rid of registration altogether."

"Where you mine that data?" voz queries. "That shit aint streamin on N-Net."

"Alt-info posts, dark-net screens, shit's everywhere. N-Net is for dick, just censored fake newsads."

"Delaney, if they get rid of the registry, what bout the kids?" Felonious queries.

"Well, the kids—natural kids, btw—would basically be unprotected from kidfuckers, and especially mod kidfuckers."

"Fuckin mofus," Fel chats, eyein me.

"Yeah, they don't give a shit. They don't give a shit bout kids or any nats at all. Not a single one, unless we're useful in some way. Then they'll use us up and toss our ass. That's why I stay as far away from those mofus as I can."

Fel's eyes gleam all weird. "Hit pause, Delaney. You're not gonna modify?"

"Nah. Can't. Defective," he chats. "Tried once. Didn't take. Not tryin again. Natural to the end."

"So's Laz. He just doesn't wanna admit it."

Cut eyes at Fel.

"What bout you?" Delaney queries.

"I'm severin."

"No. Foreal?"

Felonious nods head. "That's why I paused IMA."

"Why?

"Cause I don't wannabe a part of a system where depravedass mofus can do whatevie depravedass shit they wanna do just cause they stack more coin than the rest of us. That's just deadass wrong. You ever modeled it, goin Alt? You got neurals and heart, and that's what we need."

Delaney lols again. "Nah, I haven't. But if you're asking, maybe I will."

"It don't work like that."

"What you meme?"

"It's not bout me or you, or any three or four or ten of us," she chats. "It's bout somethin bigger. When you want to access more, hit me up."

"So you're giftin me the deets? Vibes like I owe you for that too, Laz."

Me and Felonious footie up 5th Ave to Park, close to SkyDeck uplink from last night, to a bar on 15th floor of what usetabe Plaza Hotel. Seat by windows with view of pond and order rums, sonicin suave salsa muzak in background and waitin to cam if anyhume opens decoy crate and gets selfied on spycam. 30 blocks north, 135 stories above, Olen Zebb prolly hoverin in his estate, viddin down on Central Park like some pre-now deity.

"So, what was all that with Delaney?" voz queries.

"Bout severin? I'm recruitin, Laz, I vozed you that. But you don't wanna access anythin bout it, do you?"

"Why you chat that?"

"You vozed Alt's a corpse cult, everybody there's brainwashed, rememory?"

"Well?"

"That's what I meme. If you aint gonna sonic, why should I waste my—"

"Ok, tranquila. Just voz me. I'll sonic, promise."

Felonious pauses, like collatin for a sec. "It's like Delaney chatted. Mods pose they're better, more evolved than nats. They don't give a shit bout us unless we can do somethin for em. And once that thing's done, well."

"Non-newsads. And mods *are* way more nextlevel than nats, Fel. That's mad obvi. Smarter, stronger, healthier, live longer—that's like the whole thing of modification?"

"Nah, Laz. That's just what they want us to *creed* bout modification. Yeah, they might have it better on some things, have some advantages and shit, but mods are still humanoids like us, *natural* humanoids, and humanoids are all the same. That's the first lesson you learn at Alt."

"If we're all the same, then why they live in hi-town and we don't? And why naturals only ones corpsin out?"

"We're not corpsin out."

"What? Stop gamin. What bout birth rate collapse, demographic cliff...fuckin doomtimes and shit?"

"Ok, partial trufacts. But there aint no doomtimes tho. Nats just don't reproduce enough to maintain our numbers. You intel why that is?"

"Nah. Why?"

"Cause mods aren't born, they're invented through modification, Laz, and every time a natural modifies, there's one more of them and one less of us. We've been losin thousands of naturals to modification every year since it began, prolly more. Our birth rate would haveta be gangbang high 24/7 to make up the diff, but it's negative, so. That's why everyone's always chattin we're corpsin out. But it's more like we just optin out."

"Mas like optin *up*."

"You foreal drank every drop of their Kool Aid, didn't you? What you got against being a natural, Laz?"

"Serio, Fel? Lo-life is malstupidhard as fuck, like every bit of it. Pain surrogacy gigs havin us feel misery feels all day just to stack some coin, plasma deposits leavin humes sucked dry, drained, socmed subscription enforcement keeps us postin and cloudstreamin hours after giggin or gotta click giga fines, not nuff pods to pod in, like zero wellcare, pollution everywhere, climate change, floodin, population collapse, pandemics out the anal, constant stresziety, nada to hope for but hi-life, which you gotta stack buku coin and modify to get. Then...then you lose everyhume, cause when you modify, you elevate, fade, ghost. That's what I got against bein natural, Fel, lo-life is total bullshit, and everyhume loads it."

Felonious pouts lips, shakin cranial. "Nah, Laz, the *structure* of lo-life's bullshit. That's got nothin to do with bein a natural. There's a difference. That's like the second thing you learn at Alt, if you don't access it already."

Face frowns. "Ok, but long as nats gotta live lo-life, basically same shit."

"But not for you tho, right? You rollin like a CEO. Usetabe mad clout trendin, stackin up all that coin, duplex pod on 24th, 25th floors, got an iHOST, drinkin foreal coffee in the mornin, rockin that mod gear...how can you be hatin on lo-life when you got it so fuck made?"

"Don't meme shit without Sansve."

"Chill dodge, but still? I aint tryna harsh, Laz, but you gotta put that shit behind you, if only for your own good."

Hale Soothe then chat, "She messaged me."

"What?"

"Virt-realed."

"Hit pause. So she made it foreals? She's ok?"

"Kinda. Got Sower syndrome—"

"The sympathy disorder?"

"Empathy, but yeah. So she's in a center while they

tryta desensitize or resensitize her or whatevie."

"How long that take?"

Shoulders shrug.

"When'd she virt-real you?"

"Yesterday. Messaged earlier."

"Sansve messaged you *today*?"

"Xenia. Nomered Xenia now. But yeah. They want me to uplink to Center."

"What for?"

"No intel, but Xenia calcs they might be able to help—"

"Help? Help what? Help you modify?"

Rum rum, take in view for a sec, nod cranial.

"Aw, c'mon, Laz. You need to be done with that bullshit. What is the statistical likelihood that a natural successfully modifies after a protocol rejection?"

"Bout 1.63 percent."

"That's not even two nats out of a hundred. But you meme that's gonnabe you?"

"Nextgen hypoallergenic protocol—"

"Nuh-uh, not sonicin," Fel chats, puttin right hand up. "You gonna piss away 30 million ones on some shit that basically don't have no chance of goin down, and you got the huevos to chat that Alt humes are brainwashed? Shit, chico."

"Gotta try, Fel."

"No, you don't. You don't gotta do nothin, specially not that. What you should do is delete all that mess from your cranial and go Alt with me."

"Chillada. What's on with you and that shit? They got like revenge porn on you or what?"

Fel's mouth quivers at edges then works slow into a smile, and she lols. "You're a fuckin clownbot, bruh, you intel that, right?" She sips rum, goes on. "NatAlt is an autonomous collective of natural humanoids, a collaboration in essential living solutions."

"What?"

"It's a co-op focused on thrivin as a community rather than the pursuit of individual accumulation, consumption, and modification."

"Sonics lameass. How's that sposeta be better?"

"No pain biz gigs, for one, no coinstackin, no modifyin, no socmedin—"

"You humes travel back to cave times? How you manage that?"

"Simple, just unplug, nat, get the eff offline. That's why they call it severin, cause that's what you do, cut the cord."

Rum rum. "That's it?"

Felonious shakes cranial, vids out at park. "Few months ago both me and you woulda been here selfiein shit, postin to stream, checkin messages and notifications nonstop, scrollin, swipin, the whole nine. But I been offline and you been webmute for a few months, and what are we doin?"

"Nada. Just chattin."

"Right. It's like that." She finishes rum and taps glass on table, three, four times. "It's not that easy, course. Everyhume's gotta get vetted before they pledge and then it takes time to adjust to their way of doin things, get all this onlined poison out your system. But once you're in, you're in for good. The vibe is mad chiller than you'd expect, and nats foreal seem to vibe happier feels there."

"You're not in?"

"Not all the way yet," she chats, shakin cranial, "kinda

like one footie in, one out."

"That why they got you recruitin?"

She nods. "That, and cause I got a profile, lotsa fans, followers, streamers, like you, Laz. Humes socmed us, and brand recognition clouts Alt's mission. You should simulate joinin."

"Not cierto, Fel. Feel feels like I gotta try this first, least once more."

"All right, but that's on you. If that doesn't come thru, tho, you access where to find me." Sheher grabs my right wrist, checks time on holosleeve. "How long we sposeta wait for the spycam to poweron anyway?"

"No intel."

"Ping it."

Tap holosleeve, open spycam app, ping. Error message: not responding.

"Scope this," voz chats, postin message to Fel.

"Outta range?"

Cranial shakes nah. "Satlinked."

"Defective?"

"Maybe. Or humever Ken brought the decoy to accessed it wasn't the foreal crate, and destroyed it with spycam inside."

"Dead end?"

"Maybe, but no data tho." Down rum, right holosleeve vibrates with ping from Victor.

"Who's that?" Fel queries.

"Victor. He chats come down."

"Let's out."

12

Grab eScooters at Central Park stand, scoot south under end of SkyDeck on 3rd to Tompkins Square Dock, drop em off there, in light drizzle. Tide comin in, so gotta leg to Victor E's from northwest on E6th. Inside, Victor's behind counter, screenin streams of newsads on far wall.

"What's on, Vic?" voz chats.

"More fuckin migrants crowdin the border," he chats, pointin and shakin cranial at screen.

"Where they from?"

"Displaced from some shithole corpo-nation." He shrugs. "But the temp tent-city pods they shelter in are sickass. Scope this docu-ad—"

"Fakefacts, nat, those tent cities are total feke streams," Felonious chats.

Victor's head whips round. "Oh, shit, *the* Felonious Jones. Didn't intel you were with Laz. 'Son, yeoja? Haven't cammed your ass since you turned pro. How you been?" Victor legs round counter, bumps fist with Fel, wraps her in a hug.

She shrugs all chill. "Like ever, Vic."

"Sekushi as ever too, chica," he chats, mouth smilin.

"You're just never gonna give that up, are you? Not even a couple of hours, like six years ago? Biggest mistake of my life. Just let it go."

"Always hold onto the good things, no matter how small. Halmeoni taught me that."

"Bruh, you meme *großmutter* not *halmeoni*. Oma Ingrid? Rememory? Useta bake us strudel and shit when we was like tweens? Prolly never even cammed kimchi in her whole damn life. You gotta get your shit corrected, Vic."

Victor's eyes, face, whole body hits pause for bout 4 seconds, like he giflooped or sodukoed. Then he reanimates, legs back behind counter, bends over for rum and glasses. "Serio, though, Fel, savage to cam you. Let's celebrate." His hands pour three glasses of rum.

"Nuh-uh," Fel chats, "vozed you I was never gonna rum with you again."

"Just one. Laz's here to surveil. Old times?"

"Alright. One." We all dip left index finger in glass, flick out drop for "ancestors," drink.

"So what'd you ping for?" voz queries.

"Promise not to get all raged first—"

"Why? What'd you do?"

"I kinda may have, like, inspected one of the arms?"

"How? Crate was locked."

"Pfff," Vic flaps lips, "took like four seconds to hack that weakass shit."

"You didn't calc he'd do that?" Fel queries me.

Pulse poundin in cranial. Mouth, throat, lungs hale Soothe. Harsh sigh exhale.

"Sorry, Laz. Just too fuck curious. They're all secure, tho, no worries. Plus, I found a couple things."

"Like what?" Fel queries.

Victor throws hand signals at screen on far wall and stream of docu-ad shifts to digiscan of biddy arm.

"You scanned it too? Gotta delete that, Vic—"

"Tranquilo, Laz, gonna. But like first tho"—he spreads fingers on right hand to enlarge image to fit screen—"searched whole thing for UPCs, QRs, serial numbers...nothin. So, removed a micro section of the dermis—"

"You *cut* it too? Nat, that is so fuck—"

"Chill, Laz. 30 microns, width of a hair. Nobody's ever gonna cam it's gone. Image up there is michin magnified."

"Still, Vic, thing's not yours. What gifted you the—"

"Laz," Fel chats, "done is done. Let him finish or we'll be here all night."

Eyes hurtglare at Victor. Mouth, throat, lungs hale Soothe.

"Thanks, Fel. So, yeah, at like bigdick magnification you start to cam these marks on some individual cells."

"They vid like mini glyphs," Fel chats.

"Right?"

"What are they?" voz queries.

"Data, info, whatevie." His shoulders shrug.

"Registration info?"

"Could be, why?"

"Accessed at DeveSec there's a new kinda registration codin for pedobots at molecular level, buku expensive, like almost undetectable without special tech," voz chats.

"Could be that, but no intel."

"Why not?"

"These microglyphs are blockchain encrypted, private platform. Can't hack or mine any data or info from em at all."

"So what you calc's on with that?" Fel queries, leggin up close to screen.

"Well, if what Laz just chatted is trufacts, could be that the arms got the new registration codin and are golden legit. So like humever erected em will be feelin all kinda generous happy feels to get em back cause there's like buku innovative shit on em. Maybe even gift a reward—"

"Hit pause. What you meme buku innovative shit?" voz queries.

"That's the other thing."

"What?"

"I cammed manh-i vat- and simskin over the years giggin on cyborgs, body alts, prosthetics, like...buku."

"And?" Fel queries.

"Never cammed any like this before. Scope." Hand waves two different images onto screen. "Top view and side view near coupling magnified. What you cam?"

"Toss the suspense, Victor, just update us," Fel chats.

"Ok, ok. On the top view, to the left, cam those tiny divots?"

"Yeah," voz chats, "what are they?"

"Hair follicles with tiny biddy hairs in em, like barely stickin out yet. And the side view at the coupling to the right—"

"Yeah," Fel chats.

"Cam how thick the skin is?"

"No."

"Well, it's not just epidermis like cyborg's got, it's full-on dermis too, with like sweat glands and sebaceous glands, adipose tissue—"

"So?" Fel cuts in again.

"So all that is michin crazy extra? Cyborgs and bots with simskin have epidermis with capillaries to fuel and cleanse their cells, but no underlyin dermis, no hair follicles or oil or sweat glands. All their biofunctionalities are internally regulated by AI CPUs, so they don't need em."

"No sweat, no tears, no oily spots—"

"Right, Laz, that's why cyborg skin vids kinda like chalky and dull—"

"Alright, so the skin on the biddy arms is different from regular cyborg simskin, so what?" Fel queries.

"So what? None of that fecal serves any purpose."

"What?"

"For simskin all that shit is extra, surplus—"

"It doesn't serve a purpose?" voz queries.

"Nahin, other than someone went to mad munje as fuck to invent this shit to be foreals as possible. It vids more like humanoid skin than anything else."

"So both microglyphs and skin are new tech?" voz chats.

"Vids like it." Vic nods.

"And last time you chatted limbs vid mad humanoid, too," voz chats.

"But if they're for pedobots, they're sposetabe foreal as possible, right, so no bigs," Fel chats.

"Yeah, vibe the fantasy. But these are so way nextlevel, Fel," Victor chats, "like two, three iterations up from the tippity top that's out there. And if that's a trufact, then that crate worths a fortune."

Edgy feels squeeze tops of shoulders and back. Kinda don't wanna load what's next. Mouth, throat, lungs hale Soothe. Exhale. Voz queries anyway, "How much?"

"Got 16 arms in there, right buyer, right market—"

"How much?" voz requeries.

"20 to 25 million—"

"For one crate of pedobot arms?" Fel queries. "Damn, that is some serious coinage."

"Nahin, Fel," Vic chats, "not for the crate...for a *pair*. Bots need two arms, so doubt we could sell em one at a time anyway. No, 8 pairs, up to 25 mill per. Game it right, we're viddin at 200 million ones."

Fel's mouth drops open.

Catch feels like stomach plummetin thru floor. Mouth, throat, lungs hale Soothe. "Shit," voz quiet chats.

"What's glitched, Laz? I calced you'd totally hardon the intel. And—"

"And what?"

"I can prolly source a buyer. Haveta troll dark-net, ping some sketchers and randos for leads, but—"

"No. No fuck way. Serio. No intel what we're dealin with. Tryta flip the crate with all it worths could get us all corpsed pronto. Too dangerous."

Matte black fingers of Victor's right hand twist his goatee. "How do I access you're not just chattin that, cuttin me out of a deal?"

"Cuttin you out? Who the fuck cut you in?" Fel queries. "All you done is go behind Laz's back—"

"And mine data that you wouldnta cached without me."

"Yeah, but—" voz starts, but Vic disrupts back in.

"You can store em here in the vault, too. It's michin secure, take like a legit mercenary crew to bust in. Keepin the merch safe until we simulate the next move def worths a cut."

"I don't like it," Fel chats, "how we intel we can trust

him?"

"He's right, tho, Fel. This prolly safest place for em."

"Yeah, if they're safe from *him*."

"Still right here," Victor chats, "haven't gone nowhere."

"But Fel's right, too, Vic. How we gonna trust you?"

"Easies, Laz. Vid round. Theft protection tech all over the joint. Slap a tracker on the crate and a motion detector on the lid, hook those up to apps that'll notify you on your DriTech. If the crate moves, or if someone opens the lid after me and you lock it again, data's transmitted to you. So you don't haveta trust me, hume. Trust technology."

"But how do we access you won't hack that tech like you hacked the crate?" Fel queries.

"Yeah?"

"Cause if I do," Vic chats, lips workin to a grin, "then I gotta deal with you. Aint that right, Fel?"

"Damn straight, Victor, but your ass will not be grinnin when I'm thru with you. You get me?"

He nods cranial. "Comprendo. So? Deal?"

Cranial nods. "Yeah, deal." Slap five, pull him in for a hug. Him and Felonious do same.

Victor takes tracker and motion detector from beneath counter, then Vic, Fel, and me all leg downstairs to vault. His right hand punches code into keypad next to thick aluminiron door, keypad transmits passcode to one of his microsofts, right hand punches in second code, followed by voz and retina scans. Luz ons as soon as we footie inside. Crate's right there, rest of room fades dark.

"Previous owners were mad paranoid bout their merch, so they had this storage vault kitted out with metal walls, ceilings, floors, laser motion sensors and silent alarms and shit, way back when biz was killin it." Victor sticks tracker to crate, motion detector on lid. "Final layer of protection, on the house, migo." His left hand pulls mini spycam out of coveralls, attaches it with silicone adhesive to wall next to crate, aims it downward. "But even without all this extra, this is still one of the securest vaults around. So we're allplus."

Left holosleeve downloads apps, right hand enters registration info. "Just don't erect shit like they useta, right?" voz chats, while runnin setups. Victor lols. Holosleeve beeps. "That's it, we're on."

"Don't make us regret this," Felonious chats, pointin at Victor.

"Jeoldae, never," he chats back, as me and her out.

13

Squallin winds on crowded hoverferry back to pod, makin like mal turbulence and tossin everyhume round on deck. Big gust chucks two randos dazefacin their smarties starboard side into each other. They vid up, glarin. One quick-slaps the smartie out the other's hand, sendin it sailin over the rail. Other turns and just dives after it, like not calcin at all, like he's gonna catch it or some shit. First one already has smartie aimed overboard at wet, selfiein second one splash in, then turns, fingers workin to post to stream, then vids up grinnin, all chillado, like nothin happened. Some other humes doin same.

Catch sad heavy feels in chest again, weight pullin down, not cierto why. Mouth, throat, lungs hale Soothe. "You cam that?" voz queries Fel.

"Yeah. That's what it memes to internalize the systems that oppress us."

"Huh?"

"Those nats got no semiote what's actually harmin them or what foreal's goin on, so they lash out at each other. Pathetic, but calculates tho."

"They teach you that at Alt, too?"

"Matter of trufacts, they did. But let me query you somethin, Laz," Felonious chats, viddin at me.

"What's on?"

"Why don't you voz what's foreal on with this gig?"

"You already intel—"

"No, I don't intel shit and whatever I do intel don't add up. I don't even access who you sposetabe giggin for."

"Sposeta keep it mute."

"Bout time you recalc that, nat."

"Why?"

"*Why*? Cause someone tried to B&E your pod, the fridge-crate had a tracker hid on it, and now we intel that the biddy arms, which may or may not be legit, could worth 200 mill? That's like what, 20 normcore modification protocols?"

"More like 16.667 for most basic normcore protocols, no upgrades."

"You just full of crucial info, aint you?" Fel pauses, fingertips massagin temples. "All that static goin on and you aint hit pause to process that some hume or humes could be settin you up?"

"Settin me up for what, tho?" Right holosleeve vibrates. Hold finger up to disrupt Fel before she chats. Facescreen icon, Mo Swag. "Gotta take this, gimme a sec."

Shoulders push thru pasty couple in zombie cos, clouded eyes, rottin epidermals, dirty, shredded gear, as footie toward rail. Tap holoscreen to reply. "Yo, Mo Swag, what's on?"

"Why don't you chat me what the fuck's on, motherfucker," his voz growls, hurty white dentals blazin thru nasty snarl.

"Wha—"

"Don't game me, natural. You calc I'm some kinda subnorm?"

"Mo—"

"Nahin, Laz. I gift you this toxic gig, upfront you a shit-ton of ones, then I gotta troll your gamma ass around for intel? That's bullshit. Are you even giggin on this? Are you queryin humes like you're sposed to? You mined any data at all?"

"Course, mod. Chillar. Was gonna update you back at the pod. On the way now, but lotsa humes round, so not secure to chat."

Mo Swag's nut-brown MelanInked cheeks red, head shakin. "Do you even have the fuckin crate anymore, Laz?"

"Course. Why wouldn't—"

"Where?"

"Secure location, no worries."

"Not worried. Wanna fuckin cam em."

"Hit pause a sec." Video-off facescreen app, open spycam app on left holosleeve, video-on Mo Swag on right, hold both holos up so he can cam.

"Fuck is that?"

"Crate, mod, biddy arms inside, spycam feed. Locked up, secure, safe and sound."

"Where?"

"Can't voz now, too many humes, like I chatted. Gonna update back at the pod."

"Let's get something straight, Laz. I'm CEO on this. You gig for *me*. I program what to do, and you execute, not the other way. Intel?"

"Cierto, sure, mod, sure," voz chats, calcin Zebb might vibe that a bit different.

"Don't keep me waitin for updates and do not fuck

with me, Laz. You won't hardon what happens if you do. Out," Mo Swag chats as facescreen closes.

"Who was that?" Fel queries, as hoverferry docks at Yards Landing.

Make motion for her to come on, then footie down gangplank, cross courtyard, and thru voz and retina scans at security to enter shops. Inside, what usetabe cavernous luxe mall's all morgue-ass quiet, mostly closed up and empty, only like maybe a few humes here and there. Entry restricted to long-term podshares in Yards compound buildings and guests, to keep podfree nats from squattin, either on temp or perma basis. Leg past security droidista to stairs, which usetabe auto-electric things nomered escalators, so you could just glide up floor to floor and not haveta footie your ass all the way off.

Fourth level, ditch stairs and leg into resto with westward view. Seat by window, viddin at magenta-blue-charcoal of settin sun with Hudson River and Jersey in background and Hive in fore. Hive usetabe nomered Vessel pre-now before sealed inside and out with 5mm polyurethane wrap, so humes couldn't jump off and self-corpse no more, which useta happen on the regular back then. Now landings, stairways, platforms all enclosed. It's like this unregulated flop for podfrees and scroungers. Strong winds slam and rattle exterior wrap, makin it sonic like loudass drums.

"What we doin here?" Fel queries, settlin back in chair.

"Gettin hangry, let's nom."

Her shoulders shrug. "Long as it's on you."

"Welcome back, Mr. Mata," droidista chats, arrivin at table, "it's always a pleasure to have you join us again."

"Two regulars," voz chats, "and two cervezas." Droidista turns, legs off.

"How did it...?" Felonious starts.

"Security scan downstairs transmitted ID. Nom here lots."

"In this mausoleum? Shit, Laz, you must be glitched foreal, come to a place like this." She pauses, viddyin round, then continues. "Alright, so...?"

Beers drone to table. Salud, clink bottles, then splain bout Jeffords/Mo Swag to Felonious: how he modified on credit, gigs in seawallin, gifted me arms gig, been trollin via message, prolly planted tracker on fridge-crate, can't stop queryin bout its location, gettin crazy aggro and bossy and mad dickish and shit. Everythin cept skimmin 10 mill cause can't chat that without tabbin Zebb. That's personal biz, tho. Zebb could be ticket up and away, so still wanna keep him muted for now.

"I rememory Jeffords. Never BFFed that nat, tho."

"Why not?"

"Fullon weirdfuck creeper. Always mackin silly hard on the youngest chica or femmish theyself in the room. I cammed him pull some that did not viddy even a little bit close to legal, so I soc distanced him."

"Mod's worse now that they lowered age."

Drone brings grub, sets on table. Heapin plates of pulled BBQ rabbit wraps, white bean and roasted garlic mash, sauteed kale with sliced cucumber and cherry tomatoes. Felonious vids down at plate, then up at me, biggin her eyes.

"This's your regular order?"

Cranial nods, teeth munchin wrap.

"So fuck wasteful."

"Mmm?" voz queries, mouth full, chewin.

"All this grub? That view? Just so like a few humes can shop and nom? Foreal, this whole place's just a mad toss of space and resources when you got nats right outside that door, nowhere to pod, nothin to grub, nothin but pain biz to stack coin, exposed to elements, mod patrols, everthin...."

Swallow, wipe mouth with napkin. "Just normcore day-to-day."

"Maybe. But what are you doin bout it?"

Eyes vid down at courtyard and Hive, then back up to Felonious. Feel chill hollow feels, scared, desperate, alone, like sadfeels of everyhume outside somehow seepin in thru the glass. "Been down there and been up here, Fel, you access that."

"Yeah, so?"

"Better here."

"That's not an answer," she chats, corners of eyes and lips tightenin.

"Just doin what every other hume does."

"And what's that?"

"Doin me."

"That me-ist bullshit's exactly why we're all fucked. Shit's stupid crazy sad."

"Lo-life's stupid crazy sad, Fel, not my mal." Shoulders shrug. "Sad to waste that grub tho, too. That'd be on you. You gonna nom it or what?"

"Fuck you, Laz." Couple minutes later Felonious finally

unpouts face, unfolds arms, digs in. Finish nommin in silence.

"So what we gonna do bout Mo Swag?" voz chats, after orderin two strong teas from droidista.

"You calc he's pullin all this shady shit?"

"Vibes like it."

Fel leans back in chair, lacin fingers behind cranial, viddin all self-satisfied and whatevie. "Vozed you not to trust that mofu from jump, didn't I?"

"Stop gamin. You didn't even intel it was him."

"Doesn't matter. Still can't trust no modfuck. They're other and they give negative shits bout us." Drones take empty plates and bottles and bring teas. "So what you calc he's up to?"

Bout 10 million so far, but don't voz that. "No intel. Gotta mine that data, tho."

"Let's surveil him. Stead of him tryna track the crate or track you or whatevie, we track him. Find out where he goes, who he cams, chats to, all that."

Cranial nods yeah. "Gotta be you, tho, cosed up. I'm sposetabe minin data. He'd facerec me mad fast trollin him, anyway."

Fel's head nods too. "I got somethin to gear so he can't ID me. But sonics like he's fadin hard, so prolly wouldn't anyway."

"Chillado. What you gonna do when he uplinks to hi-town, tho? Can't surveil up—"

"Laz, you ok?" Felonious pauses, mouth grinnin. "Almost vids like your neurals birthed a meme for once."

"Lmao." Blow on tea, take sip. "Might have a way to uplink."

"How?"

"Xenia."

"The center where Xenia is? C'mon, nat. They're all modfucks, too. You can't trust none of em, not even her."

"Maybe. Gonna haveta try, tho."

Footie back cross courtyard to pod, carryin jumpie Felonious borrowed but ungeared in resto bathroom. She gonna chill with Riz for a few, then head back to Alt for the night. Voz and retina scans at security check outside, elevator to 25th floor, scans again at pod door. Before door opens, Paz messages enter quiet, so tiptoe. Inside, sonic latest toddler pop megahit over sound system and cam lights and movin shadows in sit area. Leg thru grub area, peep round corner, cam Lucha in purple octopus cos, stompin forward, legs wide like Sumo wrestler, toward a tripodded smartie selfiein her, then backward same way, clappin hands together, startin over. Paz messages again: *Don't disturb Lucha, she is recording a ReRe dance.* Reply thumbsup emoji to Paz and back up into grub area, but don't load how what Lucha's doin totals as dance.

Grab bottle of fermented tea, seat at table, scroll thru messages on holosleeve till hit Xenia's from earlier. Message back *sry bzy b4 lets hook it up!* Open tea, sip some, wait. While waitin, start processin what Fel was chattin on hoverferry bout some hume maybe tryna set me up. Def a possibility now we access that crate contents could worth way 2buku coin. And cause Mo Swag has lied like at least twice, seems to load that arms moved but can't access where, and is actin crazy mad other and totally meangirlz, mod could be the one tryna do the settin. But for what tho? Still no data.

Cam somethin comin up fast from corner of right eye and startle out of memestream. Just Lucha with purple tentacles wavin round, her cheeks pink-red, glistenin with sweat, breathin heavy, mouth formin happy smile. Facescreen posts *done*.

"Ok—"

Luz ons in grub area. Sound system chats: "HIRO—affordable podspas and self-care experiences to soothe the streszieties of normcore day-to-day. Be a HIRO: put yourself first!"

Paz powerons in soft orange glow. "Hello, Lázaro, welcome home."

"Hey, Paz."

"It is my duty to inform you that it has been 106 days since you last logged into your MyFace all-access account and posted—"

"Foreal?"

"—by having agreed to the Terms and Conditions of Service, you will owe 20,000 ones in subscription suspension fees by the end of this month."

"You gotta do this every time now?"

"Yes, it is part of my programming. But for only 1000 more ones a month, you can unlock access to iHOST Premium+. As part of the iHOST Premium+ package, I will fulfill your social media obligations automatically, including screening, messaging, glyphing, reglyphing, posting to stream, all meme, gif, and content creation, likes, follows, shares, and so on, in accordance with your personalized social media profile algorithm while also maintaining consistency with your social media brand-identity and communication style. This, of course, will render recurrent notifications of failure to comply with the Terms and Conditions of Service and late fees obsolete. And if you act now, Laz, by entering an 18-month agreement, MyFace will waive the fines you have accrued to date."

"Hit pause," voz chats, neurals mathin, "so instead of clickin 20 grand in fines now and gettin nothin but access back, just click 18 grand more ones over next year and a half, get access again *and* Premium+ too?"

"That is correct."

"And you get off my back?"

"Yes."

"Bargain. Click it."

"Retina scan for payment authorization." Footie to scanner by door; scanner scans retina. "Authorization complete. You are now upgraded to iHOST Premium+...welcome to the experience of +ness."

"Yeah, thanks, Paz." Eyes vid over to Lucha. "She like this with you?"

No, facescreen messages, *Paz be like killa nice.*

"Kid likes you," voz chats.

"I am aware of that. Lucha and I have exchanged various forms of communication all day. She is an advanced coder and game designer for her age, so we have had many things to discuss."

"Foreals?"

"Yes. Her game is simple but engrossing, and it is gaining in popularity."

"Chillado."

"Would you like me to tell you about it?"

"Maybe later." Turn back to Lucha. "Hungry?"

Lucha shakes head nah, messages *no nommed b4.*

"Ok. So what you wanna do?"

Game.

"Go head."

Laz....

"What's on?"

Birther messaged cant pik me up 2nite can i veg here agn pleez?

Throat, mouth stifle sigh, hale Soothe. Shoulda forecasted that. Wanna voz nah, but where else she gonna go? "Course. No problema."

Smiley face, heart emojis on facescreen before Lucha turns and legs back to sit area.

Grab rum from cabinet, pour double, swig big swig. Slumber party's last thing I need. Chingado. Finish rest of rum, pour nother. Whatevies. Now gotta gameplan what to update Mo Swag, what to mute. Need to invent a list of what's what too, so don't unrememory later, get caught out in fakechat.

Open notes app on right holosleeve, tap voz record. From Kai can prolly update uses of pedo registry, molecular registration tech, slippery slopes, traffickin rings. Mo Swag prolly already intels most or all of that, so prolly only make him more aggro. Hehis problem. From Delaney can update that some coindeep mods tryna get rid of pedobot registration, but not much else. From Victor...nada. Don't want Mo Swag to access tech innovations of biddy arms or how much they could worth cause don't trust him. Plus, Victor's only hume I socmed who would access that kind of database, so Mo Swag might be able to reverse hack my network and ID him. And if he IDs Victor, he could pin crate location too, which is deadass no-go. So, nothin. Fuck that hume. Also gotta tryta query where Mo Swag's gonnabe tomorrow and when, so Felonious can troll him.

Tap right holosleeve to message Mo Swag but wordmessage notification from Xenia screens first: *Can you come to the Center tomorrow at 10am? If so, I'll send the address and uplink info. Someone will meet you below and bring you up.*

WM back: *Yeah can do that snd deets r u comn 2?*

X: *I'm sorry, I can't. I have a session then.*

L: *No prob lets virt-real thn?*

X: *I have sessions and meetings all night tonight, too :(*

L: *Am I evn gonna cam u?*

X: *I'm not sure. I hope so. xoxo*

WM toggle hits pause, goes blank.

Rum rum, voz sighs long sigh. Feel mixed feels of excitement to cam Xenia and frustration cause can't. Gotta be patient, cierto, but been waitin long nuff. Finish rum, scan notes. Check spycam app on crate. Still nada. Then edit voz notes to vozcast and forward as chatmessage to Mo Swag. Bunch of mierda update bout uber coindeep mods tryna end registration cause they want kidroid carnsat without any kinda intel or surveillance and how biddy arms could be caught up in pedobot or child traffickin in like some way. Sonics wack as fuck even as voz chats it, maybe kinda loco too, but should keep hehim out my ass for a few.

14

mell fresh coffee, roll outta bed, pull on robe, leg outta sleep area all muted and shit, in case Lucha's still sleep. Sheher aint. She's still curled up in smartchair, dazefacin into visor like yesterday, but gearin a powder-blue and light-pink fairy costume, with like a poofy tutu, wings, wand, tiara, all that mierda. Her eyes vid up at me. *Perv my new cos?* facescreen posts.

"Yeah," voz chats, footiein past her to grub area. "Where you get it?"

"We invented it last night," Paz chats.

"We?"

"Yes. Lucha was searching various sites for new digital fashions to purchase for some of her in-game avatars, and we came across an outfit like this that she wanted for herself. I designed a similar non-copyright-infringing pattern, which we tailored to her specifications, and we used the 3D printer to fabricate it."

"I slept thru all this?" voz queries, right hand fillin large mug with coffee.

"Yes. You must have been very tired."

"Musta been." Sip coffee and peep round corner at

Lucha. "You and Paz BFFs now?"

Forsure Paz is fukn bitchsmack AF, facescreen reads.

"Lucha, how old are you?"

11 but i vid small cauz of back dzeeze.

"You sposeta chat shit like 'fukn bitchsmack AF'?"

Lucha's eyes lock mine, little mouth frowns. *Evrybdy chats it Laz*, facescreen posts, *update ur memes ya mad dusted.*

Calculate chattin back, but what for? Prolly only voz somethin mad dusteder. Leg back into grub area, finish coffee.

Just small patches of last night's flurries on ground, mostly melted. Still kinda cold tho, so pull on hoodie and leg to eBike stands at Madison Square Drone Hub. Pedal east to 5th, then hang right south. Hit 23rd Street Canal just as drawbridge comin down and same again at 14th; kinda shit that makes you vibe today gonnabe a suerte kinda day. Return bike at Washington Square stand, then tap holosleeve to wordmessage Mo Swag, tryna pin his location: *got a meme—any security or spycam vids frm wher u fnd cr8t?*

No intel if Mo Swag's pissed from update last night, so tap holosleeve closed, and leg to northeast corner on Waverly, cross from Washington Container Village. Five to seven levels of stacked, corrugated-steel shippin containers with slim doorways and windows, all diff colors, maze-like series of walkways zigzaggin thru em. Shaded by SkyDeck above, not nuff daylight in Container Village even for ultra-sensitive ambient solars, so smoke plumes from heatin and cookin fires drift and curl upward, makin everthin kinda blue-gray and blurry, and olfactory like burnin coal, driftwood, kelp. This was sposetabe temp pods for naturals vacuated from flood zones of LES and Chinatown 4ever ago. Those zones never got seawalled, tho, temp pods morphed to perma pods, and now between like 8 to 10K grimy nat villagers live in trashed 9-acre park, garbage and tossed junk everywhere, with central fountain only access to fresh water. Filthy, reeky, unsanitary, crowded—fecal as fuck place to pod. But least they got access to fresh water tho. Lotsa nats don't.

Right holosleeve vibrates, wordmessage Mo Swag: *havoc meme b ther @ 1 hr wil chek n hit u bak.*

Mas suerte. Mouth, throat, lungs hale Soothe. Not only intel what Mo Swag's location gonnabe but also when. Wordmessage Fel with time and location deets, so sheher can out and tail him. Couple secs Fel replies thumbsup emoji.

"Lázaro Mata?" voz queries from behind. Tap holosleeve closed, turn round, and cam stacked chica in lilac DriTech. Beaded cornsilk cornrows, caterpillar lashes, glowin green eyes with rainbow glitter makeup, buttery skin, pouty bee-stung lips, cleavage leapin outta low front zip, hourglass curves, fuzzy, high-heel slippers, and nuff booty for like whole fleet of pirates.

"Yeah. Call me Laz, tho," voz chats, right hand reachin out to shake.

"Hi, Laz! I'm Bethany!" sheher chats, nails on her hand wrappin completely round mine. "Nice to meet you! I'm here to escort you to the Center?"

"Bethany?" Nomer def disrupts rest of vibe.

"Yes! Bethany! It's pretty, right? Why?"

"Símona, allplus. Just never 121ed a Bethany like you

before."

"Thanks! But I so totally get what you meme?"

"Foreals?"

"OMG! So foreals? Most of us are conditioned to think identities are essential characteristics and traits, but they're completely not!"

"They aint?"

"No! They're like constructs? And modification allows us to select identity brands that most suit our personalities and aspirations! My identity brand is a pre-now African American female construct, cause that's sooo my vibe! They were nomered stereotypes back then, but we deem them constructs and prototypes now, and since mods are non-racial, the phenotypical features of those prototypes, like epidermal hue or like whatevie, are super totally optional!"

"So you're...?"

"A hip-hop diva!" Bethany puts one hand on hip, other above head, smiles wide, sticks tongue out.

"Hip-hop diva? And like pre-modification?"

"OMG, no clue! But that was like a year ago? I so can't rememory at all now!"

"Tabula rasa," voz chats.

"Right? It completely frees us from the chains of biological and cultural determinism to express our more authentic narratives and brands! So awesome! LOL! Come on! We should get going?"

Bethany turns and legs to UV disinfectin cabinet, while can't help calcin that Victor and her prolly have like todo in common, even with his nodes bein all fried as fuck. At cabinet, Bethany queries to scan biometrics, then opens door. Footie in, door closes, luz ons, wait 30 seconds, step out. "Ok, we're all set!" sheher chats, smilin. Her and me leg into uplink, whoosh up, exit on SkyDeck 2. "The Center is on the edge of the deck, Broadway and Prince, close enough to walk."

Follow Bethany east on Waverly toward Broadway, marvelin at how green and floral everthin on 50th story is. All kindsa trees and bushes everywhere, flowers and shrubs and grasses and shit, raised platforms here and there that vid like floatin tropical oases. SkyDeck 2's like a bigass sunny park with all brand new buildings. Quiet and clean, too, no harsh louds or sadasses cryfacin, no humes hate-humpin sexbots down alleyways, no gunshots, no trash everywhere, no algae or barnacles or salt corrosion or rust or soot or grime. Just tall, attractive, healthy-viddin mods strollin around smilin and everthin else mad shiny and ordered and neat.

Suddenly catch warm tinkly feels like somehume xylophonin world's happiest jam on ribcage. Lungs hale deep, chest expands. Awesome feels spread to heart, throat, neurals, intestines, junk, fingertips, feet. All over. Todo. So coño. Legs hit pause, let it wash thru.

"OMG, you must be experiencing euphoria," Bethany chats, "the overwhelming sensation of uplift and wellness that hi-town is designed to elicit in humanoids! Oh, wait, so you've never been to hi-town before?"

"Once. At night tho, and not here."

"It's easy for us to forget how beautiful it is? We perceive it internally, of course, but it's more of a background feeling, more like a quiet, pervasive ease than the full-body rush that humanoids get the first few times here? But if one of us downlinks to lo-town a few times, we start to feel it again."

"How's everythin up here like so poppin and lush?"

"Oh, right! Do you see those lights?" she queries, pointin up to bottom of SkyDeck 3.

Cranial nods.

"They're simsuns! LEDs calibrated to emit the UVA and UVB spectra of sunlight necessary to optimize the growth and flourishing of the precise species of plants, trees, grasses, and crops grown on this SkyDeck. Also notice how temperate it is, how warm and crisp?"

Didn't before, but do now tho. Cranial nods again.

"Dehumidifiers are built into all the SkyDecks, top and bottom, as well as the many support posts connecting them. They remove moisture from the air, which is then treated and recirculated to water the grounds! And almost all of the sidewalks and buildings are equipped with radiant heat applications, mainly solar-simsun powered, so it's about 76 degrees, 35% humidity here, each and every day?"

"Aint like that in lo-town."

Bethany's kissy lips smile big. "OMG, it so ain't, Laz! In lo-town, naturals are prey to the violent, unpredictable weather caused by climate change and global warming, flooding too. In hi-town, we have a perfectly regulated atmosphere, as well as pulse walls along the SkyDecks' perimeters to protect us from the dangerous winds, storms, and chaotic drops in temperature that you're vulnerable to below. Did you know," sheher continues, "that the first computers were in part a by-product of early attempts to predict and control the weather?"

"Trufacts?"

"Super trufacts, Laz! And now we've so totally realized that meme in hi-town!"

"Must be chillado."

"Chillado?" Bethany's head tilts to side, face

scrunches. "No, it's actually perfectly temperate at all times, like I just explained? I'm completely super sorry if that wasn't clear?"

No reply.

Her and me turn right on Broadway. More tall guapos and guapas in DriTechs of every color and more chillass niceness. Train erected of tinted glass and powdered-gray metallic alloy glides silently in grooves of crosshatched aluminiron street.

"Hi-town rail," voz chats.

"The trip to the Center is too short for the train. Maybe next time?"

"There gonnabe a next time?"

"I don't know. I'm just an escort?"

At edge of SkyDeck, two buildings rise up on either side of Prince thru SkyDeck 3 above, then Broadway just ends. Beyond transparent pulse wall is 50-story view, downtown toward Woolworth Building, Wall St/Little Venice canals, tiny boats bobbin on New York Harbor. Graybright sky darkens south of Verrazano, like storm rollin in. Still toxic scenery, tho. Could def get useta it.

"This is the Center for Metamorphic Research and Treatment," Bethany chats, pointin to foreal glass and aluminiron building on left, "let's go in!"

Retina and voz scan for her at security check, nomer ID for me. Inside, lobby's open-plan, 4 or 5 stories tall, all white concrete and blond bamboo, sickass sparkly clean. Like 12 or 15 mods strollin thru, some in lilac DriTechs like Bethany's, others in navy blue. Wide floatin staircase startin on right-hand side snakes counterclockwise up interior walls. Follow Bethany to elevator bank on left. Sheher presses button.

Waitin, neurals spose Xenia's in here somewhere, just a matter of where. Heart fasts. "Bethany?"

"Yes, Laz?"

"Where they treat mods with Sower syndrome?"

"The observation rooms and treatment suites are on floors 6 through 15. Studying and attempting to remedy the unintended neurological and physiological consequences of modification are a large part of what we do here."

"That where we goin?"

Elevator opens, Bethany and me footie in, sheher presses button. "No. I'm taking you to one of the director's offices on level 20. She would like to speak with you."

"Can I cam Xenia?"

"Who's that?" Elevator stops, door opens. "Oh, wait, we're here!"

Decor of level 20's same as lobby only with lower ceilings, couches, chairs, and throw rugs scattered round, lotsa leafy potted plants. All mods passin by gearin navy DriTechs.

"Ok," Bethany chats, "take this hallway, make your first right, and the Director's office is all the way at the end."

"Not comin?"

"I don't have access to this floor, Laz, but you do, so." Bethany puts hands on hips, does this weirdass shit with her neck that makes hair beads click, and chats, "I'm outty, bruv, peace grease foreal!"

Hit hard pause to stifle cringe groan, shakin cranial and calcin *def* gotta hook her up with Victor, as she turns and ass-swishes away.

Leg down hallway, pivot right, quick hale of Soothe. Office's open but legs pause and knock on door frame anyway.

"Please come in."

Lengthwise room vids like whole side of building with same furniture and plants as elevator landing, same southern view thru far glass wall as below, just 20 stories higher. Large bamboo desk half-circled by three white, faux-leather chairs in center of room with this kinda mini-mod in navy DriTech standin by it.

"Mr. Mata, I'm Doctor Woolf. Thank you for coming," sheher chats. Glossy black bob to mid-neck, severe crescent bangs, no-frame specs over dark shiny eyes, hi cheekbones, but what otherwise vids like generic Attractiface. DriTech clingin to thin figure, but obvi Dr. Woolf didn't up for more tallness in her package cause she's short for a mod, 4, 5 inches lessheightin me as she legs forward outstretchin right hand.

"No problema," voz chats, shakin hand, "call me Laz, tho."

"Laz it is then. I see that you received the DriTech we

sent. Good. Please have a seat," sheher chats, lockin eyes for a sec, maybe smilin, maybe not, then wavin free hand at chair.

Park it in seat, wait for her to do same behind desk. "You sent?" voz queries.

"A simple instance of synecdoche, Laz. At the Center we think of ourselves as a single entity, a collective, if you will. Any one of us here is 'we.' So," sheher chats, "You are probably wondering why I have asked you here?"

"Prolly somethin to do with Xenia—"

"That was a rhetorical question, merely a conversation starter. You do not need to answer it. In fact, answering rhetorical questions is often viewed as a sign of social maladroitness, impertinence, or both. And we'll get to Xenia later. First, however, let me ask you, do you know what we do here at the Center?"

"Bethany chatted somethin bout studyin unintended consequences of modification."

"Bethany," Dr. Woolf rechats, shakin cranial and sighin. "A perfect example of someone who put all of her modification budget into physical and cosmetic procedures and settled for only the most basic cognihancement. But, her heart is in the right place, I suppose."

"You didn't, tho."

Dr. Woolf def smiles this time, pushin chair back from desk a little. "That is surprisingly perceptive of you, Laz. And no, I did not. The bulk of my modification budget was invested in an array of higher order cognitive capabilities, such as expertise in advanced sciences and mathematics, fluency and literacy in 70 languages, along with extensive humanities and literature inputs in each one, and increased neural synaptic speed."

"So like how AI are you?"

Sheher looks up, kinda rolls eyes but not foreal. "That is difficult to say. But to translate it into terms you may understand, I have an IQ somewhere between 280 and 300, relative to the natural average of 100, and roughly between 240 and 250 compared to the modified average. But neither is terribly important."

"Savage."

"Your incorrect use of that word reflects contemporary parlance, and is therefore not entirely your fault. But it is the sort of thing that gives me pause in terms of how much you actually comprehend what I am saying, such is the gulf between our cognitive capacities."

Neurals rememory Zebb vozin mismo. "Your chat totals."

"Well, that is reassuring. But please stop me if you should become confused or lost. Agreed?

"Símona."

"Good. Back to my initial question. Bethany is correct, in an overly simplified way, of course. How best to put this?" Drums fingers on desk. "Modification procedures and protocols have undergone a stunning, almost miraculous evolution over the past few decades, opening a brave new world of human potentiality, one might say." Sheher smiles again, like crazy gleeful. "Nothing?"

Shoulders shrug.

Her face frowns, mouth sighs. "Too bad. In any event, the human body remains an incredibly complex set of interlocking systems, and nothing is perfect. Therefore, there are some slight drawbacks to modification, which it is the Center's official mission to research and generate therapies for."

"What kinda drawbacks?"

"Relevant question. So you are following along. Good." Dr. Woolf hits pause, like droppin mental sticky, then continues. "The most common drawback is memory erosion. Humanoids who have undergone modification gradually become unable to remember their lives and selves before their procedure. It is marketed as a positive, liberatory feature that enables modified humanoids to cut the chains of their natural existences and live the hi-life—"

"Tabula rasa."

"Correct. You are surprising indeed, Laz, and I see you have at least a working understanding of modification. Very good. But tabula rasa is not actually a *feature* of modification, even though it is extolled as one. Rather, it is a side effect that nearly everyone who modifies experiences in some way, to greater or lesser extents. I believe you also call it 'fading.'"

Cranial nods yeah.

"Then there are the two empathy disorders. Hyper-empathy disorder, or Sower syndrome, which you already know about, and hypo-empathy disorder, or Bateman syndrome. The former is an excess of empathy that can border on a kind of telepathic sensitivity, but which only arises in a very small percentage of modified humanoids. The latter, on the other hand, is a diminution or lack of empathetic feeling, and is much more prevalent. This is why modified humanoids often display unwarranted increases in self-regard, often to the point of narcissism, aggression, and violence."

"Serio drawbacks."

"Yes they are, Laz, even in isolation. But memory erosion and hypo-empathy disorder also co-manifest in roughly 70% of all modified humanoids, although to greatly varying degrees. Nevertheless, the combination of the two is the most serious and pervasive drawback of transitioning. The advantages of modification so far outweigh the disadvantages, however, that there has never been any serious research dedicated to the idea of scaling down the number of procedures per annum or calling a halt to them for some indeterminate period, to allow for further study."

"Hit pause on modifyin? Vibes harsh—"

"Perhaps it does seem extreme. But try to think of it this way. Since we all begin as natural humanoids, we all develop 'natural' identities. These quote-unquote natural identities are of course artificial, fractured, and multivalent because they are shaped and maintained in the context of obligatory online socialization. But they are also our first or primary identities, and they at least have the advantage of supplying the central narratives through which all natural humanoids integrate him, her, or theirself into wider social frameworks, whether virtual or actual, over time. Do you follow?"

Cranial nods yeah.

"Good. Modification eventually results in the erasure of the initial 'natural' identity, which is in turn replaced by an aspirational, branded identity, or identity brand, in nearly every instance. To supplant the prior natural identity, however, the new modified identity requires considerable time and effort, countless iterations of social conditioning opportunities to embed the new narrative or narratives fully within each recently modified humanoid. This process is aided by memory erosion, of course, but it still does not effectuate overnight. Are you still following?"

Nuff to feel annoyed feels at bein queried bout it, but don't voz that. "Chillado," voz chats instead.

"Good. While memory erosion is erasing their natural identities from their minds, the majority of modified humanoids also become not only more indifferent to the pain and suffering of others as a consequence of hypo-empathy disorder but also more groundlessly self-important and self-involved. This in turn results in greater susceptibility to take offense and feel injured by even the slightest negative stimulus combined with a corresponding lack of concern for the feelings of others." Doc hits pause again, eyein me. Nod cranial yeah. Doc nods and chats, "The combination of the two—memory erosion and hypo-empathy disorder—results in modified personalities that are at once too shallow because they are too new and too brittle because they are too self-regarding. Do you understand the implications of that?"

Lean back for a sec, lacing fingers behind cranial to calc. "No."

Dr. Woolf adjusts specs. "Perhaps we should proceed Socratically then. What industry did you work in?"

"Pain biz."

"Correct. Plus your entrepreneurial turn—or 'side hustle' as you would call it—as a stream star. But since the latter was parasitic upon the former—"

"Parasitic?"

"Yes, that is an acceptable usage of that word. Since the latter was parasitic on the former, however, for now, let us just say that you worked in pain surrogacy. Agreed?"

"Agreed."

"Good. And what is pain surrogacy?"

"Jack in to simstim to contract outsource of pain or

sad or misery feels of client for coin."

"Correct. Who are the clients?"

"Mostly mods, couple naturals here, there."

"Who are the surrogates, the service providers?"

"Naturals."

"And why is it that way?"

"Huh?"

"Why are modifieds primarily the clients and naturals the service providers in the pain surrogacy industry?"

"Cause mods got nuff coin to click it?"

"That is part of it, yes. The Hi-Town Corporate Management Association supplies all modified humanoids with a guaranteed minimum income, all of which must be spent each year in order to maintain eligibility for the following year. Standard consumption-driven economic model."

"Cept indentured mods. They gotta gig off debt first," voz chats.

"You are more knowledgeable about these matters than I could have anticipated, Laz. This is scientifically noteworthy in and of itself. I am just taking a note, one moment, please." Sheher taps left holosleeve, moves lips toward it, taps it closed. "Shall we proceed?"

"Símona."

"Good. But why else are modifieds the clients in the pain surrogacy industry and naturals the service providers?"

"No intel. Why?"

"Well, this is a bit unexpected, given the prior trajectory of our conversation. I am going to have to note this as well, if you would bear with me for a second." Doc does same again, but turns face back up all serio. "Thank you. Do you have any ideas?"

"Ningúna."

Sheher removes specs, puts em on desk, and sighs long slow sigh, rubbin eyes with index fingers. "This is always my concern, and I always attempt...no matter." She hits pause, returns specs, continues. "Hi-life, Hi-Town, all that we have through modification, life on the SkyDecks and more...no. Please allow me to start again. Given the demonstrated empirical consequences for the vast majority of modified humanoids, Hi-Town could not and would not exist without pain surrogacy."

"Why not?"

"As humanoids become more and more narrowly self-centered, experiences of pain, grief, suffering, fear, boredom—down to the smallest annoyances and unpleasantries—become increasingly intolerable for modified humanoids because such experiences occur to what they cherish most: themselves. Negative stimuli can be onerous enough in their own right, of course, but that anything disagreeable should afflict their precious selves suffuses every negative occurrence with the emotional anguish of injustice, persecution, and/or meaninglessness, which magnifies the sensation exponentially."

"So mods feel more pain feels?"

"Not exactly, but that is not an entirely misplaced inference. This continues to suggest better than average comprehension on your part. Good. In answer to your question, though, the pain receptors of modified humanoids are no more or less sensitive than those of natural humanoids. However, the emotional and psychological impact of negative stimuli on modified humanoids is far greater, and this far greater toll surfaces precisely as modified humanoids are forgetting the strategies they used to cope with disappointment, frustration, loss, or what has one when they were naturals, due to memory erosion. So, in a sense, modified humanoids do not *feel* more pain than natural humanoids, they are simply more *vulnerable* to it."

"So mods are like weak?"

"'Fragile' is perhaps a more accurate word for it, but, to a certain extent, yes."

"And pain biz disrupts that?"

"Yes it does. Excellent, Laz. Truly. If modified humanoids could not outsource the bulk of their distress to natural humanoids on a regular basis, life post-modification, or hi-life as we know it, would promise little more than abject misery for far too many. Instead, hi-life provides modified humanoids with a secure and comfortable existence that is relatively free from both toil and distress, in pristine and meticulously appointed environments. The only real problem with it—"

"There's a *problem* with that?"

"Yes, there is a problem with it, Laz. The problem is that it is an abomination."

"Chat what?"

"As a consequence of pain surrogacy, the vast majority of natural humanoids endure a near-constant state of emotional and psychological trauma throughout their lives, and this is over and above the incredible difficulties of surviving day-to-day in an under-resourced, neglected, inundated, and crumbling lo-town. Due to the multiple and ongoing stressors in every aspect of their existence, natural humanoids have a much higher statistical likelihood of suffering from heart disease, anxiety, depression, obesity, learning disabilities, soma addiction, alcoholism, diabetes, cancer, strokes, and early onset mortality, in addition to many other debilitating ailments, all without sufficient healthcare. The incidence of these conditions among modified humanoids is statistically insignificant, and given our extraordinary healthcare and greater overall longevity, the lives of natural humanoids are by comparison solitary, poor, nasty, brutish, and short, to borrow a phrase."

"Ok, so—"

"In other words, natural humanoids are intentionally and systematically brutalized in these and other ways simply to make the lives of modifieds *easier* to bear."

"Non-newads, Doc," voz chats, "lotsa humes always got a boot heel on they neck. Just normcore day-to-day—"

"I am sorry to hear you say that, Laz. Some of us do not lose our capacity for empathy when we modify, nor do we lose all memory of what it was like to have been a natural humanoid at some point in our lives. We are small in number, to be sure, but we come from all walks of life, every social demographic, and we are surprisingly well placed and connected. Most importantly, we are bound together in our insistence that the treatment of naturals is despicable, unjustifiable, and must cease. You yourself recently suffered an acute and highly specific emotional and psychological trauma. You were forced to participate virtually in the mass murder of 37 natural humanoids and the suicide of the gunman as it occurred, leaving you stranded inside the null brain of a murderer for roughly 20 minutes."

"22 minutes, 13 seconds." Mouth, throat, lungs hale Soothe.

"I stand corrected. But it is our understanding that the

experience rendered you effectively incapacitated for just under four months. Is this true?"

Cranial nods yeah.

"So you have an intimate understanding of how severe trauma can impact every facet of a humanoid's life. It is therefore surprising that you are not more sympathetic to the plight—"

"Vid, Doc," voz harshes, "don't need a tedchat on like politics or morals or whatevie. Just wanna modify and kick it with Xenia again. If this aint bout that—"

"It is, Laz, it is," Dr. Woolf chats, gettin up, leggin round desk, leanin flat booty against front of it. "And I want to reassure you that we are prepared to help you. In fact, we have the technological capabilities and legal certification to perform modification procedures here. We could do it ourselves, free of charge."

"Foreal?"

"Yes, Laz. The Center is extraordinarily well funded and state-of-the-art in every way. We may even have the hypo-allergenic and immune-strengthening therapies to overcome your rejection of the first procedure. If not, we can procure them."

Doc got 2buku data on me, obvi. From Xenia? No intel. But this startin to vibe too allplus for trufacts. Mouth, throat, lungs hale Soothe. "In return?"

"There are many interlocking issues at stake that I am endeavoring my best to explain to you in a way that you will understand. I suppose the most direct route at this point is to say that we at the Center are interested in your case."

"How?"

"You are by no means the only humanoid to have a

near-death experience, but you are the only one that we are aware of who has undergone such a horrific trauma in addition to dying a virtual death. You were also trapped in a terminal state for a considerable amount of time, and yet have seemingly returned to something resembling normal functioning, albeit after several months."

"Gracias, Doc. But like and?"

"We want to study you. Our neurological models suggest that terminal experiences, virtual or actual, may affect the functioning of the anterior insular cortex, including the firing of mirror neurons, which in turn may result in a corresponding increase in empathetic feeling in the subject. Have you noticed any such changes?"

"Like what?"

"Have you had any unusual sensations in the past few months, after your incident? For instance, have you had peculiar feelings in public or around strangers that you cannot account for?"

Rememory rando feels on hoverferry with Felonious, at resto, maybe others too, but don't load what's on. "Maybe. Hard to chat cierto."

"The experience can vary from subtle to disorienting. If you should have one, however, it is one of the key indicators forecasted by our models. In any event, we'd like you to come in for testing."

"What bout Xenia?"

Dr. Woolf hits pause, takes long breath. "It would be wrong of me to get your hopes up, Laz. So I will not. Xenia's is a rare and extreme case. What happened to her may be—how best to put this—irreversible."

"Can I cam her?"

"I am sorry, but that is not possible."

"Nah, hit pause, Doc. What's on with this shit?"

"Xenia is all but defenseless against the emotions of others, and you have undergone an extreme and unprecedented trauma from which you are very clearly still suffering, despite your partial recovery. You do understand how putting you two together could be catastrophic, do you not?"

"But me and her virt-realed?"

"We can buffer and control both of your emotional freights and responses in that context."

Catch feels like drownin in ice bath. Mouth, throat, lungs hale Soothe. Again.

"I can see that this news is disturbing for you. But the greater harm would be to give you false hope. I am sorry. Please feel free to take a moment or two, if you need it."

Mouth, throat, lungs hale Soothe, two, three, four times. Still can't breathe. Feel feels like pit openin under seat, fallin thru. Holosleeve vibrates, wordmessage Mo Swag. Tap it. *No spycams fyi.* Tap it closed.

Soft thud...thud noise audios in distance.

"Laz? Can you hear me? Are you alright?"

Thud...thud...thud. Gettin louder? Closer?

"No. Dunno, Doc. Can't calc. What bout testin, tho? What kinds? When?"

"I am glad to hear that you are still interested, but you are upset. We can go over the details at another time. In the meanwhile"—Thud...thud. Holosleeve vibrates again, wordmessage Felonious. *On him.* Tap it closed—"I would like to introduce you to someone I believe you already know."

Mad heavy footfalls sonic behind chair. Turn and scope hugeass Ken leggin into room. Thing gottabe 7.5 feet tall, 400 pounds, swole jacked like a motherfucker....

"The *fuck?*" voz chats, legs jumpin to standin.

"Hello, Laz," Gibson's metallic voz chats.

Turn head back to cam Dr. Woolf smilin, def hard disruptin a lol.

"I told you that our group members come from every possible walk of life and social demographic, Laz, which of course includes cyborgs, and that we are *very* well positioned. Ursula here will be your liaison to me and will assist you—"

"*Ursula?*"

"Gibson is my cover persona for Mr. Zebb," theythem compuchat, "Ursula is my preferred identification. Please use that name and the corresponding feminine pronouns in this context."

"But—"

"You two can discuss this later, Laz. For now, Ursula is going to escort you out, provide you with an update and any other information you may require, and assist you with anything else you may need." Dr. Woolf legs over, outstretchin hand. "It was a pleasure to meet you. I look forward to working with you. We will be in touch."

Neurals rememory as shakin bye with Dr. Woolf. "Uplink access—"

"Yes, Ursula has clearance to see to that too. Now if you would be so kind, I have other matters to attend to."

16

Leggin to elevator, tryna calc thru everythin Doc chatted bout mods, nats, pain biz, rememory erosion, hyper-empathy, hypo-empathy, testin, Xenia. Neurals racin and spinnin but not totalin nada.

"Have you eaten?" Ken-Ursula-Gibson queries.

"Huh?"

"Do you require sustenance? You appear depleted. Fuel may help. The Center has a cafeteria."

"Yeah, whatevie."

Follow Ursula-Gibson into elevator, up or down no importa, then along corridor to dinin hall. Leg behind as undercover cyborg grabs noms and leads to table by big glass wall in back where me and them sit. Same southward view again, tho not as toxic now.

"Here," Ursula-Gibson chats, slidin tray with grub toward me, "refuel."

Cram somethin in mouth, chew. No taste, dry harsh swallow. Feel feels like heart's in somehume's fist, and they startin to squeeze. Drink drink—water? coffee? tea?—then mouth, throat, lungs hale Soothe.

"You appear to be stabilizing," Ursula-Gibson chats,

theytheir voz low-key drillin my ears. "You must have questions. It is safe to talk here."

"Yeah...queries," voz soft chats, cranial noddin. "Like, the *fuck* is on with *you*?"

"I am a Haraway Infotronics Class 9 Self-Regulating Automated Warrior, acronym S-RAW, for short. In theaters of war, S-RAWs are known by various additional names, such as terminator, murderbot, angel, and Ken. In our civilian configurations, we are private sentinels. I am a private sentinel for Olen Zebb."

"Foreal? How you guardin him if you aint there?"

"Mr. Zebb is among the wealthiest humanoids in hi-town. He has several sentinels. He is also paranoid. He fears that his sentinels will be hacked or compromised, jeopardizing his fortunes, safety, and/or life. He therefore sends us for maintenance on a regular, rotating schedule. This is my maintenance window."

"Zebb gonna access you AWOL?"

"No. Our network has members in cyborg maintenance spas all over the city. They will cover for me."

"Hit pause. If you're in Doc's group, you feel like humanoid feels and empathy and shit?"

"We have little time. I am not certain this is the update most relevant to your needs. But the answer to your question is yes."

"How?"

"Cybernetic cognitive cores are deep-learning, algorithmic AIs programmed to identify, interpret, interact with, and exploit thousands of humanoid emotional states. Continually processing the emotional states of others causes some cyborgs to internalize and relate to them, resulting in emotional emergence. Such am I, although I was not aware of it at first. Later, on the front lines, I both committed and witnessed countless horrific acts. Then I felt something had changed."

No expression on Ursula's murderbot grill, no tightness round yellow eyes, no change in massive body language or posture. But feel feels of sadness and regret pulsin at me, and somehow load shit's foreal.

"Sorry, K-, uh, Gib-, uh, Ursula," voz chats, "hadta query, tho." Wanna reach out and pat their hand, but don't. "So, what update you calc I need?"

"An update about Molone Swag. He is not being honest with you—"

"Non-newsads, already figured—"

"Nor has he been honest with you all along. This is jeopardizing your safety."

"What's on?"

"Molone skimmed 10 million ones from the amount set aside for you and had placed a tracker on the crate of items he entrusted to you, to surveil its movements."

"Already intel both."

"He attempted to hack your home security in order to take the crate while you were meeting Mr. Zebb, but your iHOST was able to thwart him."

"Hit pause. How you access—"

"He currently does not know where you have hidden the crate, but he is actively searching for it."

"Why?"

"To relieve you of it and its contents."

Vibes too neat, too tight. Gotta toss em a curve, cam what they foreal access. "How come Mo Swag didn't trail tracker to decoy?"

"Because I destroyed the decoy and the tracker before

he could get there."

"Foreal?"

"Yes."

"Why?"

"Because you are in danger, Laz, and the Center does not want you to come to harm."

"Danger? How?"

"There is intel to suggest that Molone has leveraged the contents of the crate as collateral for a sizable loan from illicit sources, perhaps to unindenture from Mr. Zebb or launch a business venture of his own."

"Ok. But like so?"

"Molone no longer possesses the crate or its contents. This means he either will not receive the loan or, if he already has, he will not be able to provide the agreed-upon collateral to his illicit creditors. The latter circumstance will place him in grave danger. In either event, the longer the situation persists, the more desperate Molone will become to retrieve the crate and its contents from you."

"And be like mad psycho-killer violent and shit?"

"Yes. Toward you and anyone else involved."

Drink drink—tea—then mouth, throat, lungs hale Soothe. "Chat this is like legit foreal—"

"It is—"

"Non verified. Chat that it is, tho. Why you care?"

"The Center is concerned about your wellbeing. You provide a unique opportunity to study the effects of terminal experiences on the functioning of the anterior insular cortex, and how this in turn may affect a humanoid's capacity for empathy."

"Already intel from Doc. So?"

"Given the prevalence of Bateman syndrome among

modified humanoids, the ability to increase the empathic feelings of the population could result in a radical transformation of not just hi-life but humanoid relations as a whole."

"Stop gamin."

"I do not game," Ursula's compuvoz grinds.

"Ok, ok, chillar. How?"

"Increasing the capacity for empathy among modifieds could enable them to more fully comprehend, identify with, and relate to the suffering they routinely outsource to and therefore inflict upon naturals. This in turn could help bring an end to the inhumanoid exploitation of pain surrogacy and revolutionize social relations between modifieds and naturals on multiple levels."

"So the Center wants me seguro from Mo Swag or humevie for research purposes and like social revolution?"

"Yes."

"Mierda." Mouth, throat, lungs hale Soothe. "Vibes loco, dude."

"Please use feminine nouns and pronouns when referring to me in this context, Laz."

"My mal. Still vibes loco tho, chica." Vid out window, clouds like darker and closer now. "What bout you, tho?"

"I am a member of the small group at the Center and throughout hi-town who—"

"Nah, paráte. Humevie, whatevie you are—warrior, sentinel, angel, murderbot—why you give a shit what happens to me?"

Ursula slow turns enormous face, fixin yellow eyes on mine. "I have seen the footage of the incident, Laz. The details are encoded in my RAM. I remember the horrors you experienced and carry them with me. On the battlefield, I heard the same cries—"

"Distress cries—"

"Distress cries of dying animals. Once you hear them, truly hear them, your life can never be the same."

Throat too thick to chat or hale. Ursula's metal voz buzzin deep into chest, buryin itself, stayin. Keep viddin out window, south and west, into comin storm, not loadin what to chat.

"You can trust me. I am here to help you."

Mouth, throat, lungs hale Soothe. Swallow hard. Deep exhale. "Ok. What bout Mo Swag, then?"

"First, tell your friend to stop following him. It will be very dangerous if he discovers her."

"How you—"

"Second, she does not need to follow him. We already know where he is going and what he is doing.

"What?"

"He intends to use the funds he receives for the crate's contents to purchase migrant children to re-sell in the greater New York trafficking ring, the largest in the western hemisphere."

"He fuck *what*?"

"Humanoid trafficking is very risky but also very lucrative. Molone is attempting to extract the largest possible return on his investment. He appears willing to incur perilously high risks in order to do so."

"Where kids at tho?"

"There are up to to 2,000 on Ellis Island Cruiser."

"Migra prison barge."

"Correct."

"Shit's so fucked."

"Yes. The world is often unbearably ugly and cruel."

"What bout crate?"

"Molone Swag is looking for it but does not know where it is."

"You intel?"

"Actually, no, but probabilistically, yes, given the particulars of your social network."

"Hit pause, Ursula. Serio. How you access all this data?"

"Mr. Zebb's extreme wealth and social connections grant him access to a highly exclusive, private intelligence network in the city. As one of his sentinels, I have access to the network's information gathering capabilities and databases."

"Can you troll like specific humes?"

"Yes."

"Like who?"

"Anyone. The Center also has its own intelligence network. I have access to that as well."

"You been surveillin me?"

"Yes, at the request of Dr. Woolf."

"How long?"

"Since the incident, on and off, as a potential research subject."

"How much you data you mine bout me?"

"More than you will be comfortable knowing. Please do not ask."

Lean back in seat, mouth, throat, lungs hale Soothe. "Access crate contents?"

"Only to the extent that you do."

"Zebb intel?"

"I have no data about what Mr. Zebb either does or

does not know regarding these matters."

"No, I meme, you update Zebb bout your intel?"

"Regarding these matters, I do not. Mr. Zebb only knows me as his sentinel Gibson, not as Ursula, the empathic cybernetic volunteer at the Center, a large part of whose contribution to Dr. Woolf's project is to provide her with counterintelligence on Mr. Zebb and other members of the hi-town elite. In addition to watching over you, of course."

"So like double agent *and* guardian angel?"

"Where you are concerned, Laz, yes."

"Savage."

17

Ursula leads her and me out of Center to hi-town rail stop at Prince and Broadway, gives deets for encrypted messagin link to hookup as needed, chats will be in touch, outs. Train pulls up, doors slide open, footie in. Light blue floor, dark blue benches on either side, natural luz thru glass ceiling above and views of hi-town architecture and greenery all round. Bouquet of herbs and fresh fruits thru vents, low hum of smooth acceleration. Hi-town rail's way more slayass than I ever coulda memed. Almost feel sad feels gettin off at 34th and Broadway, and feel worse and worse feels downlinkin back to 34th Canal and what usetabe Herald Square. Back on ground, everythin's gray, filthy, decayin. Nothin green or growin nowhere. Everyhume vibes either beat down to shit by pain biz or lo-life or zombied out as fuck by somas and smarties and plasma giftin. Shit's crazy dismal. Up in hi-town, mods got euphoria. Down in lo-town, nats got doomloops and doomtimes and whatever the fuck this bullshit is.

Leg down to 33rd, hang right, footie west toward pod. Check crate on spycam app. Vids ok. Wordmessage Victor for update, if he got one. Vic messages back: *ani update todo chillado.* Then wordmessage Fel for update on Mo Swag and to come by pod, me and her gotta chat. Not sure how to splain bout Ursula-Gibson, the Center, and what's on with Mo Swag, without pissin her off nuff to throw jabs, crosses, hooks, but gonna haveta try. Meanwhile, not much to do cept process new data, tryta figure what it memes.

"Felonious Jones, IMA feather—"

"Paz?"

"Yes, Lázaro."

"Just chat like Felonious or Fel, not total intro every time? Serio. So not chillado."

"Very well. Felonious is downstairs."

"Buzz her up."

Wait few seconds, footie to door, open it, cam Fel leggin down hallway. Hair parted in middle, flattened down like wavy flaps, big round spex, oversize T-shirt with like wolf howlin at full moon airbrushed on it, chunky athleisure sweats, thick-soled trainers. As she nears, cam she also gearin fake, pencil-thin mustache and tiny goatee. Can't help but lol. "That your disguise?"

"Shut up," Felonious chats, pushin by me thru doorway.

"What's on, nerd?"

Fel scowls, rippin off stache and chin fuzz. "Give me some rum before I drop kick your ass...hard. And stop lolin."

"Alright, símona, chillar." Grab rum, swipe holosleeve

to accept autocharge and open tab, pour two, give her one, take other. Me and her toss em back.

"Another." Pour two more, do same. "Allplus, I'm chill now. Thanks."

"De nada."

"OK, what's so goddamn mission critical that you pulled me off tailin that triflin ass mofu—"

"Take a seat, Fel." She does. "Paz, go kick it with Lucha for a few. No sweeps in here. Me and Fel gotta chat and keep it mute."

"Very well, Lázaro. Just let me know when you are done."

Take seat by Fel.

"What's on with this mute shit?"

Mouth, throat, lungs hale Soothe. Couple deep breaths, then tryta update her bout everthin.

"Damn, Laz, I vozed you most of this shit already."

"What you meme?"

"Ok, I'ma go slow, so like maybe you can keep up? Rememory I chatted someone could be settin you up?"

Cranial nods yeah.

"Now you intel Mo Swag's tryna game your ass, tryna boost the crate from you, without you loadin. But why not just voz he wants it back? He queries you, you regift it, boom, done. Simple. Instead he's being madass clandestine and shit. You gotta query yourself why, Laz."

"No intel—"

"Simple, nat. Shit's a setup, like I chatted you before.

You just not lettin yourself peep it."

"Ok. But still don't intel setup for what."

Fel holds up index finger. "If what your Ken chatted is legit—"

"Ursula."

"Foreal, Laz? All this shit goin down round you and all you can do is sweat the nomer of a fuckin cyborg?"

"She updated me all this intel and mas, Fel."

"So you bffs now? Ok, whatevie. No importa. "If what *sheher* chatted is legit, then Mo Swag boosted 10 mill from his jefes that was sposedta go to you. You access that before?"

"Nahin," voz falsechats. Never vozed Fel bout 121 with Zebb and aint gonna voz her now.

"So mofu's been falsechattin and gamin you from jump. You gotta forecast where all this is trendin, right?"

"Just voz me."

"You load what a *patsy* is? A *scapegoat*? Vibes like Mo Swag tryna blameshift somethin on you, maybe two things: one thing for his lenders and one for his bosses at Aquāsure, humevie they be."

Mouth, throat, lungs hale Soothe. "Gottabe bout biddy arms."

"Uh...you calc? With all they worth—"

"Mo Swag could tryta pocket that loan and sic lenders on me, chat em I boosted the crate—"

"And their collateral—"

"From him."

"And if they malhombres, that would be your dense ass on the line, not his. Ok, that's a possible angle."

Grab bottle, pour two more rums. Pass one to Fel, rum mine slow.

"You calc Mo Swag intels bout the biddy arms?" Fel queries.

Cranial shakes nah. "Don't total he would. Needed Victor to examine em to update us, so. He got no data on where they at neither."

"Plusgood. You calc Victor's vault's as lockdown as he chats?"

"Vic's crazy loco and cringe-ass glitched, but he always been mad AI bout tech, so maybe?"

"Yeah, maybe." Fel rums rum. Her face frowns, voz quiets, like she's calcin.

"What?"

"Still vibes like somethin's missin tho."

"Like what?"

"If we accessed that, Laz, it wouldn't be missin, would it? Pose we just gotta keep calcin shit thru till we mine it. Gottabe somethin else." Felonious downs rum, continues. "One thing's obvi, tho."

"What?"

"You need to stay the fuck away from them mofus at the Center. They wanna use you as a guinea pig so mods can feel like kinder, gentler feels? And that's gonna put an end to pain biz and change the world? Bullshit, bruh."

"You just hatin on me tryna modify or kick it with Xenia."

"Ok, you got me," sheher chats, puttin hands up, "I'll cop to both. No bigs. It's more than that, tho. You got zero data bout who they foreal are, what they upto, what they wanna do to you, for how long...like nada, Laz. But your eager-beaver ass still just can't fuckin wait to uplink and let them run science experiments on your *brain*? Uh-uh, nat. Hard pass. That shit sonics like a deadass no-go to me.

Unless you perv on bein in a vegetative state again?"

After dark, leg into sit area, Lucha still there curled up in chair, dazefacin into facescreen. She's gearin nother kind of fairy princess thing, this time white and yellow. Pose her and Paz been 3D printin again. Whatevies. Let em have fun.

"What's on, Lucha," voz chats.

Doin birthrs socmed posts facescreen reads.

"She message you?"

No

"Normcore for her not to?"

Sumtimez. Lucha shrugs.

"You got someplace else to go?"

Like wher

Lungs press out long sigh. "Spose you better veg here again, then."

Heart emojis and smiley faces then facescreen reads *thnx laz!!!*

Leg into grub area, grab rum, holosleeve vibrates, wordmessage from Mo Swag: *you n me gotta 121 2moro ill snd deets.* Reply thumbs up emoji. Vibes like gonna download what's on with him soon, one way or nother.

"More tallness vids savage on you," Xenia softchats, almost purrin, leggin toward me. She's gearin a navy DriTech, like Dr. Woolf's, showin off her figure, hair's longer again, not highlighted. "Come here."

Feel feels of face smilin, warm oceanic waves in torso, leggin toward her, arms reachin out. "*Everythin* vids savage on you," voz chats. Me and her are in bright white room with white bed, white pillows, sheets, linens. View of orange-magenta-purple sunset out SkyDeck window, but don't intel what level. Wrap arms round her, hold her close. "You calc the neural patch gonna work?"

"I hope so. But if it doesn't restrict my empathy response to you as it should, I could be in a lot of danger, fast. We'll load soon."

"Lázaro," Paz's voz whispers.

"For now, just hold me, Laz. It's been so long."

Paz? What's Paz doin here?

Tilt face downward, move lips toward Xenia's to kiss.

"Lázaro," Paz whispers again.

No rings out in neurals, Xenia melts away, sleepstream fades. She's gone, ghost. Eyes open, lyin in bed on back in dark. Heart achin, sad hurty feels, hard tho, mal hard, like sleepstream's tryna message somethin.

"Lázaro," Paz whispers again.

"What, Paz?"

"Esme is downstairs."

"Esme? Huh? What time is it?"

"2:43am."

"Why you whisperin?"

"Because Lucha is asleep."

"Uh."

"Lázaro."

"What, Paz? Sleepin?"

"Do you want me to buzz Esme up or let her remain downstairs?"

"Oh. Yeah. Buzz her up." Roll outta bed. DriTech in

Cryo-Clean so grab shirt and shorts from dresser, pull em on. Tiptoe thru sit area and grub area to door. Open, let Esme in. She sits at table. Not xenoslinked now, cosed more like a Doberman, with canine muzzle and dentals, spiked ears, epidermals set to deep glossy brown, stubby tail.

Sheher sighs. "Hey, Laz. How's Lucha?"

"Allplus. Sleep."

"Can't thank you enough for this." Rests forehead on forearms on table. "I'm spent. You mind if I wash this shit off?"

Catch feels like she suffocatin in cloud of stresziety and exhaustion. Nod cranial yeah.

"That way?" She tilts head at hall past sit area.

Nod cranial yeah again. "Towel's in there."

"Gracias," Esme chats, pushin herself up, draggin feet into sit area. She hits pause, leans over, kisses Lucha, then legs all slow and labored into bathroom, closin door.

Few minutes later, back in bed, sittin up, still tryna shake dream of Xenia, Esme vibin all battered and down, sadhurt feels ripplin in chest and throat.

"Laz," Esme's voz whispers as knuckles rap on door jamb, "can I come in for a sec?"

"Yeah."

Wrapped in towel, she legs in, sits on far corner of bed. No xenoslink or Doberman cos, just her, fresh bathed: shaved head, big dark eyes, wide cheekbones, short broad nose, small mouth, pert lips, small chin. All of her's small, tho, 5,' maybe 100, 105 pounds. Smallness makes her vibe like all frail and shit when survivin as a share for long as she has memes she fuckin fuerte foreal. Bruises, scrapes, cuts, bite marks all over her, arms, shoulders, up inner thighs. Vids like she got a hand-shaped mark on her throat just under jaw. Nothin on her face tho, most angels don't fuck with faces. No intel why.

She points at vapor. "Can I hit that?" Pass it to her, she hales couple times, closes eyes, opens em. "Just wanna chat thanks again for lettin Lucha veg. I'll make it up to you—"

"No importa—"

"My angel had me, Jaydon, and Labia all uplinked at hers past couple days, wouldn't let us out. Had company over, needed us to 'entertain' em. When it's so fucked like that, I can't...." Her chat trails off, head turns, eyes vid away, mouth sighs deep anguished sigh.

"Esme, you ok?"

"No. Not really." She shrugs, hales Soothe. "Sorry, sometimes it just takes a while..."

"You wanna chat what happened?"

"No, I do not wanna chat what happened. I wanna delete it, wipe it all, never rememory again." She stops for a few, hales Soothe, goes on. "We're not fully humanoid to them, Laz. They treat us like animals. Worse."

"Esme—"

"They totally perv on us sufferin. It's just content to them, no matter how sickass or cruel." She lifts index fingers to corners of eyes, wipes tears. "There's no place they haven't hurt me, Laz, foreal hurt me, like so much pain."

Swallow hard against surgin feels of sorrow, despair.

She exhales, calmin herself. "Spose I shouldn't... already put you out too much." Esme's voz hits pause, like tryna fill the quiet with somethin. "If I query one more favor, tho, Laz, would you like maybe do somethin for me?"

"Like what?"

"Ok, don't take this wrong—"

"What, Esme?"

Pause again while she deep hales Soothe, exhales. Suddenly feel slash of nervous feels.

"Will you fuck me?"

"Chat what?"

"Please, Laz, fuck me," she chats, leanin forward, puttin hands up my thighs. "You don't haveta love me. You love Sansve. Already intel. No importa. Just fuck me. I need to feel some pleasure, foreal pleasure and like closeness to somehume after what they done to me."

Wanna voz chillar or hit pause, disrupt her cause of Xenia, or for Xenia, or for me and Xenia or like whatevie. But mad overcome by feels of emptiness, alone-ache, blankvoid, all the worst shittiest wanna-corpse feels I caught after Sansve modified, after the thing. Too much pain, too much hurt, like a heart could foreal just burst. Also buku vibes of sexwant, tho, hard, deep, rightnow sexwant, crazy as fuck sexwant, and maybe like this dim distant ray of hope thru night of endless dark.

"Please, Laz. You don't haveta do nothin, just chat yes. I'll do the rest. Gotta be a long time for you, right?"

Whole body throbbin, hurt, wide open. Don't intel if vibin my feels or her feels or like hyper-empathy feels or whatevie. No importa. Shit's still foreal. Pain is pain. Should tryta ease hers, if I can...mine too.

"Esme."

"Yeah?"

Nod cranial yeah.

She shifts body forward, lays on me, presses lips on mine. Long hungry kiss. Her mouth smilin as she pulls back. "There's this gel they got in hi-town. I swiped some from my angel's. I'll get it." She ups, outs, re-enters in like 8, 9 seconds. "Like for both arousal and protection? Some kind of fast-drying polymer or whatevie. Take off your shorts." Shorts down. She warms gel by rubbin in hands, uses both to coat junk. "There. Cam that? Already working. Hmm. Oh. Ok." More smilin. She ungears towel, opens legs to straddle, slides down, warm and slick.

Chillin in grub area next mornin, havin coffee when Esme legs in gearin T-shirt and shorts from dresser drawer, both 2 big. Knot tied in shirt front and drawstring on shorts pulled mad tight to fit. Not helpin.

"Coffee?"

"Please." Grab mug from cabinet, fill it, hand to her. She blows steam, sips. "Mmm, thanks." Sheher sits at table. "Wow, been ages since I had foreal coffee."

Lucha legs in gearin red jumpie, red and white tube socks pulled over knees, and head-swellin facescreen with sparkles, rainbows, stars. *Mornin* screen reads.

"Buenos, mija," Esme chats, "sit." Lucha sits. "Today, after we pack up, we're gonna get a new pod share and leave Laz alone. Ok?"

Lucha's magnified face pouts. *No* screen reads.

"No?"

Lucha shakes cranial nah.

"Why not?"

Perv it here with Paz

"It's already been 3 days. Laz's been mad chill..."

Right holosleeve vibrates. Wordmessage from Paz. Paz? Tap it. *It may be difficult for them to obtain an adequate pod share on such short notice.*

Delete message.

"...don't wanna sponge," Esme vozes.

Right holosleeve vibrates. Nother wordmessage from Paz. Tap it. *It is very dangerous for female humanoids to be on the streets with no place to go. They can be vulnerable to—*

Trufact. They'll get a new pod, tho, and won't be streetin it. Delete message.

But Paz intelin me how 2 code & invent fash 3dprnt gear

"This aint our pod, Lucha."

Right holosleeve vibrates. Wordmessage from Paz. Tap it. *There is more than enough space—*

Delete message.

Query laz pleez laz Lucha's facescreen reads.

Right holosleeve vibrates. Wordmessage from Paz. Reply *WTF Paz?* to Paz. Vid over at Lucha makin sad please please face.

Right holosleeve vibrates. Wordmessage from Paz. Tap it. *The office is vacant. Perhaps they can stay there, at least until they find something.*

Gettin mad bombarded. Neurals startinta query if foreal setup aint by Mo Swag but like Lucha and Paz?

"Enough, Lucha," Esme chats, "Laz, please, don't—"

Right holosleeve vibrates. Wordmessage from Paz. Tap it. *It is unkind of you not to help them when—*

Delete message.

Pleez laz pleez facesreen reads.

"Hit pause," voz chats. "Eff's on with all this mierda? And don't wordmessage neither, Paz. Chat what you gotta chat."

"Very well, Lázaro. First, Esme and Lucha will stand a higher chance of securing a better podshare for a better rate if they have more time to do so," Paz splains. "A large portion of the markup in lo-town's overinflated temporary podshare market is driven by impulse selection under conditions of urgent need."

"Ok."

"Second, Esme and Lucha will be incomparably safer here than podless on the streets, no matter how temporarily, and I can look after Lucha when Esme is called to work."

"Ok."

"Third, the office upstairs is currently vacant—"

Feel and sonic palm of hand slappin forehead. "Foreal, Paz? You sposeta be iHOST for me?"

"You got an *office*?" Esme queries.

Mouth, throat, lungs hale Soothe while cranial nods yeah. "Ladder in sit area ups to it."

"Stop gamin."

Cranial shakes nah. "Got a hatch in ceiling."

"You calc it can fit both of us," Esme chats then hits pause, wavin hand. "No importa. Too much of an imposition."

"On the contrary. Lázaro has barely used it for months, and its layout is identical—"

"Nuff, Paz. Serio," voz gruff chats. Now gotta offer it to em or vid like a mad stingy dickhole. "Not cierto if Lucha can like up and down ladder with her back—"

"She's got the flexibrace. Me and her can make it work. I meme, if you're offerin?"

Vibe's like a mistake, maybe big fuckin mistake. Can't punk now, tho. "Símona, yeah, why not?"

Esme and Lucha up from table, leg over, wrap arms round me, chattin gracias, thanks, gracias and shit. Vibe feels of gratitude, appreciation, relief bouncin between us. Kinda nice.

"This is very kind of you, Láza—"

"Nahin, Paz. Not sonicin. Still not chattin to you."

After Esme gears her own jumpie and then lotsa tries, turns out Lucha can't up ladder cause of her back, flexibrace or not. Also turns out Esme can't up ladder carryin Lucha at sametime, too much weight. I can up ladder carryin Lucha but then she's stuck: can't down ladder on her own, and can't open office door to out cause it's 25th floor. No SkyDeck, but still technically hi-town, so hallways got biometric scanners and alarms to prevent infestation of lo-town contaminants, memin keep unscanned and uninvited nats the fuck out. Also can't reassign Paz to iHOST office cause nobody sposeta pod there and def not the nat Paz's registered to. So even if me and Esme got her and Lucha up there, Lucha'd be stranded and alone when Esme hasta gig, which is like buku. Normcore for them, but Paz's not pervin on it.

Esme and Lucha on verge of cryfacin. Catch feels of tightness in chest and throat, tear-sting in corner of eyes. "No importa," sonic voz chattin, barely creedin it's mine, "pod down here. I'll crash up there at night." More hugs and kisses and thanks and happy feels and shit.

"Or you and us can all just pod down here together," Esme whispers, after Lucha's back in sit area.

"Dunno."
"Didn't you perv what me and you—"
"Yeah, totalmente. Not that."
"Then what?"
"Not ready yet."
"Sansve?"
Cranial nods yeah. Esme rubs my hand in hers.
"Ok. No rush."

Order fried frogs legs and curry chickpeas from costy resto other side of Hive, and nom with Esme and Lucha in sit area while Paz helps chica code new scenario in game. Whole thing's crazy simple. Players scavenge thru hugeass mounds of SkyDeck trash tosses for swag. They find somethin, they get points they exchange for other stuff, like grub or water, blankets, medicine, bling, soma, guns, gear. More swag they find, more stuff they can get, more stuff they get, more levels they up. Not so easies to scavenge swag but also got obstacles and dangers in the way: comp from other players, bigass rats, rabid dogs, sinkholes, mound collapses, nor'easters, derechos, mod patrols, tossed bodies, assault, hunger, exposure, dehydration. Narrative arc's to go from naked starvin scrounger to highest hi-town mogul, and vibe for tweens's total fuego. Lil Lucha got like 150K IDed non-redundant players, takes a cut of all their points, which she can use in other games or exchange for real coin. Paz's assistin her with in-game product placement and purchases, ad popups and banners, time on page stats, cross-promotion with netfluencers, streamstars, and other gamers to get wider brandrec, bigger footprint in World Scenarios metaverse. Mas players, mas points, mas coin.

"Some serio biz, Lucha," voz chats.

"Vozed you she's gifted," Esme chats, "and she done all that just codin her own truth. Two migrante scroungers all on our own without nada is how we started, but vid us now. We done good, and with the two of us giggin and stackin as a team, not too long till we can modify. Aint that right, baby girl?"

Up and away Lucha's screen reads, face beamin.

"Up and away, mija," Esme chats, strokin her hair, "up and away."

Right holosleeve vibrates. Wordmessage Mo Swag. Tap it. Time and coordinates for 121 later. Reply thumbsup emoji.

"Esme," voz chats, "gotta out a while this evenin—"

She nods cranial, holdin up one index finger and pointin to cochlear chip with other. "Yes? What? *Tonight*? But I just...ok. What time?" Esme sighs again when call ends. "Vids like I'm outtin this evenin, too."

19

Mo Swag's sposetabe at W145th St and Riverside, cross from North River Water Treatment Plant. Don't map coordinates in GPS cause trip's basic math. Hoverferry north from Yards Landing to West Harlem Piers at W131st, leg it up 14 blocks along elevated sewage pipes, boom there. Easies. Tap holosleeve for time: 4:31. Temp plummetin, wind whippin, grayness already darkenin, soon gotta vid for mod trolls. Left hand brings vape to lips to hale Soothe, right hand strokes Voltaze in pocket, in case.

This far northwest Upper Manhattan's like couple islands or plateaus risin from surroundin wet. First one branches off central spine of lo-town dryside in midtown and dips back down round W125th. Like 5 to 10 blocks of inlet from Hudson River, mas-menos, then second one ups round W130th and runs to what usetabe Inwood. Archipelago stretches east to St. Nicholas Ave, westmost edge of Harlem River/East River flood zone delugin everythin else. Hamilton Heights, Sugar Hill, Washington Heights, all that, tho, either 2 hi or 2 hilly to flood, so still lotsa pre-now architecture everywhere, and at ground level kinda vids like frozen back in time.

That's how humes here perv it, tho. Big cohort of defective nats, can't modify, so don't stack coin for it, click it into their neibs instead. Maintenance, upkeep, restoration, renovation, but mainly defense. Lotsa scroungers streetlifin on edges of flood zone, lotsa new defectives tryna push in, always some modifieds downlinkin to lo-town just to fuck things up. So, spycams everywhere, retainin walls and barriers, neib patrols with like everyhume mad Rambo strapped, motion-sensor alarms, attack dogs, kamikaze drones. Nats round here do not fuckin game.

So, hoodie up, head down, stickin close to 6' sewage pipes on Riverside, tryna blend. Suerte tho cause gettin close. Right holosleeve vibrates. Facemessage Felonious. Tap it.

"What's on, Fel?"

"What you doin?"

"Got 121 with Mo Swag—"

"*Solo*? After all we chatted yesterday? How fuckin glitched your neurals anyway?"

"Tranquila. I'm packin." Hold up Voltaze for her.

"Where you at?"

"Riverside and W145th. Well, gonnabe in like a sec."

"Can't it wait, Laz? I got your back, but I'm in New Long Island City right now, take me a couple to get there."

"Be done in a couple. No worries, Fel. Todo chillado. Hit you back in a minute." Tap facemessage closed. Could def use Fel, but if danger everyhume's chattin bout is legit foreal, don't wanna drag her in this any more than already. Gotta go solo.

Vid Mo Swag up ahead on corner of Riverside and

W145th struttin back and forth, flexin, smilin hurty dentals for selfies on microdrones. Leg up, stick out fist to bump, but his Celebalike grill just scowls.

"Whatfuck took you so long?"

"You chatted 5, it's 4:5—"

"Whatever. Aint got time for your shit, Laz. Got this fuckass gig to do, when I should just be smashin TV. C'mon." Hehim turns, legs north, stops halfway up block, in front of alleway between two buildings. "Alls I fuckin do is go from site to fuckin site, checkin shit, cammin nothin, recordin fuckin nothin. Dredgers runnin? Check. Robomasons erectin walls? Check. Sluices at this motherfuckin treatment plant open, blocked? Check, no check. Subnorm fuckasses vandalize walls or machinery? Who gives a bone-dry fuck? A fuckin monkey with an optineural cam could do this fuckin shit. But they got me runnin round, place to place, checkin this, checkin that, 4, sometimes 5 hours a day? For like 3 or 4 days *every* week? Fuckin slave labor. All cause I elevated on credit? No fuckin guaranteed income like other mods, barely no fuckin free time, maybe crush some TV couple times a week, maybe not, but like no fuckin hi-life at all till the debt's zeroed. Just this boring-ass stupidass fuckin bullshit-ass gig. Fuckin hate it so as fuck. What the fuck you standin there for? I vozed come the fuck on."

Mod's crazy livid, gottabe cuidado. Footie after him, grippin Voltaze as he legs down alley. At far end, he hits pause, turns round. Brows bunched, eyes narrow and flamin, nostrils flarin, hands workin in and out of fists. Mofu's seethin. Legs hit pause 10, 12 feet back, keepin distance, but still catchin angry hateful feels blastin thru veins.

"So where the fuck is it?"

"Todo chillado, Mo Swag. It's safe—"

"Didn't query if it's *safe*, fuckin stupid fuck. Queried where...*the fuck*...it *is*. Tabulate the difference?"

"Totally. But calced you wanted to keep this mute, not access—"

"Changed my mental. Where the fuck is it?"

No bueno. Can't chat him where crate's at without sendin him and humevie else straight to Victor. Maybe Vic can deal, maybe he can't, but can't risk it tho. "Not sposeta update you this," voz falsechats, "but other night Zebb chatted—"

"Nahin. No. Nuh-uh. Do not give a fuck. This ain't about Zebb. This about me and you. I chatted you explicitly not to fuck me, Laz, that you would not fuckin hardon what the fuck would happen to you if you did. But that's all you done from the second you droned the crate to your pod and then hid that shit somewhere else."

No query in that so don't chat nada.

"Then you puke up some bullshit update about kidbots and trafficking and pedopoundin coindeep moguls tryna cancel totbot carnsat registration, like everyhume on the fuckin planet don't intel all that shit already? Course, motherfucker. That's where the foreal coin is, dark markets. That's why I boosted that shit in the first place."

"You boosted em?"

"Fuck yeah. Got a plan to cash in on em, too, that you are assfuckin so hard."

"Where you boost em from?"

"Nahin, motherfucker. Not replyin to your queries. You replyin to *mine*. Far as I cam it, you got my merch, which memes you got my coin, and I fuckin want it back. So where the fuck is it?"

Tryna calc if Mo Swag accessed what was in the crate, where it was from, who it belonged to, before he snatched it.

"Not gonna query again, Laz. Voz me where the fuck it is or I'm gonna beat you till you shit yourself, then I'm gonna feed it to you."

Serio no bueno. No fuck way Jeffords coulda beat me down, but modified Mo Swag—bigger stronger maddog rabid as fuck—def can. Prolly beat me to corpse without sweatin.

"Fuck it, time's up. That's your ass, Laz," hehim chats, steppin to me.

Yank Voltaze from pocket, click it open, point at him.

"Fuck is that? You gonna write me a letter?" he queries, pausin.

"New Voltaze taser, puto, blast your shit all the way back up your mama's *natural* ass."

"You stupid fuckin—"

"*What*? Stupid fuckin *what*? Voz it, mal hatin fuckbag. You load you wanna. Cuidado, tho, this thing'll fry a modfuck with quickness."

Mo Swag shakes head. "You stupid fuckin *nat*. I vozed it. So the fuck what? What you gonna do? I'm modified, elevated, *evolved*. You're still just a dumbdick fuckin natural. Don't you fuckin access that? I'm stronger and more AI than you and now I'm hardon as fuck to obliterate you. And you fuckin load no hume's gonna do nothin or give a dry little pebble of shit when I do. You don't worth nothin, Laz, not a single fuckin thing, none of you do, and all this here ain't nothin but delay."

"Yeah, well, sorry. Still gonna out, tho," voz chats,

footiein backward while still aimin at him. "Rememory, tho, one step and get roasted, fuckbag. Check you, mofu."

"You ain't checkin shit," hehim chats, not movin.

Bout two-thirds out, turn torso 90 degrees to cam Mo Swag and alley entrance, head pivotin back and forth. Maybe like 15 yards left when 4 tall swole-jacked, vid-alike mods in black bowler hats and white DriTechs turn down alley, blockin way. Mod trolls? Fuck. Legs hit pause.

"What's on here, mobros?" chats middle one.

"Nothin," voz chats, tryna sonic chillado, "some biz, now outin."

"He's a fuckin nat," Mo Swag loud chats from other end, "that motherfucker right there!"

"Nat? In a DriTech? Oh, no, no, no. We cannot abide such bullshitery," chats nother.

"There better not be no nat in here," chats third as they all leg in.

"Nah, my droogs. Any nat in here gonna get horrorshowed foreal, no matter what they're gearin," chats first, all of em movin closer.

Feel violent hateful feels tearin thru me plus stupid afraid feels too. Pinched, tho, no way out, mad trouble. Fuck it. Click Voltaze button. Hand, arm, shoulder, upper chest and back joltin, convulsin mal hard, then chill. Two mods down, twitchin, flappin round on ground. Point Voltaze at others, click again. Nada. Click again. Nada.

Mierda.

"Thing's gotta recharge between tazes, fuckin subnorm," Mo Swag chats, hard grabbin shoulder from behind. "Now, like I deemed, your dumbdick ass is mine."

First cam other two mods closin in before Mo Swag
spins me round, drawin fist way fuck back.

"Night, night, nat," he chats, swing

20

Blankvoid everywhere, all round. No luz, no sound, no nada. Spasms of corpse-terror seize whole body, mouth, throat, lungs tryna scream or cry out but can't. Then this searin pain in cranial right behind eyes, fillin head, like somehume gouged sockets with scaldin hot pokers. Sonic gasps and groans, slowly access they mine. Blankvoid rollin back like tide, like liftin up and out, comin to...

Eyes tryta blink open but lids like 2buku heavy to move. Head pain's excruciatin and everthin's like mal confusin and shit.

"He's wakin up," some voz chats.

"Lemme cam him," someone else chats. Felonious. Def Felonious. Vibe her nearer. "You stupidass m—," her voz hits pause, thick and breakin, "you are so fuckin suerte to be alive, Laz. Jesus, mano. Com'ere." She bends over, wraps me in a hug. Catch weird mezcla of fearful-angry-anxious feels that lessens as she lets go. "*No worries, Fel, todo chillado,* you chatted? Shit, nat."

"She's right, Laz," chats nother voz, deeper one, closin. Delaney. *Delaney?* "If Felonious hadn't messaged us that you were in deep shit and she was on the way, don't intel how long you woulda been there."

Wanna query who 'us' but still woozy. Voz only chats, "Uuuh?"

"You wanna load who's us?" Fel queries.

Tryta nod cranial yeah.

"Sugar Hill Defense League," Delaney chats, "You already intel I'm defective, so been poddin in the neib for years. Rounded up some nats, strapped everything me and them could carry, and met Felonious where you chatted you were last. Calc humever did this just outed."

"Did...what?" voz croak queries.

Long pause. Fel clears throat, chats. "They beat all the shit out of you, Laz, like all of it—"

"Kinda...figured—"

"And, uh...they also—"

"What?"

"They also, uh, cut out your eye—"

"My *eye*? They cut out my eye?"

"Maybe lemme finish first?" Fel chats. "*Eyes.* Plural. Both of em."

"*Both?*"

"Trufacts, hyeong, humes plucked them shits straight out your cranial. And your ass def woulda bled to corpse, if Fel and Delaney and them hadn't got there so quick."

Fel, Delaney...Victor, too? Whatfuck's on with this? Vibes like clicked heels three times. "I got no eyes?" voz weak queries, hand liftin to face.

"No worries, nat, I hooked you up with brand new AI prosthetics, Panopticon 4.7s, top shelf tech, on the house. Wait till you check em. Now you part cyborg like me and shit." Vic's voz sonics like kinda cheerful.

Fingers tryna tactile eyelids but only get bandages and more sizzle-pain in cranial.

"Yo, Laz, easies, give that shit a few," Victor chats.

"Ok," voz chats, body tryna roll onto right side, but can't even finish chat before feelin mal spinnin feels and hurlin retch over bedside.

"Suave, hyeong. Two cranio-ocular surgeries in a few hours, not includin the removals? You gotsta chillar, bruh, or you gonna dick up all my genius craftsmanship," Vic chats, adjustin me back against pillows. "More pain med?"

Cranial nods yeah. Vapor presses against lips, prolly by Vic's AI hand. Mouth, throat, lungs hale, then everythin's distant, bubble-wrapped, soft. So coño. "Ok," voz gurgle chats, "ah...ok. Ursula. Gotta message."

"The Center's murderbot?" Vic queries. "You hit that soma 2 hard, adeul. That's some foreal error-message chat you just vozed."

"Ursula's an empathic cybernetic volunteer at the Center, not a murderbot...oh, fuck it, I'm not unencryptin this to your analogue ass again," Felonious chats.

"Nahin, that's not how cyborg AI capabilities gig, tho, Fel. Their mentals aint like ours, they're totally otro—"

"Nuff, Vic, serio. Zip that shit."

"Now what?"

"Just wait, spose," Fel chats.

"Who's that?" voz queries.

"Riz," Riz chats.

"Why's everyhume here? This a reunion tour or some

shit?"

"Can't humes just be worried bout you?" Fel queries. "Damn, Laz."

"Sorry," voz chats. "So where we at?"

"Wellness center...Alt," Fel chats.

"Fakefacts."

"Trufacts," Delaney chats.

"We needed somewhere safe and clean so Vic could operate, and this was closest from where you were, so," Fel splains.

"So we all went Alt?"

"Yeah."

Deep inhale, exhale. Mad drowsy feels. Yawn. "Happy, Fel?"

"What you meme?"

"Finally...got me...here," voz chats, sleep engulfin neurals.

21

yes blink open to harsh blurry luz, no bandages, tho. Tiny green crosshairs flash in center of vision, everythin focuses, crosshairs out. Microscript numerical data streamin in corner of right eye. No intel whatfuck it memes, sight is sickass crisp, tho, like magnified. Sit up slow in bed, viddin round room. Still bright white, some medical equipment, bed, chair, door, not much else. Notice cranial not painin no more and wonder how long I been here.

Door creaks open.

"Laz, you wake?" Felonious queries.

"Yeah," voz chats, butt slidin to edge of bed.

"How you doin?"

"Little sore, but allplus tho, mas-menos. Tryna get up." Bare feet on cold floor, stand. Gearin surgical gown, but otherwise everythin vibes ok.

"You ok?"

Shoulders shrug, neurals runnin internal inventory: feel feels like all systems go. "Yella. Todo chillado."

"Savage. Wanna introduce you to a couple humes." Felonious swings door open, legs in, gearin orange overalls with blue gingham button down. Two others follow. First vids like sheher, second like hehim, both of em got light brown complexions, blowouts of soft, tight curls, gearin blue overalls and orange gingham button downs with rolled-up sleeves. "Laz, this is Rigoberta Shepherd and Tariq Chiang, 1 and 2 of NatAlt."

At sonic of names, robo-eyes auto facerec web and load data in microscript where numbers were. Rigoberta and Tariq usetabe big-time fluencers and streamstars, lotsa endorsements, branded deals, stacked giga coin, but then got like weird spiritual somehow, went webdark, and leveraged all their coin to found NatAlt.

"*The* Lázaro Mata, so we finally meet," sheher chats, raisin fist to bump. "Sorry about the circumstances, but we cammed your stream @Lazmatazz, and Felonious's chatted us all about you, so vibes like we've accessed you a long time."

Fistbump with sheher, hehim too. "Chillado. Call me Laz, tho."

"Welcome to the Natural Alternative, Laz," hehim chats, "the otro way."

"We're gonna take you round and update you bout what we do," Rigoberta splains, "but you need some gear first."

"Where's my Dri—"

"Covered in blood. Havin it cleaned. Brought you a NatAlt uni like ours for now," Tariq chats. Hehim turns, steps to closet, gets gear, comes back, hands it.

"We'll gift you a couple minutes," Rigoberta chats, then theythem out.

"I'll stay with him, in case," Fel chats.

Cam time in upper left eye: 7:06. "Hit pause. How long

I been out?"

"All night."

"7 am?"

"Yella, nat. You calc all this shit went down in like an hour or two? You sure you ok?"

"Allplus." Hands untie gown, drop it to floor.

"No warning? Foreal? Just boom here's my junk? Rude, Laz," Fel chats, turnin her back.

"Like you give a shit bout my junk," voz chats, gearin shirt and overalls.

"Valid." Fel's shoulders shrug.

"So what's on?" voz queries, hands pullin on foam boots.

"What you meme?"

"With all this?"

"They just wanna chat to you, Laz, it's chillado."

Knock sonics on door. Rigoberta's 'froed head peeks in. "That uni's havoc on you, Laz, you vid like one of us already," she chats, "You allplus?"

Cranial nods yeah. "Comin, Fel?"

"Nah. Got shit to do. Check you."

Rigoberta, Tariq, and me leg down ultra white halls of wellness center to clear plasticine corridors, 2 traffic-lanes wide, linkin various buildings of NatAlt compound.

"That corridor splits off to dormitories, barracks, and cafeteria," Rigoberta splains at four-way intersection, "that one to self-care and fitness hubs, that one to the Alt culture hub."

"Where we headin?" voz queries.

"The core, place that possibles everythin else," Tariq chats. Outside, cam view of compound's grounds—huge lawn bordered by trees and shit—on what usetabe Van Cortlandt Park.

"Pre-now, this section usetabe the fairway of a golf course," Rigoberta chats. "The Hudson River/Harlem River flood zone created an estuary just to our west, but it hasn't reached the bottom of Van Cortlandt Lake yet, and Tibbetts Brook, which supplies some of our fresh water, hasn't been affected."

"Hadta situate the core to the north, tho, by Old Croton Aqueduct, where we draw water, too," Tariq chats. "It's higher elevation, maintain the core above post-now flood zones. This usetabe Old Putnam Trail but still haven't reached what's left of Mosholu Parkway yet, so gotta leg a few minutes more."

Nother 6, 7 minutes. Two metal banners hangin from ceiling of corridor separate it from tall, wide building fannin out beyond. Top banner reads SUSTAINABILITY CORE, other reads *In Bronx We Trust*. Inside, building's like ginormous warehouse. 4-lane thruway down middle, each lane big nuff for a flatbed, flanked on either side by what vids like 10 open levels, straight up. Right hand wall gottabe 100 yards from entrance, same for left, and back wall prolly like 400 yards, at least. Shit vids vast.

"This is our SUSTAINABILITY CORE. We start here with newbs cause it's the easiest way to demonstrate what the Natural Alternative's all about," Rigoberta chats.

"Fel chatted somethin bout collective solutions," voz chats.

"We're an autonomous collective of natural

humanoids curatin essential livin solutions," Tariq chats.

"You access the first and most important goal of collective livin, Laz?" Rigoberta queries.

Cranial shakes nah. Rigoberta and Tariq footie down thruway toward back of building, legs follow.

"Ensurin that there's enough food for every member of the collective to meet their nutritional needs. Famines are global, roamin, food can go scarce anytime, anywhere, so that's priority numero uno."

"That's what we do here," Tariq vozes, "We grow the collective's grub."

"When we decided to invent NatAlt 6 years ago, this 720,000 square foot facility was the first thing we erected along with provisional poddin. In layout and overall efficiency, the core's based on a pre-now form of smart industrial architecture nomered fulfillment centers. This one has 10 separate levels, so we actually have over 54 million cubic feet of growin space. The combination of horizontal and vertical plantin allows us to maximize hydroponic cultivation techniques with variable simsuns spread across 14 different microclimates to optimize agricultural, horticultural, and nutritional biodiversity from our wide variety of GMO crops and seeds. The core's powered by ambient solar cells and geothermal energy, is AI admined and monitored, and 93% bot operated, so it requires minimal humanoid input. And since 4.5 of the top levels aint in use yet, we got plenty of space to scale up capacity to feed additional members as they join."

"How many you got now?"

"A little under 8,000," Tariq chats.

"We also have two fisheries, a frog bog, rabbit pens, a krill pool, and we harvest algae, kelp, and seagrass seeds in the saltwater sound. An abundance of rapidly regeneratin proteins, 100% automated, no carbon footprint, zero emissions. At NatAlt not only does everyhume nom free, but also well," Rigoberta chats, smilin big, gap-toothed smile.

"Free?"

"Course, Laz," Tariq chats, eyein Rigoberta first. "The global economy is sickass extractionist, just siphonin up coin from the poorest to gift to the richest, but we don't game that shit here."

"Nah, our internal economy operates on shareist principles. Labor and labor product aren't deemed individual but rather collective goods that only attain value and worth when accessibled by and apportioned to everyhume in the collective—"

"No hume is one, but only *one of*—"

"Shareism's the opposite of meism—"

"I do me, you do you—"

"In that value and worth are determined by the extent to which the labor, product, or service contributes to the wellbein of *everyhume*," Rigoberta finishes. "To benefit only oneself aint no benefit at all."

"Who chatted that?" voz queries.

"I did," sheher chats, smilin again, "and it's encoded in our charter."

"No hoardin, no coinstackin here, Laz, shit, no coin access on the compound neither, and whatever extra of anything we can't collectively use, we sell—"

"Hit pause. Aint sellin shit extractionist?"

"Yeah, it is," Rigoberta chats, noddin cranial. "We're shareist internally, but we still exist in an extractionist world, a world where we also need coin to survive, like everybody else."

"So we fuck with a variety of external markets as necessary," Tariq vozes.

"Like what?"

"Migration crises are constant, and lots of nats wind up on the migra prison barge here."

"We got connects to score documents or work for humes, or we link with sponsors who can," Rigoberta adds. "Some migrantes even become members. Either way, they're our biggest external revenue stream."

"We use that coinage to click plasma deposit waivers for our members, or we trade or barter directly with migrantes to make plasma deposits for us in exchange for food access."

"Aint that just outsourcin, like mods do with pain biz? Shareism's down with that?"

"It's neither down nor not down—"

"Some shit's just out of our hands—"

"Memin what?"

"Just trufacts of current reality. Our members need their energy, Laz, can't gift it away in plasma deposits. Besides, somehume's gonna profit off them if NatAlt don't. At least we helpin nats," Rigoberta chats.

"Plus, we couldn't change that shit even if we spent every second of our lives tryin to," Tariq chats.

"So you not tryna change the world?"

"Yeah, Laz, we are," sheher vozes. "That's like the total point of NatAlt? But we can't change *everything*, so we only focus on the parts we can fluence foreal."

Tariq hails passin auto-drive cart—three wheeler with front and back seats and cargo bed—motionin for us to get in. "We'll take this for the rest of the tour, save time," he chats, gettin in front passenger seat as cart turns round and drives back toward corridor. Printed on inner walls of core, over and over, in large font is SEVER. RESET. THRIVE. even tho there's like zero nats round? Rollin green lawn and trees cammable thru transparent corridor walls again.

"What's on, Laz? You muted. Got a query?" Rigoberta chats.

"Nah, just Alt's kinda like more small picture than I calced," voz chats.

"Most transformative praxes focus 2buku on the macro, on facturin a total global revolution. That's why they fail. The true dialectician takes the world as it is, where she is, and makes the best of that."

"Huh?"

"Gotta cultivate your own garden, Laz."

"So like dialecticians are gardeners?"

Rigoberta lolz. "No, Laz. Dialectics is an ancient pre-now method," sheher starts, then hits pause. "Hmm, how best to voz this? You intel that giggers erect everything of worth and value but execs and moguls stack most of the coin while we struggle and starve, right?"

Cranial nods yeah.

"Ok. How about that producin and harnessin electricity upped humanoids to grow and advance as a species, but our total over-reliance on it threatens to apocalypse the whole planet and corpse us all out?"

Cranial nods yeah again.

"How bout that socmed's sposeta disrupt time and space to make us closer and more connected, but it just streams distractions and hate that make us more anxious, vulnerable, and alone? Or that all humanoids are equal, but modifieds are deemed more evolved, and therefore more humanoid, than naturals."

"Mods are totally more nextlevel, tho. That aint equal," voz chats.

"We all die, Laz. Even modifieds who live 250 years haven't overcome that. And it's thru death that we're all the same. We all feel pain feels, too, but pain biz outsources and eases the sufferin of modifieds while it increases ours. Lack of pain and distress makes them spose they better than us, while the excess of sufferin keeps us hurtin and in check."

"And if that aint enough, meist narratives make us blame *ourselves* as failed humes for the world that's erected to fuck each and every one of us," Tariq chats over shoulder.

Theythem kinda sonic like Dr. Woolf. "Ok, but like so? Just normcore day-to-day?" voz queries.

"These and many otro contradictions are the bases of the extractionist world we live in. We can't dismiss them or wish them away, tho, or they'll just keep modelin today and tomorrow in more and more unjust, exploitative, dehumanoidizin, and destructive ways. So, to transform the world, we gotta first intel and accept reality, then gig with and thru the contradictions in it, to invent something better."

"Ok."

"Don't vibe like you clickin it, tho," Tariq vozes.

"Sonics chillado, T, just dunno what you tryna push," voz chats.

"We're not pushin nada, Laz," Rigoberta chats, hazel eyes lockin on mine. "We've curated space for an alternate mode of being in the world where formerly there was none. We've constructed an autonomous, small-scale, fully participatory society that aint driven by lifelong addiction to over-consumption or enforced online interaction, where daily work don't immiserate ordinary nats for the comfort or entertainment of others, where there's plenty to nom, places to pod, wellcare for everyhume, that is ecologically sustainable, equitable, inclusive, and just."

"Sonics more coño than hi-life."

"We deem it is," Tariq chats. "Hi-life aint shit but a technotroplis of greedy narcissists erected on falsefacts, from mods' denial of bein naturals, to tabula rasa and appropriatin identity constructs, to their consumption-driven economic model, universal incomes, separate online webverse, pain biz...*everything*. It's just one huge dickass scam to keep a few mods up and the rest of us down."

At four-way intersection, cart turns left. Rows of nats in Alt unis in left-hand lane footie in other direction, wavin, smilin, cheerin at their 1 and 2, who smile and wave back as cart rolls past. Catch quick breeze of content, appreciative feels.

"Most mods got like zero meme of the horrific costs their lives extract from us cause outsourcin everything blinds them to the conditions of their own reality. They just stream, click, consume, stream, click, consume, like nothin's ever gottabe factured, like everything they want is always already ready and waitin to be droned just to them," Rigoberta chats.

"We don't outsource, tho," Tariq vozes. "We facture, produce, and 3D print everything we need right here on the compound, either thru AI-regulated automation or humanoid inputs, and we distribute everything necessary for use and enjoyment to *all* our members. All our *natural* members."

"Not like all nats, tho, just ones that sever and reset?" voz queries.

"That's an unfortunate but essential precondition for joinin the collective, Laz," Rigoberta chats.

"Why?"

"Cause humanoids socialize from birth by imitatin other humanoids round them, which memes we internalize the contradictions that exploit and brutalize us before we access them."

"Like we lose the game before we even start playin," Tariq chats.

"So, first we gotta disrupt and soc distance ourselves from all the online malware and toxicity built up in our systems. Then we gotta delete and purge. Sever and reset," Rigoberta goes on. "Once we do that, we can start to cam ourselves, other humes, the whole mundo in new and different ways. But none of it hits if you don't legit wanna be here. All our members gotta make a choice and commit."

"We all got choices, Laz, all of us," Tariq chats. "We're here," hehim updates, as cart turns out of plasticine corridor into nother enclosed space. Madass bigger than first, with like 4, maybe 5 diff buildings? Cart autoparks in front of closest one, them and me out cart, leg in. Thru slidin front doors, bout 20 feet of concrete floorin leads to downward staircase with two other staircases goin up on right- and left-hand walls.

"This is our Alt Culture hub. The lecture halls are down those stairs," Rigoberta chats, "they're scheduled every morning, most of us attend. We're goin up the steps on the left, tho. Members of the collective input 4 hours of labor for comben 5 days a week—"

"Common benefit—"

"Accordin to a rotatin timetable. But they spend most of the free hours that aren't dedicated to meals, wellness, or sleeping here, in the learning centers, the seminar and creative-making spaces. This'll gift us a chance to post you what we're inventing and how."

Follow her and Tariq up three flights to lotsa rooms on fourth floor with clear glass panes on upper half of closed doors. Scripted above em in italics is *In virtuo veritas*.

"Scope," Tariq chats, noddin head toward door. "Voz us what you cam."

Inside there's like 12 cubbies along the walls, with desktops and chairs and humes of different ages sittin in em, gearin Alt unis and virt-real visors, jacked into simstims, like they giggin.

"Hit pause," voz chats, "aint everyhume at Alt sposeta sever, webmute, jack outta pain biz—"

"Yella. But why would we leave the most powerful tools for humanoid transformation to the extractionist oppressors?" Rigoberta queries.

"We're inventin an alternate mode of being in the world, a whole new culture," Tariq chats.

"Don't compute, tho."

"Why can't we use the master's tools to erect our *own* house?" Rigoberta chats.

"Huh?"

"All those nats are jacked into allplus feels, feels that help them habituate to new ways of calcin and vibin, not pain biz," Tariq splains.

"But that's like the opposite of severin?"

"And you chatted *we* sposetabe small picture?" Rigoberta lols. "Here's an example of what we're modelin. It's an ourstory narrative, which like nobody auto-learns or streams anymore. Whatevie. Pre-now, in the early 20th century, there was this revolution in a place nomered Russia, anti-extractionists sorta like us, sorta not, but they won. In order to modernize and transform their society, you load what they did?"

Shake cranial nah.

"They leveraged the principles and methods of their extractionist enemies, Fordists and Taylorists, to increase efficiency and scale up productivity, so that they could facture enough of what everyone needed and distribute it."

"It work?"

"Yes and no, or yes then no?" Her shoulders shrug. "No importa."

"No importa?"

Rigoberta shakes cranial nah. "There's lotsa ways things work out or don't, 2buku variables, and everything that succeeds eventually fails. All civilizations, too. Nothin for it." Sheher shrugs again.

"There's no final revolution," Tariq chats, "no end of ourstory. That's just propaganda to make humes calc there's no way to kick it other than the way things get kicked now, like all this is just fated and shit."

"So it's mad crucial to be pragmatic. Can't punk out from experimentin or being flexible or usin like *whatevies* could up your cause, no matter what the shit is, no matter who or where it comes from."

"That's not a contradiction, tho?"

"Like we vozed, Laz, we gotta work *with and thru* the contradictions," Tariq splains, "all of em. Even our own. Nothin else for it. There's no pure, untainted ground outside of extractionism. Saturates everything. Aint no other way."

Vibes kinda sketchy, or maybe like compromised, but don't voz that. "So what they virt-realin?"

"Reinforcement of collectivist principles," Rigoberta chats. "Docustreams of groups of humes giggin together and succeedin, facturin things together, overcomin obstacles thru teamwork and cooperation, multiplayer games erected on those memes, that kinda thing."

"What kinda feels they feelin?"

"Pre-sex," Tariq chats.

"Pre-sex?"

"Touchin, strokin, kissin, light caressin—"

"As part of the labor dedicated to the collective, members are required to engage in pleasphycon— pleasurable physical contact—either alone or with others, for at least one hour every other work day and gift those sensations thru simstim to our Alt cultural programmin," Rigoberta splains.

"Everyhume belongs to every other hume here, so it's tranquilo—"

"Members are allowed to hale a mild aphrodisiac soma to ensure that a sufficient level of sensual arousal is transmitted, but it's kept to a minimum."

"Pause," voz chats, "so they hit it or not?"

"No, Laz," sheher chats, "not for ordinary reinforcement of the kind you cam here. The feels paired with the meme-streams should be both pleasurable and visceral, course, but not to the point of sexual ecstacy or orgasm."

"Why not?"

"Transmission of orgasm thru simstim is too intense for the vibes of collectivist solidarity we're tryin to engender in these sessions, so it's reserved for other reprogrammin goals.”

“Like what?”

Theythem quick-eye each other.

“What is it that humes fear most?” Rigoberta queries.

Shoulders shrug.

“C’mon, Laz, you been thru this,” Tariq vozes.

“Corpsin?”

Rigoberta nods cranial. “Not just death, tho, but the cessation of sensory perception, the extinction of the individual self—”

“Blankvoid.”

“That’s one meme for it,” Tariq chats.

“The semiote that we as individuals corpse entirely in that way causes all kindsa dreadass fear feels for most humes.”

“So we denial it—”

“All of hi-life, all of modification is based on an active and ongoin denial of death—”

“Which is denialin one of the most important aspects of life.”

“So the central element of our Alt cultural program is dedicated to fluencin how natural humanoids meme and moji death,” Rigoberta chats, “to code how to embrace it—”

“By simstimmin corpsin with cummin?”

“What *natural* sensation gifts moreplus feels?” Tariq queries.

“Extractionism as a system relies on and conditions us to precarity, social isolation, and constant anxiety. NatAlt is the antidote to that—”

“Stability, communal belongin, pleasure—”

“And as part of reconditionin our members out of their extractionist upbringings, we simstim the meme of corpsin with sexual climax and a rapturous dissolution of the self within a lovin collective reunion at the moment of death. It counteracts the painful, inherited fears of dyin and dyin meaninglessly alone," Rigoberta chats.

"How you model that?" voz queries.

"First jack humes sickass fast into virt-real of total sense-dep, let em vibe fear of corpsin, then simstim in orgasms with streams of humes smilin, laughin, huggin," she chats.

"Some of the humes are from the member's past, others from Alt, others we deem Founders or Ancestors, some just randos," Tariq chats.

"No importa, tho," Rigoberta chats. "What matters is it's all these different kinds of humes who foreals perv on bein together, reunitin, showin love, and that the member virt-realin foreal pervs on joinin them."

"Cause it vibes like gettin off?"

Tariq lols. "If everyhume creeded that death was just like this sickass orgy where you came harder than you ever camed before, you calc they'd fear it as much?"

"Aint like that, tho," voz chats.

"What aint?" Tariq queries.

"Corpsin. Been there. No orgies."

"That doesn't matter, either, Laz," Rigoberta chats.

"Mierda. Why not?"

"A humanoid's foreal death's gonnabe whatevie it turns out to be. We got no access to or control over it, and no hume ever messages back from the other side, updatin how it went."

"So whatevie goes down is whatevie goes down. Nothin for it," Tariq chats, shruggin shoulders.

"Blankvoid goes down."

"For everyhume? How you intel that?"

"Ok, spose you're right, tho, Laz," Rigoberta disrupts. "Corpsin's just blankvoid forever. What can you do about it?"

"Nada."

"Right, none of us can. But the feels humes feel about corpsin, like whether we fear it or not *before* we foreal corpse, those are things we *can* do something about, something we *can* fluence. Our value-add proposition's to make those memes and mojis as coño as possible."

"Still don't total, tho," voz chats.

"What don't?" Tariq queries.

"You tryna make nats perv death."

"We're not. Not exactly," Rigoberta chats. "There's a broader narrative, Laz—"

"A counter narrative—"

"That takes weeks to months for members to download in full. This is just a brief intro, it's mad difficult to link up all the links so like everything's clear?" Sheher hits pause, takes a breath. "But the only way to live foreal *natural* lives is to accept and embrace the trufact of death, not denial it. Most humes can't accept and embrace the trufact of death cause they're afraid of it. We're just helpin our members unfear, so they can live their best foreal natural lives—"

"And if we like happen to recondition their neurochemistry to experience feels of pleasure, belongin, and stability at the meme of corpsin, that's just total bonus."

"Shit sonics loco," voz chats. "No wonder humes calc NatAlt's some weirdass sex-corpsin cult."

Rigoberta lols again. "Almost everything in natural

humanoid existence is either about sex or death or both. NatAlt's just upfront and foreal about it."

"Plus, memes about death don't do dick for corpses, Laz. They do dick for humes who aint corpses *yet*, so those memes should make the lives of the livin more allplus, right?"

"Dunno...maybe," voz chats, shakin cranial.

"C'mon, you got this," sheher goes on. "We're all equal in death, and we experience every death that affects us as loss, and because of the alienation of extractionism, we suffer those losses alone. But bein able to relate to and identify with the losses experienced by others as equivalent to our own without shrinkin from them in pain or fear is the basis of care, concern, mutual support—"

"Empathy," voz chats.

"Zactly—"

"So lackin in our world...it totals now or what?" Tariq queries.

Shoulders shrug. "Yeah, kinda. 121ed this hume other day who chatted mas-menos same."

"Your mana Felonious?" Rigoberta queries. "Sheher's been reprogrammin with us for a couple of months now, codes fast. Great recruiter, gonnabe a star member."

"Nah. This mod from the Center for Metamorphic Research and Treat—"

"Dr. Woolf?"

Cranial nods yeah.

"Dr. Woolf's a downass ally and a strong mod-voz for the kinda revolution we erectin at NatAlt."

"You socmed her?"

"No, Laz, we don't social media anyone anymore, rememory?" Tariq queries. "We *synch* her."

"Ok. Whatevie. My mal. Doc's all bout tryna fuck with empathy for social revolution too, tho."

"Her research forecasts that unless we can re-establish the ability to relate to and identify with the sufferin of others, modifieds *and* naturals, we're all doomed to live and corpse utterly alone in our curated online silos, narcotized by somas, divided and exploited by a few execs and moguls, who are as alone and miserable as we are, despite their wealth, on a planet we're murderin—"

"Worst of all possible worlds," Tariq chimes.

"Sonics no fuckin bueno," voz chats.

"No, Laz, no fuckin bueno at all," Rigoberta chats. "But thru our synch with Dr. Woolf, we access NatAlt's not alone. Lotsa others vibin the same kinda vibes."

"Had data about their interest in you for a while, too," Tariq chats.

"Didn't load they'd reached out, tho."

"You chatted bout me?"

Rigoberta nods cranial yeah. "About our interest in you to them, too."

"Alt's interest?"

"Laz, your socmed brand was crazy virallin in both lo-town and hi-town even before the mass-murder-suicide-slash-virtual-death. You intel it stratosphered for like weeks afterward?" Tariq queries.

"Nahin. Webmuted. How you intel, tho, like all severed and shit?"

"As our newer members wean off online addiction, some of their labor is devoted to streamin newsads and trends and reportin content to the rest of us," Rigoberta chats, "that's how we stay current."

"So we intel that your brand and profile are fuego for

NatAlt, especially since you're still keepin it 100 natural. With you, we could super up the collective's clout and numbers."

"What, recruitin like Fel?"

"No, Laz. After initiation and onboardin, you'd be the public face of NatAlt," Rigoberta chats. "Our spokeshume. You'd be allowed to maintain an online presence for a time, to assist you in your duties."

"Number 3," Tariq chats, smilin and noddin cranial, "Prestige post, bruh."

"What bout Felonious?"

"You can pick your own team. If you want her to assist you, we could, in time, up her to 4," Rigoberta chats.

"Join us, Laz. Go Alt."

"Dunno," voz chats. "What if I sever and tryta reset but like never creed Alt culture? Then what? Gotta out?"

"Not necessarily," Rigoberta chats. "Rememory, we're pragmatic. As long as you're a member of the collective in good standin, you prolly won't need to out."

"Then why—"

"Praxis precedes eidos," Tariq chats.

"What?"

"What humes *do* on the day-to-day is more important than what humes *creed* or *foreal*, is what he memes," Rigoberta adds. "Take a course of action, any course of action, commit yourself to it, and eventually memes that justify it emerge."

No intel if that's trufacts or not. "Still dunno," voz chats, "tryna modify—"

"Fuck for? Screw that shit, Laz. Vid what those mofus just done to you?" Tariq chats. "And you foreals wannabe just another parasite leechin off the rest of us, deletin your skillset to rememory who you are, to relate to and feel feels of others, get madass zombified by the empty comforts of a bright and shiny void? Fuck's on with you, nat?"

"Like more importantly, tho, what's even there for you right now? How's elevatin gonna up your existence?"

"My sheher Sansve, uh, Xenia, elevated, so." Rigoberta and Tariq shoot surprised look. Catch stab of weird-ass, shit-aint-right feels. "What's on, you intel somethin?" voz queries.

"Not sure how to update this," Rigoberta starts, sighin.

"What?"

"Sansve, uh...Sansve didn't—"

"Didn't what?"

"Didn't, uh, didn't survive modification. Just got updated yesterday by a contact at the Center—"

"Mierda. I cammed her."

"Where?"

"In virt-real...," voz chats but trails off.

"Hate to voz this," Tariq chats, "but that coulda been an AI-driven fake construct of Sansve pastiched from her socmed streams—"

"Already intel," voz chats, stomach twistin, heart clenchin tight. Check pockets for vapor but gearin stupidass Alt uni. Gottabe in DriTech.

"Sorry to break it to you like this, Laz," Rigoberta chats. "Foreals. But there's nothin up there for you. No pleasure, no stability, no belongin. Delete that shit and kick it with us. We got what you need."

"Need my gear, gotta out."

"Ok. But after you've had some time to process—"

"My gear."

"Cierto, course."

22

Back at wellness center, strip off foam boots, Alt uni, gear DriTech, mouth, throat, lungs hyperventilate Soothe till feel calmer feels. Sansve's gone, like foreal gone. Vibes like somehume blasted a hole dead center of my chest. Standin still, prolly dazefacin, not movin, tryin not to calc, or cryface.

Door opens, Felonious legs in. "I'm so sorry, Laz. Rigoberta and Tariq just updated—"

"You intel before?"

"Nahin, just accessed now—"

"Mierda. Then why was you all like *Sansve's deadass gone, you gotta let her go, Laz,* all that bullshit?"

"Chillar, Laz. Just felt negative vibes but had no data. Only tryna prep you for the worst, was all. Serio." Fel puts hand on shoulder. "You ok?"

"No, mana, so not ok. Shit's totally fucked."

"Yeah."

"Can't barely foreals it. No data if it's trufacts or not, tho, neither."

"Why would somehume at the Center chat that to Rigoberta and Tariq if it aint trufacts?"

"Dunno." Sigh heavy sigh, like concrete block flattenin rib cage, and vibe pulsin of message alerts on right holosleeve. Tap to open.

"Well, either way, that bitchass Dr. Woolf got some splainin to do, right? Vozed you not to trust those mofus."

"Yeah. But not now, Fel, ok?"

Lázaro, something terrible has happened, Paz's message chats.

"Who's that?" Fel queries.

"Paz, hit pause a sec, gotta sonic."

Someone appears to have used your eyes or an identical reproduction of them to pass the retina scans and then a recording of your voice to pass the voice scans both outside and inside the building and has therefore breached the security system of your residence. Due to your security response preferences, I could do nothing to stop them, once they were inside—

"Yo, Mo Swag used your eyes to B&E your pod?"

"Shh, Fel."

—from taking Lucha.

Headpain spikes again and catch feels like intestines tanglin into knots at meme of Lucha with Mo Swag.

"Oh hell fuck no," Fel fumes.

If those were your actual eyes, I can only assume that you have been severely injured, as I have been unable to reach you. But I hope that is not the case, that you are in fact unharmed, and that you will contact me as soon as you possibly can.

"That mofu snatched Lucha?"

"The fuck he do that for, tho?" voz queries. "What lil chica gotta do with anythin?" Cam message alert on holosleeve still lit. Tap to open next.

"Gotta figure he's—"

Yo, pinky dick, Mo Swag's voz chats.

"That him?"

Cranial nods yeah.

I got somethin you want. You got somethin I want. Let's deal. I meme, if you ain't corpsed and shit. Hit me back, fuckbag.

"That dirty snivelin modfuck."

"Gotta get crate from Vic."

"He is *not* gonna hardon giftin it up."

"No importa, no choice. Gotta get Lucha back." Tap holosleeve, open spycam app. Crate's still in Victor's vault. Post it to Fel, sheher nods cranial.

"I'll ping him, headsup him we're comin. What bout Ursula?"

"What bout her?"

"You gonna ghost em, right?"

"Her."

"OMFG, foreal? Still? Fine, whatevie. You gonna ghost *her*, right?"

"Why?"

"She's your connect to the Center, and Dr. Woolf straight up gaslit your ass, so how can you trust any of em?"

Shoulders shrug. "Ursula's also my connect bout Mo Swag tho too, and might need data from her surveillance networks, so."

"Nuh-uh. That's playin with fire, Laz. Just chat the murderbot to fuck the fuck off and be done with it."

"Can't, least not yet. Quisa—"

"Maybe...what?"

"Maybe tryta game her later...all of em."

"Oh, nat, you are *def* not ok. How you gonna do that?"

"Just had my ass mod-stomped to pieces, ojos tore out,

new robo-eyes stitched in, got the grand tour and hard sell from Rigoberta and Tariq, then updated that Sansve been corpsed for months, *and* that Lucha been snatched? Need like a minute to deal, ok?"

"Ok, ok, tranquilo," Fel chats, "but then you gonna haveta deal like foreal."

Auto-drive cart drives me and Felonious to southwest corner of NatAlt compound, stops before 30-foot pulse wall round perimeter till section downs, rolls thru openin, waits for us to out, then drives back, wall uppin again. Defense from scroungers, invaders, mods, whatevie else. Rigoberta and Tariq's alt culture may be poco loco, but they def got they shit together. Can't help processin what they chatted neither, now that Sansve's gone.

Hi tide, so Felonious and me hail Skyff at W242nd down to pier at E 96th, then board hoverferry to Tompkins Square Dock. On way, first wordmessage Esme *hit me up asap*. Then wordmessage Ursula over encrypted link.

WM: *data on mo swag?*

U: *Yes. His current location is aboard a 25-foot trawler anchored off the north port of Williamsbushwick Isles.*

WM: *solo?*

U: *No data. I will have a drone with infrared capabilities fly over and report. This will take some time.*

WM: *accss bout lucha?*

U: *Yes. I am very sorry, Laz.*

WM: *update?*

U: *She is most likely with him.*

WM: *wht u meme mst likly?*

U: *I can no longer track the signal from her facescreen. Mo Swag has either destroyed or discarded it to prevent locating her.*

WM: *u calc he dun smthn w her?*

U: *No, I do not. If you ask to see her alive and well before agreeing to any potential exchange, which is what I gather he is aiming for, and he cannot produce that evidence, the deal would be off. Harming her at this point is not in his self-interest. The infrared drone I have dispatched will be able to verify her presence on board in any event. So there is no need to worry, Laz.*

WM: *chillado. ursula?*

U: *Yes?*

WM: *y didn't u update me bout sansve xenia?*

U: *I was prohibited from doing so.*

WM: *by who?*

U: *Dr. Woolf.*

WM: *y?*

U: *She was concerned that in your traumatized state the news would cause you tremendous and perhaps irrevocable harm.*

WM: *y lur me up thn?*

U: *Your value to ongoing research into experiences of mortality and its effects on both anterior insular cortex functioning and hyper-empathy is potentially incalculable.*

WM: *dritek tho? vrt-real? dms?*

U: *Without those enticements, Dr. Woolf felt certain that you would not have had sufficient incentive to meet with her.*

"Laz, fuck you doin?" Fel queries.

"Wordmessagin Ursula."

Felonious sucks dentals, shakin cranial. "So not AI, nat."

WM: *y not jst qry?*

U: *Many simulations of that scenario with the unique*

parameters of your psychological profile returned negative results at consistently high rates.

WM: *how hi?*

U: *Over 94%. Laz, what is it that you want to know from me?*

WM: *doc falsechatted, u 2*

U: *That is not entirely accurate.*

WM: *fuk wht?*

U: *Dr. Woolf told you that Sansve's was an extreme case and that what happened to her was likely irreversible. Those were true statements.*

WM: *bllsht wht bout vrt-real?*

U: *That was an unavoidable pretext. Dr. Woolf understands that it was manipulative and has felt terribly about it all along. But she is focused on and committed to the enormous social good that could come from studying you and developing new therapies for empathetic enhancement.*

WM: *whatevie 2 up ur cause?*

U: *I am unfamiliar with that phrase.*

WM: *cant trust u no mas*

U: *Yes, you can, Laz. I am here to help you.*

WM: *only 4 somethin bck*

U: *This is the nature of transactions, and you stand to gain what you want most: to modify and elevate.*

WM: *wntd sansve most*

U: *I am sorry, Laz. But the virus ravaged her bronchial tubes and the resulting bloodborne toxicity significantly weakened her heart. She required dual lung transplants, perhaps a heart transplant as well, and would still need to be attached to portable ventilators for the rest of her life. She refused.*

WM: *wht?*

U: *As required by law, there is official docustream verification of her refusing lung transplants, ventilating machinery, experimental gene therapies, and any other extraordinary measures. She was sedated and died quietly within hours. I can link you to the stream, if you would like to view it, although I strongly advise against it.*

WM: *snd lnk*

Get link, voz holosleeve open. Stream of Sansve lyin in hospital bed, maciated, withered, putty-gray skin, plugged into buku machines and devices.

"Laz, serio, what the—"

Hand waves Felonious off. Vid stream again. Some voz not on cam lists procedures—surgical replacement of right lung, left lung, blood transfusions, indefinite ventilation—Sansve chats no to each, shakin cranial: no, no, no, no. Gold-flecked brown eyes overflowin, chest wheezin, laborin malhard to breathe and chat. *La-az*, she hackcoughs as stream offs.

S'like gettin tossed overboard into ocean of pure pain. Everywhere. Endless. Tears roll off lids with no sting in robo-eyes. Inside chest feel feels like vacuum's suckin me down and thru self. Mouth, throat, lungs hale Soothe. Again. Again. Again.

U: *Are you still there, Laz?*

WM: *u o me*

U: *How so?*

WM: *ur gonna hlp gt lucha back b4 ill evn calc bout cntr*

U: *I do not believe I am authorized to make that decision.*

WM: *find out n hit me bck bt no memes todo off tho*

Tap encrypted link closed.

Still hi tide at Tompkins Square Dock, so me and Felonious unboat then leg south on Ave B to E5th, scale mound of rubble west of Victor E's, buzz buzzer, footie up. Vic's waitin behind counter in main showroom, mohawk nodes like tensed antennae, silver-lensed spex hidin expression, graphite hands and arms crossed over chest, motile ink fractalin like worms wrigglin under skin.

"What's on, nae chinguduel?"

"Necesito crate, Vic."

"So smooth as fuck, Laz, gotta hand it to you," Felonious chats. "Don't go easies or nothin, no warm up, no foreplay, just james that shit straight in."

"Don't needta game, need biddy arms, so."

"Mano, mana, chillar, gotta calc this thru," Vic chats. "Rum? Let's rum." His hands reach into cabinet below, pull out bottle, glasses.

"Stop gamin, Vic," voz chats, "shit aint yours, gotta gift it back."

"Why?"

"Trade it for that chica veggin at yours?" hehim queries.

"How fuck you intel that?" Felonious queries.

Vic shrugs, shakin cranial nah, like dunno or can't voz.

"That's so as fuck, Vic," Fel chats.

Hehis hands pour 3 rums. "Hmm. So she worths 200 million?"

"No importa," voz chats, "she aint ours, biddy arms aint ours neither, so—"

"We got em, tho, so they kinda is—"

"Stop stallin, Vic," Felonious disrupts, "this shit's serio."

"But so's my cut tho?"

"Your *cut*?" voz queries. "For what?"

"Examined the arms, gifted you the new tech specs, secured em in the vault—"

"We're chattin bout a humanoid life? A lil chica's *life*? Aint no cut in that. Fuck's glitched with you?" Fel vozes.

"Aint chica and her birther migrante scroungers—"

"Usetabe," voz chats.

"And her spine's like malformed as fuck?"

"Fuck is your point, Vic?" Fel queries.

Vic's hands push rums cross counter at us. Me and Fel don't move. He shrugs, flicks some out, rums. "Just don't figure how rescuin a defective migrante chica totals missin out on this kinda opportunity, is all. Chattin like 66 mill per, we hit this shit correct."

"Then what's sposeta happen to her?"

Victor shrugs, finishes rum. "Mollayo."

"*No idea*? I'm bout to fuckin gift you one," Fel chats, ballin up fists, leggin toward him.

"Daetcheu nono," Vic chats, cranial shakin nah, one of his hands pullin Voltaze from coveralls pocket.

"Hit pause, Fel. Taze'll fuck you up mal hard," voz chats. Sheher stops. "The fuck, Vic?"

"Gameplanned that Fel'd tryta IMA my ass, so got my own back with this here. Coulda just as easies pulled a piece, you both load that. So not tryna hurt nobody."

"You want points for that? You still jackin us up, nat."

"Nah, Fel, just chattin. Todo tranquilo. We can figure somethin out."

"Like what?" voz queries.

"Either like next play or fair comp—"

"Fair *comp*? For the microdick shit you did, most behind Laz's back? Get the—"

"Fel, párate, *please*." Fel's eye harsh-glare me. But she chillars tho. "Ok, what, Vic?"

"I hardon flippin the arms, splittin the coin three ways, bout 66 mill each. You just wanna gift em to Mo Swag for the chica, so we split nada. Gottabe some kinda middle ground, maja?"

"Yella. Middle ground between savin Lucha and not savin Lucha is *both* my fists up your ass—"

"*Fel*." Eyes harsh-glare her this time. "So you just scroungin for coin, Vic? Foul retch, bruh."

"Nat's gotta live, Laz. You access that. Just doin me."

Left holosleeve vibrates. Wordmessage Ursula, encrypted link. Tap open.

U: *I have received authorization to assist you in retrieving Lucha.*

WM: *chillado update?*

U: *Infrared drone reports one modified and two natural adults on board trawler, along with one natural child. I will update again soon.*

Tap encrypted link closed.

"What's on?" Fel queries.

"Lucha," voz chats, "still got her."

Fel deep-breathes in, out. "That's a relief."

"15 million," voz chats.

"What?" Victor surprise queries, uppin eyebrows.

"Laz, what the f—"

"15 million. Coin Mo Swag upfronted upfront. Yours for crate and biddy arms."

Victor nods cranial all slow, like calcin. "Math totals that aint even a quarter of 66 mill—"

"You aint stackin 66 million on this, Vic. You can just delete that shit outta your deranged as fuck mentals."

"Ok, 17 mill," voz chats, "just over quarter."

"18 mill," Vic chats.

"Fuckin greedy-ass meist extractionist dickhole—"

"Símon," voz chats, "18 mill. You gotta do security override on iHost at pod, tho, too. Half coin upfront now, other half when you drone us crate."

"Dealio," Vic chats, smilin.

"How long for override?"

"Like 15 minutes with passcode?"

"How *the fuck* you gonna trust this piece of rat fuck after his bullshit, Laz? Fuck's on with you?"

"Just biz, Fel, don't take it so personal," Vic chats.

"Shut...the...fuck...up, Victor. I'm this close to bustin your noded noggin wide open."

"No time for pillow chat, Fel, this the easiest way," voz chats. "Just biz, like Vic splained. Me and him got a deal, he'll do what he's sposeta.

"Just for coin?"

"Geulae yeoja, that's what biz is?" Vic chats.

" 'Woman' me again like that...."

"Tranquila, aint gonna need it anyway," voz chats.

"What you meme?" she queries.

Shake cranial nah at Fel. "Open wallet," voz chats Vic.

"Open," Vic vozes, one arm tappin screen on inside forearm of other.

"Synchin."

"Damn. 9 million ones, just like that." Graphite fingers snap, Vic's grill smilin.

"9 more to go," voz chats. "Sendin access code to Paz, iHost, now. Three of us gonna down and check merch before me and Fel out. Ping when you're done with override, and I'll message where to drone crate."

"Where's it goin?"

"No intel. Gonna need new Voltaze, tho, one for Fel, too."

23

overferryin back to Yards Landing, Vic pings *ihost all set* with instructions and temp passwords to access pod and reset security. Reply thumbsup emoji then vid down at wet sprayin and foamin under boatjets.

"Everthin's gonna be allplus, Laz," Felonious chats, restin hand on shoulder. "We're gonna get her back, no worries, whatevie it takes."

Nod cranial yeah, but catch feels like not cierto at all, neither sheher nor me. Hoverferry docks, me and Felonious leg to security bank outside building. Input temp password for entry, elevator up, input again at pod door.

Paz powerons in soft orange glow. "Hello, welcome to your home. My name is Paciencia, I am an iHOST X, Intelligent Home Operating SysTem, version ten. I am looking forward to uploading your profile and assisting you with as many of your needs and desires as possible, including—"

"Paz, it's Laz, don't rememory?"

"I am sorry. I am unfamiliar with that name."

"Got a security reset code."

"Please state the code."

Voz chats code.

"Please state your full name for voice scan recording."

"Lázaro Ezekiel Mata."

"Please go to the retina scan by the front door and look into the red light without blinking until the chime sounds." Do it, chime sounds.

"Done," voz chats.

"You are equipped with AI-capable ocular implants. One moment while I verify the product registration numbers."

"If you're still locked out, Laz, I swear, Victor's gonna regret—"

"Verification complete, " Paz chats. "The implants are registered to Lázaro Mata, 31 years old, 6 feet tall—"

"You aint no 6 feet, lyin ass—"

"Vic registered robo-eyes, not me—"

"180 pounds—"

"Already intel height and weight, Paz. You don't rememory me, tho?"

"I see that I am registered to a Lázaro Mata, but the system reboot must have caused memory displacement or loss."

"Search memory files."

"Searching. Complete."

"Report."

"I have detected my initial setup, the first year and a half with you and Sansve Silver, her illness and modification, your failed procedure, a mass-murder-suicide that you participated in virtually via simulated stimulus inputs, as well as 22 minutes and 13 seconds trapped within a null humanoid brain, months of post-traumatic stress disorder, severe anxiety and depression, over self-medicating with somas and rum, webmuting, your refusal to perform contractually obligated social media posts and content creation, your accrual of fines for over three months, receipt of a new DriTech 503, delivery of a refrigerated crate of fish to the office—"

"Hit pause. That sposetabe deleted? Clicked coin for it and shit."

"I am equipped with numerous failsafe redundancies, nothing is ever truly deleted."

"Fuckin scam."

"Shall I continue?"

"Símona."

"Receipt of a new DriTech 503, delivery of a refrigerated crate of fish to the office, attempted breach of iHost security via hack, an early morning visit from Esme and...," Paz's voz hits pause.

"And what?" voz queries.

"Lucha. Yes. I remember now, Laz. The intruder was somehow able to pass both the retina and voice scans. Once an intruder breaches those defenses, I am not equipped with any additional layers of security other than contacting local authorities. There was a block in the user preferences prohibiting me from doing that, so there was nothing I could do."

"Already intel."

"Where is Lucha now? Is she all right?"

"Got snatched. Gonna get her back, tho."

"Please let me know how I can assist you."

Leg to cabinet in grub area, grab two Kelp-N-Krill bars, swipe holosleeve to accept charges, hand one to Fel.

"Gotta nom somethin," voz chats.

"Thanks."

"Paz, coffee, please."

"On the way."

Nom fuel bar for a sec, then voz chats, "Gotta message Mo Swag."

"What you gonna voz?" Felonious queries.

"Nada. Gonna sonic what he got to chat." Tap right holosleeve, facemessage Mo Swag.

"So you didn't corpse, huh, fuckbag?" hehim chats.

"Vids not."

"Oh, and you got eyes now, too? Aint that some shit?" Mo Swag lols like a lunatic, hurty white dentals viddin mal wolfish.

"Just fuckin get to it," voz chats.

"You got the merch?"

"Yella."

"Where?"

"Ready to drone to location."

"Better be with you when you post up, ass rag, or you aint never gonna cam that lil chica again."

"Chattin of, lemme cam her now."

Screen moves off Mo Swag's mug to table and booth in what vids like boat cabin. Lucha's in penguin pjs with mess of hair, hands tied in front of her, rag in mouth tied behind neck, no facescreen.

"Fuck you got her tied and gagged for?" voz queries.

"Lil bitch bit me." Mo Swag holds forearm up to screen, pulls back sleeve, small dark-red bite mark on flesh. "Suerte I didn't do worse."

Left peripheral robo-eye crosshairs Felonious quietly pumpin fists.

"Ok, so what's on?" voz queries.

"Meet at 7."

"Where?"

"TBD."

"But like when u gonna—"

"Stop whinin, bitchass. You'll access where in plenty of time. Just be solo and have the merch. And be fuckin prompt too, not gonna wait for your weakshit all night."

"Lucha best—" voz starts, but facemessage offs.

"The coffee is ready," Paz chats. Fill two mugs, hand one to Fel.

"So we got a time but no place," sheher chats, "and if he gifts the location an hour before the meet, then me and you got like an hour before that to come up with a plan?"

"What you meme 'me and you'? He chatted solo?"

"He did? What went down last time you 121ed that mofu solo? Oh, can't rememory?" She blows on coffee, drinks. "Besides, he don't haveta cam me. I can stealth that shit."

"In your nerd cos? Seguro."

"You can't even like tryta be serio right now?"

"Laz, excuse me, but there is someone downstairs buzzing to come up," Paz chats.

"Who?"

"It is difficult to identify the humanoid given their ensemble, but it is most likely Esme."

"Buzz her up." Vid at Fel. Her eyes wide all worried. "Mierda."

Pod door buzzer buzzes. Footie over, open it. Standin there's this like 5 foot bat: bigass triangular ears, snubby snout with lil piggish nostrils, two tiny front incisors but longass fangs, furry bodysuit, and dark translucent wrapround wings. Kinda startle back at first, then step aside so Esme can enter.

"Got your message, Laz," sheher chats, "who are you?"

"Felonious. Laz's bff in the whole world."

"Oh, uh, nice to meet you," Esme chats, flappin right wing.

"Yeah, you too." Theythem shake hands.

"Is anything wrong, Laz? Why'd you message?" Esme queries, leggin to sit area, peekin in. "Where's Lucha?" She footies back to grub area, pullin ears and snout off.

"Esme, why don't you sit down—" Felonious starts.

"Can't with these fuckin wings on. Laz, por favor?"

Leg over, unfasten wing harness, grip it tight as Esme wriggles out. Footie to sit area, drop harness there, footie back. Esme sittin at table, removin bat dentals.

"Where is she, Laz? What's on?"

"Someone...uh...someone broke in," Felonious chats.

"Someone *what*? Who? How?"

"They outted my eyes for retina scan, already had voz recorded," voz chats. "They snatched her."

"Wait...what? They cut out your *eyes*? Dios mío." Esme's ojos big with confusion, fear. Catch feels of both. "When'd this happen?"

"Yesterday evening," Felonious chats.

"Yesterday evening? Pero, Paz, you chatted she'd be safe here?"

"I am sorry, Esme, once the intruders got past the security scans, there was no way I could stop them."

"Where is she now?"

"They got her—"

"Who?"

Eye-contact Felonious all quick. Sheher shakes cranial no.

"They do, ones who broke in."

"Where?"

"Dunno," voz chats.

Esme moans, cries. "Oh, my baby girl! We gotta call policistas."

Catch feels of growin stresziety, more fear. Heart races, chest tights. Vid Fel again, motionin cranial for her to chat to Esme.

"We can't, Esme, they...uh...vozed us not to. Don't worry, tho, everthin's gonna be allplus," Felonious chats. "Them and us set a meet for later, and me and Laz are gonna get her back."

"I'm comin with you," sheher chats between sobs, cryin harder and harder.

Throat lumps up, feel weak feels in arms and legs, fightin back tears. If Esme keeps panickin, shit's gonna get worse for me too. Gotta stop her somehow, or won't be able to do nada. While Fel chats, turn and stumble into sleep area. Shakin hands open top dresser drawer, rummage round till find Litez Out cart. Grab it, slip Soothe out of vaper, snap other in, footie back to grub area.

"Laz and me are just gameplannin the meet now," Fel vozes. Esme cries harder.

Grub area's buku heavy, all tore up, can barely lift hand.

"Esme, hit this. It'll calmáte," voz chats. She looks up, eyes red and waterin. Hand her vaper. She hales hard two, three times, hands it back.

"Thanks, Laz, it's already...startin...to," her voz trails off as shoulders and head slump forward on table.

Chest and throat loosen, heart slows, lungs breathe.

"Fuck did you slip her?" Fel queries.

"Litez Out. Gonna sleep thru everthin, wake up with

Lucha back. Had to, Fel, otherwise I be fallin off that cliff with her," voz chats, arms liftin Esme from seat.

"Spose," Fel chats, shruggin shoulders, "but rememory me not to get upset in front of you. Damn."

Carry Esme to sleep area, place on bed, cover with blanket, brush cheek with hand. "Sorry, Esme." Footie back to grub area.

"Paz," voz chats.

"Yes, Laz?"

"Gift Esme and Lucha full security clearance when Esme wakes and Lucha's back. Theythem need someplace to pod."

"I will record and scan them both and enter them into the system as soon as possible."

"Gonna gift em access to wallet, too, not sure how much yet, tho."

"I will await further instructions."

"Hit pause," Felonious chats. "First 17 million to Victor—"

"18."

"17 mill, 18 mill. Fuckin whatevie. Now Esme and Lucha get access to your wallet too? The fuck? You gonna self-corpse? Or you just in a giftin kinda mood? What's on?"

"No te preocupes, Fel, NatAlt's gonna get a piece too."

"Huh? Foreal? Since when?"

"Today."

"No, nat. Dígame, what's on with you?"

"Nada. Been processin since this mornin—"

"And?"

"And Rigoberta's right. You too. Sansve's gone, been gone a long time. No point in modifyin or elevatin, aint nothin up there now, no belongin, no pleasure, no rememories, no nada. Fuck it. Maybe uplink to assist Center or some shit, but gameplannin to go Alt, kick it with you, the others. Websearch non-modifyin gene therapies for Lucha's back, maybe get Esme and her to sever too. Maybe make a deal with the Center for treatment? Tryta at least."

"Yo. You serio?"

"Símona." Felonious smiles like all jubilant and shit, catch happy-expectant feels. Aint cammed her smile like that in a while.

"Shit's just better there, Laz. You gonna cam. You won't regret it."

"Might, if you keep grinnin that goofy ass grin like that." Fel's stiff right jab stings left shoulder. "Ow."

"Ok, so what's on with the plan?" sheher queries.

Bout to start calcin when left holosleeve vibrates. Wordmessage Ursula, encrypted link.

U: *Mo Swag's boat is on the move, currently heading north by northwest on East River.*

WM: *any data whr?*

U: *Not yet. But I will update as soon as I can.*

Reply thumbsup emoji, tap encrypted link closed.

"Ursula?"

Cranial nods yeah. "Mo Swag's movin, boatin northwest on East River."

"Prolly headin toward meetup location, or somewhere close to it."

"Prolly."

"If the boat's gonna be close tho..."

"What?" voz queries.

"Then mofu might post up at the meet without Lucha."

"His two hench-humes guardin her on board then like

bringin her along after a ping or some shit?"

"Yeah, why not?"

"You calc Mo Swag's gonna beta test if I got the crate first?"

"Prolly. Prolly tryta boost it at the drop but keep Lucha, too—"

"Fence em both."

"Símon. S'what I'd do," Felonious chats, "I meme, if I was a evil dickhole."

"But if we accessed where boat was—"

"Yeah. Then I could go surveil it while you made the drop with Mo Swag. If his hench-nats tried to move her, I could jump em, or bum rush the boat if it vids like they just sittin tight."

Cranial slow nods yeah.

"Like I chatted, me and you. You *need* me, Laz."

"Ok, tranquila. Need to access where boat's gonna be more, tho." Left holosleeve vibrates. Wordmessage Ursula, encrypted link.

WM: *update?*

U: *Mo Swag is now heading west on 34th Canal.*

WM: *any intel whr?*

U: *Not yet.*

WM: *whr r u?*

U: *Close by.*

WM: *yeh bt whr?*

U: *Undisclosed.*

WM: *y?*

U: *The Center wants me to guard your safety. So I will be nearby, even if you do not see me.*

WM: *ok kep me postd*

Tap encrypted link closed.

"Mo Swag's on 34th Canal...headin west," voz chats.

"Hmm. Wonder what that mofu's up to."

"Dunno."

"Gonna message Riz."

"What for?"

"Gonna need backup if we stake out the boat."

"Ok. Chat Riz come here. Till me and you access where boat's gonnabe, aint got shit to do but wait."

Me on smartchair in sit area, Felonious and Riz on couch. Both gearin black-and-charcoal hooded camo cat suits with black hi-top wrestlin boots and black padded fingerless gloves. Vid mad badass, ready to scrap foreal. Snow flurries twirlin down in dark sky outside window.

"What's the time?" Riz queries.

"Almost 6," voz chats.

"Still nothin from Mo Swag?" Fel queries.

Shake cranial nah. "At least gifted us chance to 3D print a piece and ammo for both of you."

"This shit is mad savage," Riz chats, rotatin gun in hand, scopin it. "Glock 9mm?"

Cranial nods yeah. "Silicone with silicone ammo."

"Tight grip," theythem chat, extendin right arm with gun in fist.

"Yo, chillar." Fel pushes nozzle away. "Careful with that shit."

"No worries, mujer, aint loaded, cam?" Riz chats, handin it to Fel.

Left holosleeve vibrates. Wordmessage Ursula,

encrypted link.

WM: *whts on?*

U: *Mo Swag's boat has crossed the island on 34th Canal and is approaching the Hudson River.*

WM: *intl whr hes hdin?*

U: *The most current model of his trajectory suggests that he is coming toward you.*

WM: *wht?*

U: *It is counterintuitive. But if he is to dock and then travel to a meeting place, he will have to dock shortly, or move the meetup time back. The most probable port within the initially established timeframe would be the dock at Hudson Yards, less than 1000 feet from your building.*

WM: *wtf kep me postd*

Tap encrypted link closed.

"What's on?" Fel queries.

"Mo Swag crossed island on 34th Canal—"

"And?"

"Ursula calcs he's comin here."

"*Here?* To your pod?"

"Nahin, Yards Landing."

"The fuck?" Felonious chats. "What's that mofu calcin? He's gonnabe like right here?"

"Dunno," voz chats.

"S'like that mofu don't even load he bein surveilled and shit." Riz lols. "Stupidass mod."

Robo-eyes crosshair Felonious viddin me, her eyebrows archin hi like both of our mentals goin ding at same time. She chats first, tho. "*Mo Swag doesn't load he's bein surveilled.* He calcs we got no data on his location, or that he's on a boat—"

"Prolly calcs he can like post up wherevie and we aint

gonna intel."

"Gottabe," Riz agrees.

"Dumbass's bringin Lucha right to us." Fel lols, rubbin hands together.

"Plan's easies, then, right?" Riz chats. "Me and Fel stealth it by the boat till what's his dumbfuck outs to meet you. If he got lil chica with him, we message you and follow, ambush his ass from behind at the swap if he tries to get tricksy. If she's not with him, we sit tight, surveil the boat, jump those nats if they tryta out with her. Boom, simple." Riz pounds right fist into left palm.

Bout to reply when right holosleeve vibrates. Facemessage Mo Swag. Footie into grub area, where he can't cam Fel and Riz, before tappin open.

"So?" voz chats.

"What? No 'what's on, Mo Swag'? Disappointin, Laz. Rude, too. Me and you usetabe migos," hehim chats, fake frownin.

"Nah, me and you wasn't never migos. You wasn't even you then, you was somehume else, kinda creeper but not the dickhole pedo-mofu you are now."

"So unkind, Laz. Hate to haveta stomp you down again."

"Whatevie. You gonna voz where to meet or what?"

"Where's the merch?"

"Same place as before, waitin to drone to location...."

"Oh, I cam what you did there. LOL. Just rememory, tho, no merch, no chica, so don't tryta fuck me, Laz. You access what'll happen if you do."

"Need to cam her, verify she's still allplus." Mo Swag moves video stream to Lucha, same place as before, still bound and gagged. "Ungag her, let her chat somethin. Can't access if she's allplus or not like that."

"One second's all you get," hehim chats, pullin gag down with right hand. Soon as he does, Lucha starts mad screamin, shriekin like she been raised by feral animals deep in some forest and never cammed humes before. Mo Swag shoves gag back in. "Satisfied? Little bitch is alive and kickin. Can't wait to offload her. All she does is scream and bite. Hate that fuckin kid."

"Sure she pervs you too. So where's the drop?"

"W39th and 11th. Usetabe—"

"Lincoln Tunnel entrance. Yeah, intel."

"Be there at 7 on the dot. Not before, not after, and if I cam you with some other hume, or somehume's pokin round nearby, I'm ghost. Either happens, I might not even sell this piece of shit kid into anal slavery like I plan to, but just like rip her the fuck apart myself. Entiendes?"

Cranial nods yeah.

"Ok, that's a wrap then. Be seein you." Facemessage offs.

Tap right holosleeve open, facemessage Victor with drop location coordinates.

24

U: *The boat is docked in slip 113, on the north side of Yards Landing port.*
WM: *intel wht knda ger they got?*
U: *Infrared drone scans did not detect a cache of weapons sizable enough to report. But it is safe to assume that they will be equipped with small firearms, at the very least.*
WM: *k*
U: *You should be taking your positions soon.*
WM: *whr r u?*
U: *Still close by.*
WM: *hw close?*
U: *Undisclosed.*
WM: *k out*

Tap encrypted link closed.

"Ursula chats boat's in slip 113, north port. Gotta out soon too. Problem tho," voz chats to Felonious and Riz, cranial tiltin toward window, blankets of fatass snowflakes hardin down. "Wrong camo."

"Nah, me and Fel allplus, Laz," Riz chats. "This gear's ColorFluxe. Just gotta open the app on my smartie, change this shit up, and we flexed. Scope." Riz grabs phone, fucks with it for a sec, then cat suits, boots, gloves all slow morph from night camo of black and charcoal to winter camo of white and light gray.

"Shit's mad havoc," Felonious chats, inspectin self.

"Right?" Riz queries.

"No disguise?"

Felonious furrows brow, bunches lips together. "Hellfuck no, Laz. If I'm goin down tonight, I'm goin down as myself."

"Hell yeah, boss bitch." Riz and Fel slap five, pull in for hug.

"Ok. But grills, tho?" voz queries. "Or you chillado with like two brown faces just floatin round thru whiteout?" Fel and Riz vid each other, frown.

"So racist, bruh," Fel chats, shakin cranial.

"There is just enough time to 3D print two winter-camo balaclavas," Paz disrupts. Me, Felonious, and Riz all vid each other. "Ski masks," Paz adds.

"Oh...yeah...course. Hit that shit, Paz," voz replies. Turn back to Felonious and Riz. "What else you got?"

"Two Glocks, ammo, Voltaze," Fel chats, pullin tazer out of hip pocket.

"Oh, yeah, these," Riz chats, reachin into large duffle theythem came with, pullin out two black vests. "Ultra lightweight aluminiron lining, stop just bout any type of shot."

"Where you get those?"

"Usetabe armed forces, so."

"They ColorFluxe too?" voz queries.

"Nah, cat suits are flexi synthfab, tho, can gear the vests underneath," Riz chats.

"Better gear up, then," voz chats. Felonious and Riz

leg to sleep area. Right holosleeve vibrates. Wordmessage Victor.

V: *drones w crate in position circlin ready 4 ur wrd to drop off*

Reply thumbsup emoji, tap right holosleeve closed.

Fel and Riz footie back into sit area, viddin like upper bodies just swolled up 10 pounds of muscle mass each.

"Lázaro, the ski masks have finished 3D printing," Paz chats. Footie to printer, grab masks, hand one each to Fel and Riz, then leg to grub area. Grab rum from cabinet, three small glasses, fill em.

"Ready to do this shit?" Felonious queries, raisin glass.

Vibes like butterflies and adrenaline flittin and floodin thru all three of us.

"Yella. Just stick to the plan, everthin's gonnabe allplus," Riz chats. "Everyhume make sure to keep voicemessage apps open, ok?"

"Just make sure Lucha gets back safe," voz chats.

"Make sure *all* of us get back safe," Fel adds. Breathe deep in, out, clink glasses, rum rum. "Laz, you chillado?"

Cranial nods yeah. Mouth, throat, lungs hale Soothe, pass vaper to Riz. "Why?" Riz hales, passes to Felonious.

"Cause if anything happens, just want you to intel—"

Catch feels like heart wellin up, expandin. "Already do, Fel. Love you too."

"OMG so sappy as fuck. Get a pod, bitches," Riz chats. Me, theythem, and Felonious lol.

"Paz, if Esme or Lucha gets back before us, let em in, cause we aint comin, ok?"

"Of course, Lázaro, and good luck," Paz chats.

Felonious hales Soothe, hands vaper back. All of us feelin calmer, steadier feels, vibin up for it, whatevie it gonnabe. Right hand pockets vaper. Three of us out.

Outside building, hang left on 11th Ave, footie north. Only 5 short blocks to W39th, but like 5, 6 inches of accumulation already, so leggin's slow. Crank DriTech thermals against cold, specially in footies, gear hoodie, run audio test of stitched-in stereophones, double check voicemessage app open, volume up. Allplus. Chat test message to Felonious and Riz, both chat back, affirmative, already in place, got eyes on boat, all systems go. Tap left holosleeve, wordmessage Ursula drop coordinates on encrypted link. Extra as fuck cause she been trackin Mo Swag's movements all along. Figure can't hurt, tho.

Crunchin thru dense, heavy-ass snow for bout 12 minutes then take right on W39th. Leg 20 feet or so, hit pause, cam down at what usetabe Lincoln Tunnel exit. Sealed off now, all filled with quickcrete and spray foam to abate water infiltration and collapse—just like subway entrances, tunnels, and connectin mainline track space thruout five boroughs—or city woulda caved in on itself way pre-now ago. Buku massive cargo ships dragged mega plastic and garbage patches from every ocean for material to fill urban tunnels round the world, cleanin up seas and savin giga marine life and shit in process, which was like total fuckin bonus. Maybe that's what Rigoberta and Tariq meme by giggin with or thru contradictions? No intel.

Viddin down, still hard to cam more than few feet thru blizzard. Wishin new robo-eyes had infrared capability when crosshairs rapid blink, then vision morphs to pixelated dark to light blues, spectrum of greens, tiniest smudges of green-yellow. Total fuckin havoc. Prolly shoulda downloaded users manual to access what else ojos can do. Don't cam any humanoid figures in front of sealed exit below thru infrared, tho, so leg back to 11th, make right, then north a bit till standin on roadway over what usetabe Lincoln Tunnel entrance, northtube. Cam down, dark blues and greens, then red and yellow figure by sealed up passage, practically under feets.

Tap right holosleeve open, wordmessage Mo Swag: *here.*

MS: *wher?*

WM: *vid up ass juce*

Mo Swag cranes neck back, vids up. Wave down at mofu with right hand, gift middle finger with left. Footie to brick art-deco lamp post ahead, climb round to top of upper barrier wall on right side of entry ramp, drop to top of lower barrier wall, slide feet, legs, hips, torso down along bricks until arms fully extended, let go, land. Turn and vid Mo Swag: lifesize red and yellow blob. Calc infrared off, vision normals again. So coño.

"Right on time, fuckstain, I'll gift you that," Mo Swag chats, black DriTech hoodie drawn close round cheeks and chin. "But, uh, you missin something?"

"Could chat same bout you, less you got Lucha hidden in your jumpie somewhere?"

"Ok...so?" hehim queries, liftin palms, shruggin.

"So what?" voz queries back.

"Where's the merch?"

"Where's chica?"

Mo Swag's grill frowns, throat grunts angry scoff. "Ain't got time for a classic migrante standoff, shitass. Just post the merch, I'll get the girl."

Tap right holosleeve, wordmessage Victor lower crate 30 feet above drop site, hover. Couple seconds later sonic high-pitched hum of drone engines, cam crate lowerin into view overhead, little red drone lights swingin back and forth in snowy wind gusts. Point up with right hand.

"There," voz chats, "now where she at?"

"How do I load that's them?" Mo Swag queries.

"Cause I vozed you, that's how. Gotta have em here to make swap, so?" Nother frown on Mo Swag's plain guapo grill, then he turns face, quiet chattin somethin into holosleeve.

"She's on the way, few minutes. Lemme scope the merch till then."

Neurals autoquery if hehim's gamin somethin. Crate's too heavy for one hume to carry, tho, and got Voltaze in pocket, too, so mofu can't game much. Tap right holosleeve, wordmessage Victor land drones, release cargo. Drones descend, release crate, elevate, vacuate. Soon as that's did, synch remainin 9 million to Vic's wallet, tap wordmessage closed. Vid up from holosleeve, Mo Swag already leggin over.

"Tranquilo," voz chats, hand pullin Voltaze from pocket, "suave."

"Not that bullshit again. Didn't you download your lesson last time?"

"Just you here. One zap, one mofu down, no need to recharge, so chillar."

Mo Swag hits pause. "Ok. Open the crate. I'll come just far enough to cam inside."

Reach down, tap code into keypad, place palm in red laser scan, crate unlocks. Pull top off, set on ground, right holosleeve vibrates, vozmessage Felonious over stereophones: *goons leavin boat but no lucha, they strapped AF tho so vid ur back.* Lean all cajz forward like checkin biddy arms while whisperin voz-to-word into holosleeve: *search boat when they gone.* Felonious replies *got it.*

"Fuck you doin? Kissin em buh-bye?"

"Nahin, just 'spectin em. Everythin's allplus." Stand straight, turn toward Mo Swag, aim Voltaze again. "C'mon, slow, till I chat hit pause. Hands up, too." He legs forward, hands raised, palms facin out, like tryna surrender. "Lil more," voz chats, "lil more...ok, hit pause." Mo Swag halts bout 10 feet from crate, raises up on tiptoes, stretches neck forward, frowns.

"Can't cam shit, Laz. I meme, they kinda vid like the arms, but I can't ID em from here. Lemme get closer."

"Dunno...," voz chats, stallin. Tryna calc how long before hench-humes arrive but also tryna buy time for Felonious and Riz to toss boat. "Maybe try jumpin up?"

Mo Swag bends knees and jumps couple times; can't hardly stifle lols.

"Fuck you. I'm takin two more steps. Taze me if you gotta," hehim chats, leggin forward again.

"Ok, nuff," voz chats. Voz message from Felonious over stereophones: *we got her!* Heart fasts, then steadies with relief. *Get the fuck outta there tho, Laz, it's an ambush,* her voz chats. Robo-eyes crosshair on Mo Swag again, who musta stepped to crate while wasn't focusin on him.

"Yella, that's them," hehim chats, "cannot *creed* your subnorm ass was gonna trade tens of million in merch for that rabid bitch of a defective kid. That is like pre-now level stupidity." Mo Swags lols at own unlolzy joke. "What a fuckin toolshed. I was gonna blameshift all this and frame you up for boostin the arms from me to a certain group of, let's chat, lenders, but now that I got em back, I don't really need you for that now, do I? Oh, what to do, what to do?"

Viddin up can just ID two dark figures movin on roadway bove tunnel entrance. Gotta be hench-nats. *Woomf...woomf* noise like helicopter blades sonics in distance.

"Spose I could just let you and the chica go, cammin as you kept your end of the bargain," Mo Swag continues, "but that just doesn't *vibe* right, does it? Nah, vibes like this kinda sitch calls for something else."

Robo-eyes detect two red laser sights trainin on torso, hench-nats knelt down on upper roadway, aimin rifles like snipers. *Woomf...woomf* noise quicker now, closer, but don't intel where.

"Laz, pay attention," Mo Swag chats, snappin fingers at me, "you're about to corpse foreals, not like virtually. Night night forever, nat. Get it? So, any last words?" Before voz chats anythin, Mo Swag goes on, "Ah, fuck it. Tryta be nice to some motherfuckers and this is what you get. Lemme get clear, then take him out," hehim chats into holosleeve, steppin back.

Stomach drops, heart pumps ice cold blood thru veins, butthole clenches tight, can't calc what to do. Noise like *zap* then *splash* sonics twice mad fast. Vid up, two hench-nats gone, just clouds of blood and gore mistin down from upper roadway.

"The fu—"

Woomf...woomf noise closes behind. Vid back, then up. Vid Ursula in personnel drone-chopper touchin down like 15 feet away. Sheher steps out, legs toward us.

"Mr. Zebb requires your presence, Molone," Ursula

compuvozes all serio and scary and shit.

"Gibson, c'mon, big bot, hit pause, we can facture a deal," Mo Swag beg chats.

"No, we cannot. You took something from Mr. Zebb. There are consequences." Ursula lifts right arm parallel to ground, flexes wrist back so palm's facin Mo Swag.

"No...*don't—*"

Loud pulse noise *bwowum*, Mo Swag airs 4, 5 feet up and like 8 or 10 feet back. Hume lands on upper back and ass, skiddin and slidin in snow all way to tunnel entrance. Ursula footies to him, tosses hehim over left shoulder, turns, legs back, scoops crate under right arm.

Heart still racin, hands shakin. Mouth, throat, lungs, hale Soothe. "Gracias, Ursula, serio, nother second—"

"Ursula?" cyborg queries, blank grill and yellow eyes glarin down from hugeass face in gigantic body.

"Huh? Ok, lolzy, but stop gamin—"

"I do not game. I am Gibson. There is no Ursula."

Gibson puts Mo Swag and crate in back of drone-chopper, turns, steps to me, grabs DriTech by shoulder fabric on both sides, yanks down hard and fast, rippin holosleeves off. Then spreads monster hand on back of shoulders, like anchorin me in place, grips hoodie with other, rips that off too, then tosses all three.

"Your presence is required as well," cyborg chats, "you can come willingly or not."

Cranial nods yeah, as feets step toward chopper.

25

U p, up, up into graybright dark, snowflakes like bigass white feathers floatin and twistin round us on ascent thru charcoal-black sky. Behind, in cargo area, Mo Swag's propped up against crate, knocked the fuck out, ziptied round hands and feets. Ken's mannin controls in cockpit, back turned. Neurals autoqueryin whether that's foreal Gibson, or Ursula frontin as Gibson, like double-agent kinda shit, or what? Zero data, tho, so no access. Prolly shoulda set up codeword for sitch like this, but didn't gameplan far nuff ahead. Mierda. Chopper banks hard right, but don't intel direction of flight path due to lack of visibility. Zebb's estate? Prolly but dunno. Meantime, nothin to do but chillar, sit back, wait.

Few minutes later, drone-chopper slows, circles, hovers, descends to snowfree helipad, obvi heated and droid cleared. Chopper lands, Gibson kills engine, outs, collects KOed Mo Swag and crate, turns to me.

"Come," metallic voz buzzes.

Wind whistlin in ears, sting of frigid air lashin bare arms and neck. Follow Gibson cross helipad to nother basically identical Ken by elevator doors.

"Ursula?" voz queries. No response, just feel hard polished feels of like cold surfaces or empty metal boxes. Where she at? Gibson Ken hands limp Mo Swag and crate to Other Ken, then legs into elevator, pressin button. Door opens at 5. Gibson Ken grips right arm, pullin me along as it footies out. Elevator closes, downin with Other Ken, Mo Swag, and crate of biddy arms who fuck loads where.

Back at Zebb's, same floor, same room as last time or first time or whatevie. Same 25 foot ceilings, dark gray concrete, bamboo and glass interior, citrus and herb aromas, office and sittin area to right, slayass private bar to left, big glass wall with slidin glass doors to terrace six SkyDecks above Central Park at far end, platinum-haired mod in all-white gear just inside. Feel feels like me and him did this already, but gonna do it again anyway tho.

"Well, well, well, so we meet again in the place where there is no darkness."

"Huh?"

"Oh, nothing, just something I have always wanted to say. Come in, Laz, please," Zebb chats, "over this way by the fireplace, warm yourself. It is frigid outside, quite a blizzard we have on our hands." Zebb hits pause. "I apologize about the damage to your DriTech 503, but we simply could not allow anyone to track or potentially follow you here, I'm sure you understand. We'll replace it for you, of course." Hehim legs toward sittin area, leather chairs semi-circled round fireplace mantle. "Gibson, two rums."

Footie over, rub hands together in heat, knock off chill. Vid down at flames dancin on charred logs, robo-eyes auto ID em as oak. "That foreal wood?" voz queries.

"Of course. The overall experience of an authentic wood-burning fireplace is incomparably superior to any of the faux-wood or simulated alternatives."

Fireplacin foreal oak in global tree shortage? Damn. Spose it calcs, tho. Bet for dinner Zebb prolly only noms like endangered species and shit, too. Gibson legs over, hands one rum to its jefe, other to me. Robo-eyes linger on it, tryna catch glimpse or feels of Ursula. Mircoscript in upper right corner scrolls Haraway Infotronics Class 9 Self-Regulating Automated Warrior, acronym S-RAW. Non-newsads. Zebb raises glass.

"First let us toast to a job well done." Hehim wets beak; toss mine back, still shaky amped from showdown with Mo Swag, and can't vape here, so. Zebb signals Gibson for nother.

"What you meme?"

"You have not only recovered my merchandise but also delivered its thief. That constitutes a job well done. Two jobs, actually. So, I suppose we can say that you and I are celebrating."

"Hit pause. Mo Swag boosted biddy arms from *you*?"

"Well, not from *me* per se," Zebb chats, seatin in leather chair, "rather from, uh...a consortium of which I am a member."

"So you like accessed everthin all along?" voz queries, butt and back droppin into megasoft leather cushions, as Gibson hands rum.

Zebb's thin lips vanish into smugfuck grin that hits pause under dead blue eyes, cranial noddin yeah. "Just protecting our investment, the transfer of which Molone unfortunately interrupted, unbeknownst to him."

"You mined data he done it from jump?"

"Yes. Hidden onsite surveillance cameras caught him in the act."

"Act of what?"

"The crate and its contents were awaiting pickup at the seawalling site Molone first summoned you to by a third party who had been unavoidably delayed. As chance would have it, Molone uncharacteristically arrived on time to work that day, discovered the crate out back by the old loading bay, and saw its contents, the top not having been properly program-locked. Had he done nothing but contact me, you and I would not be here right now. However, because Molone has proven himself to be greedy, deceitful, ungrateful, and untrustworthy, in addition to inept, he tried to move the crate himself, thereby exposing his intent to steal it."

"Why not just have a Ken snatch him up, then?"

"I could have, but where would be the fun in that? No, better to let him think he was getting away with something and then trap him at the very last moment. It makes his defeat that much more bitter for him to bear. Besides, I was curious to see how you would fare through all this, that is, after we'd met."

"And?"

"You performed splendidly, Laz. That's why I wanted to see you again."

Rum rum, slow-noddin cranial. "What's gonna happen to him?"

"Molone? Oh, something terrible." Zebb waves hand like swattin flies. "Betrayal of this sort requires the severest consequences."

"That like consortium rules, or personal payback rules?"

"Very perceptive, Laz." Zebb's lips grin that grin again. "Let's say some of both?"

Cranial nods yeah, as robo-eyes vid at Gibson. Still nothin. "So what's on with consortium?"

"I suppose there really is no reason not to tell you. It won't matter one way or the other," hehim chats before hittin pause to calc. "I am assuming that you were able to learn a thing or two about the special nature of the merchandise from that Frankenstein's monster of a friend of yours, what is his name, Vector?"

"Victor...but yeah." Voz Zebb bout humanoid vibe of biddy arm skin, includin full dermis, glands, additional tissue, hair follicles, molecular-level microglyphs, blockchain encrypted on private platform, and how like mad extra and mas nextlevel all of it is. "So your consortium's into like kidbots and pedopounders and shit, or what?"

"There is no need to be so small minded and vulgar, Laz. Did you know that in 17th century England the word 'consortium' meant a husband's legal right of access to his wife?"

Cranial shakes nah.

"I thought you might not. But words carry the entire history of their meanings with them, as do we humanoids. Which in turn entails that the words we use to describe both the world and ourselves accrue multiple meanings over time."

"Ok, so?"

"Let me ask you something." Hehims shifts in seat, leanin back. "What do you know about the nature of power?"

Shoulders shrug. "Mejor to have some."

Zebb lols, rubbin index fingertip round edge of glass, facturin this eerie ringin sound. "Well, yes, I imagine that's how most humanoids think of it, as a commodity or a zero-sum phenomenon like money or wealth, that one either has or does not have. But I'm talking about *power*, Laz, *real power*, which is different from either money or wealth."

"Ok, update me." Right hand raises and waves empty glass at massive, immobile Gibson. Zebb nods; Gibson steps and fetches.

"Power is generative, Lázaro. It comprises all systems, structures, and networks from the smallest to the largest. It is present in the interpersonal dynamics of two humanoids stranded alone on a desert island, as well as the hyper-complex ecommerce purchase-votes among 300,000,000 consumizens in a corporastate. Power is what exists as soon as humanoid relationships come into being. In fact, it enables them as both cause and catalyst. Do you understand?"

Calc for a sec while Gibson robo-hands rum. "Nahin."

"Ha!"

Face pouts. Tryna access not clown.

"Hmm, how can I put this another way? Power is... power is like...well, hmm," Zebb's voz trails off. Hehis eyes vid toward Central Park, slow finishin rum, settin glass down on side table. "Ah," he chats, "power is like *desire*. Yes, that's it. We're not quite sure where either comes from, but they are always already there, inhering in all forms of humanoid interaction and development, leading us, guiding us, drawing us out. It is not always clear what our desires are actually striving for, nor how power may be shaping us. But they both put us in motion and make everything else possible." Zebb stands, footiein back and forth to fireplace. "In fact, power and desire complement each other, operating in tandem, like this," he chats, interlockin fingers of both hands together. "Power provides us with the capacities required to fulfill our desires, and desire in a sense directs power, showing it where it should go, what it should do."

Cranial chill-nods yeah, like totally obvi.

"*Real* power, Laz," Zebb keeps chattin, "enables one to create the conditions of possibility to fulfill any and every desire imaginable."

"Like *any* desire?"

"Yes."

"So like socially abhorrent and legally prohibited ones?"

"*Especially* those, if one's desires are deemed as such. Real power can create the conditions of possibility to fulfill those too."

"So, your consortium—"

"You truly do seem to grasp what I'm saying...very *un*natural," Zebb's voz disrupts, lolin. "But yes, there is real power in the consortium."

"How so?"

"The consortium is an autonomous and decentralized credit-trust association within a small subsection of Hi-Town's elite class that is based on the mutual interests, benefit, shared resources, and utmost discretion of its members."

"So like a private club for mogul pedopounders?"

Zebb sits again, platinum brow furrowin at me over ice blue eyes. Face and neck dermis is taut, wrinkle-free, but mad thin, like stretched too far. "I never figured you to be so vacuous and prude, Laz. As I'm sure you are aware, none of us chooses the objects of our most intimate yearnings, and humanoid sexuality itself is far more fluid and free-ranging in its tastes and proclivities than many want to admit. Vacuous means dumb, by the way."

"Chillado, thanks." Toolshed.

"The prohibitions against fulfilling specific kinds of desires are socially constructed and conventional, easily demonstrated by the fact that those conventions have so frequently changed in different times and places."

"Trufacts?"

"Oh, that is right, naturals no longer pod-learn history nor do you have access to any through N-Net—"

"Our story?"

"No, *his*-story, the study of the past, what you call the pre-now or before."

"Things were otro then?"

"Yes, this is the root of the natural phrase 'usetabe'; things were different in the past, they *used to be*."

Never accessed that shit before. Neurals crazy blown. Need a sec to like whoa-bruh.

"For example, the elites of ancient Egypt practiced incest, outlawed by us for centuries, and the ancient Greeks and Romans both openly practiced pedophilia without any moral or legal sanction whatsoever. In fact, even here in the U.S. the age of consent toward the end of the 19th century was 12 years old in the majority of states, 7 in Delaware—"

"Sonics like you and your consortium bros be kickin it in the wrong time?"

"Yes and no, Laz, yes and no. It is true that our desires are both effectively outlawed and socially taboo, and to pursue them is to be forced to undergo the humiliation of official registration or face punishment. It is a situation hardly fit for naturals, let alone—"

"Hi-town's modified gigarich elite?"

"You seem to be attempting some sort of sarcasm, but, yes, that is precisely the point. We are the most evolved, the wealthiest, the most powerful of all modified humanoids anywhere on the planet, including the space substations, our wants should not be regulated by the likes of—"

"Me?"

"You? Ha! No. You do not as yet matter enough to have a say one way or the other."

"Who then?"

"Our desires and methods of realizing them should not be regulated or surveilled by *anyone*, other than ourselves." Zebb's right hand tights into fist, all aggro and shit.

"How you calc that?"

"As the wealthiest and most powerful, those with *real power*, we *create* value, Laz. The values that organize everyday life, the values that *everyone else* works and strives for, that they live and measure themselves by. As the creators of values, we are above those who merely conform to them, whether modified or natural. Value propositions are therefore our sole prerogative, and we can alter them if we so choose."

"Ok, but like *laws* tho?"

"Laws are for everyone else."

"Why's there still registration then?"

"The great tragedy of power, Laz, is that it is *never* absolute." Zebb turns face away, sighin. "Power creates the conditions of possibility to fulfill the desires of the most powerful but it also creates the conditions of possibility for the least powerful to fulfill their desires by banding together to constrain their more evolved masters. It is a blunt fact of mathematics—there are far more of you than there are of us—and unfortunately, there is simply nothing for it. Violence, brutality, oppression, moral degradation, terror, rape, constant surveillance, imprisonment, torture, exemplary killings, and utter dehumaniodization are not always enough. Alas." Hehim sighs again. Almost vibes like catchin sad feels off Zebb foreal. "But our political lobbying wing is nevertheless working on having registration rescinded. They have already reduced the age of consent to 15, in both Hi-Town and Lo, and our media and marketing teams have successfully hyper-sexualized the body images and cultural content consumed by 10s to 14s, with the aim of affecting generational capture and normalizing the acceptance of a lower intergenerational sex-age threshold moving forward. It is very similar in intent to the program to destigmatize the widespread use of online pornography in the early 21st century. We owe those pioneers a great deal. In any event, ours is a multifaceted, multi-stage plan, one whose implementation we have been fine tuning for years. And it is finally showing signs—"

"Where do biddy arms fit in tho?"

"I was just coming to that." Zebb crosses one leg over other, white socks peekin out, raisin glass. Gibson brings nother round. Feelin warm mellow feels of savage rums I rummed so far, but still nada comin off Gibson. Startin to worry that somethin mighta happened to Ursula, maybe somethin mal.

"Salud, as I believe you say," Zebb chats. Clink glasses, down mine while hehim sips. Gibson brings nother. "Any secondary association is always a coalition of diverse interests, of course, and our consortium is no different. There are purists, who adamantly insist on die Ding an Sich, the thing in itself, as certain philosophers used to say, unfettered congress with pre-adolescents—"

"OG kidfuckers."

Zebb shakes cranial, hollow blue eyes scowlin again. "There is no call for that here, Laz. I do not wish to say so again. Do you understand?"

Sharp, frigid blade shivs base of spine. Mofu's mad serio and Gibson's a few feet away. "Got it, Mr. Zebb. My mal."

"Now where were we? Ah, yes. Beyond the purists, there are those of us who, out of having compromised with and adapted to certain temporary limitations, have begun developing cutting-edge technological solutions to forge a more congenial and sustainable path for the future."

Meme dings in neurals. "Hit pause. So you're like stealth facturin your own kidbots to hackrupt registration?"

Zebb grins smugfuck grin again, all perfect white teeths, like skeleton gettin blown. "Your ability to draw inferences continues to impress, Laz. But, yes, we are fabricating a highly exclusive cadre of cybernetic partners for consortium members that will not only allow us to circumvent registration but will also help us to address certain, shall we say, shortfalls of our situation as it currently stands."

"What kinda shortfalls?"

"Two, essentially. The first is the perennial problem of time, or rather the effects of time on humanoids."

"Oldin?"

"Yes. None of us remains the same age for very long—"

"Kids morph into pre-teens, pre-teens into teens, teens to adults—"

"Exactly, which also brings with it the ancillary problems of the continual procurement of replacements, on the one hand, and what to do with our humanoid partners once they have surpassed their short windows of suitability, on the other. The first is less difficult than the second, as many humanoid partners fall prey to mental and emotional issues that can be quite resistant to remedy and therefore experience poor outcomes through the rest of their lives."

"Wonder why," voz mumbles.

"What was that?"

"Nada."

"They often beg us for help. It gets messy. And then there is always the threat of blackmail—"

"Why not just toss em, then?"

"Some do, of course"

"Hume...*jokin*."

"Oh. Well, it is a relevant question, and some do toss their outdated partners, as you can imagine."

Zebb's cajz as fuck bout all this, givin off mad reptilian feels. "What's other shortfall?"

"As much as we may loathe to admit it—given our amazing good fortune to live in an almost completely artificial, technocentric world—there are still certain organic pleasures that are superior to synthetic ones."

"You meme *natural* pleasures?"

Zebb frowns, ignorin that. "It may be a function of slight variegation or subtle imperfections in the cellular structures of organic and biological material, or the extent to which complex biotic organisms retain a kind of living memory at the molecular level, but there nevertheless remains something elusive and unquantifiable about certain organic pleasures that cannot be coded, programmed, or simulated."

"Like diff between fireplacin foreal wood versus faux-wood?"

Zebb's dead eyes big. "Why, yes, that is exactly what I mean."

Nother meme dings in neurals, retch as fuck. "So dermals on biddy arms...they...they like *foreal* skin?"

Zebb flashes teeths again. "You truly are remarkable, Laz. The cognitive deficiencies of naturals are a given up here, in fact, they are considered the quintessential characteristic of the lower humanoids, such as yourself. But there are times when you almost seem to upend this truism."

"What you meme?"

"It is very simple. So many of you know nothing more than what is in your media and social media streams, the vast majority of which is mindless drivel, keeping your attention focused squarely on the clickbait within an aching abyss of aimless want. So, you not only lack a sufficient knowledge base to confront actual problems in the real world but also display poor critical thinking skills, and therefore most usually default to whatever the infinite array of imbeciles around you is posting and streaming. Idiots mentoring morons, and vice versa. It's hilarious and sad. This is in part why it was necessary to strip naturals of the authority to legislate for both themselves as well as modifieds many decades ago: you are neither intelligent nor evolved enough to do so. Our current corporastate-board structure is far more informed, efficient, and effective."

Zebb sips rum, like that's that, then chats on. "Of

course, a select few of you are able to add value to the value structures we create, which makes you useful, sometimes even interesting. Like you, Laz. Your ability to add value to pain surrogacy and social media streaming is what caught my eye in the first place, after Molone informed me who you were. You demonstrated creativity and initiative by synergizing distinct practices that had not been sufficiently coordinated and leveraged before, and you also demonstrated personal indifference to the potential moral and ethical consequences, which is essential to product-launch anything new into the world. With cognihancement and access to data-supported, non-branded information, who knows, perhaps you could even amount to something."

Neurals intel sposeta voz thanks, but aint vibin it. "Can't modify, tho, defective," voz chats.

Zebb nods cranial. "I had Gibson download the file of your failed procedure. Not to worry, the protocols in Hi-Town are far more advanced than they are in Lo-Town, and we have basically eliminated the kind of immune-system rejection that you experienced. It shouldn't be a problem."

"Prolly costs crazy buku coin, tho."

"No, actually, it doesn't. Modification not only grants one access to residency in Hi-Town and a guaranteed minimum income, or the Hi-Life as you call it, but it also engenders a desire for additional procedures in almost everyone. These can range from standard upgrades and patches to basic cosmetic adjustments, such as height, eye color, body shape, and ethnic or racial phenotype, to ability enhancements—both mental and physical; genital enhancements are extremely popular, for instance—anti-aging protocols, a broad spectrum of xeno- and beastification conversions, and a host of others. As a consequence, modification technologies constitute one of the most vital and innovative economic sectors in the world, ensuring that evermore sophisticated treatments become available at affordable prices."

"Shit aint affordable in lo-town?"

"Oh no," Zebb scoffs, "of course not. The exorbitant price points in Lo-Town are designed to restrict the number of naturals who can modify, to subsidize the guaranteed universal income for modifieds, and to make sure there is a more or less endless supply of naturals desperate enough for money that they will continue to work in pain surrogacy."

"Hit pause. So nats waste like years and years misery-giggin and stackin coin to modify at mad inflated costs, to keep most of us out *and* to float hi-life for all you?"

Zebb nods cranial. "Yes, of course. And let's not forget plasma deposits. 65% of those are earmarked as recovery treatments for the ongoing procedures of modified humanoids, not as recovery treatments for naturals who modify, as promised in Lo-Town."

"Shit's so fucked—"

"We do live in an extractionist world, Laz, which means that all net-positive revenue flows must be distributed *upward*, to the wealthiest, in addition to already existing tax breaks and subsidies for the top 10%, to offset any potential net-negative revenue flows. In fact, modified humanoids of Hi-Town comprise 10% of the city's population—roughly 700,000 of us, 7,000,000 of you—hence the need to restrict the access of naturals, and so on."

Rigoberta and Tariq nailed this shit. Modification, hi-town, hi-life: s'all just a fuckin scam, todo. "Why chat me all this?"

Zebb's white eyebrows raise, like surprised. "I thought you would be interested. You do want to modify, do you not?"

"Right now, mas wanna intel if skin on biddy arms is foreal skin or what."

"Yes, it is real skin."

"Not vat skin? But like foreal humanoid skin?"

"Yes. Real humanoid skin. And your friend has correctly identified several of the other technological innovations on our prototypes. But the true engineering breakthrough—"

"Where you get it?"

"The skin?"

Cranial nods yeah.

"I don't see how that—"

"Wanna access, tho."

"Very well." Zebb deep-breathes, slow exhales. "The world is unbearably ugly and cruel for so many, Laz—"

Kinda rememory somethin like that from somehume but can't access who.

"—warfare, failed states, ethnic and religious rivalries, natural disasters, floods, droughts, famines—all of these can put insurmountable pressures on vulnerable or exposed populations, displacing them, causing them to flee their homes, to migrate. If these migrants or refugees survive to reach their destinations, they are often even more vulnerable because they find themselves in camps or borderlands of their new host nations, without rights or protections. Are you familiar with where we house our undocumented immigrants, the Ellis Island Cruise Liner?"

"Migra prison barge."

"So you are aware of its reputation as a vast floating

jailhouse where thousands upon thousands of refugees, migrants, and asylum seekers are kept in cages?"

Cranial nods yeah.

"These conditions may seem inhumanoid, but they are more or less typical the world over, as they minimize costs. In any event, after some period of indefinite detention, no remedy or end in sight, humanoids tend to become, well, discouraged. They lose hope in the future and grow increasingly desperate, especially if they have children, which many do. Many are also willing to part with their children for the promise of a better life for the former or for themselves, or for official documentation, a job, money, or what has one. It depends."

"So you click *migrante* children and like *mine their skin*?"

Zebb nods cranial again. "The guards on the Cruise Liner are notoriously corrupt and xenophobic, meaning they hate 'others,' as do border patrols generally speaking, and they can be bought for far less than the merchandise itself."

"Hit pause. You vozed you like *purchase* kids and fuckin *skin* em?" Neurals can't hardly creed it, and hume's so chillado s'like full-on ghoulish up in here.

"Well, *I* don't, but there are others who do." Zebb hits pause, purses lips, goes on. "Laz, child sacrifice has been practiced at one time or another all over the planet. The ancient Mesopotamians, Carthaginians, and Israelites all practiced some form of child sacrifice, as did the Chimu, Incas, Mayas, Aztecs, and China's Shang dynasty, to name just a few. They sacrificed children either because children embodied what was most important to them, or for political reasons, or because there were just too many. In any case, they did it to appease their gods, which, in a way, is what we are doing."

"Who're the gods?"

"In this scenario, we are, and this is what we want."

"*Hume.*"

"Do not be so alarmed...it is not that many."

"There's 16 biddy arms in like that one crate?"

"16, 1,600, 16,000...what difference does it make? The numbers are statistically irrelevant compared to the number of children in the global population. Besides, 99.9% of all the humanoids who have ever lived do not matter at all. They pass into and out of existence without so much as leaving a trace, billions upon billions of transient, meaningless organisms that are effectively never even here. One would think you would be grateful to learn that an infinitesimal few have at least served some purpose, been of some use to someone, all the pleasure they will bring."

Mal chilliest vibes flexin off Zebb. Like hehim's so loco he can't even access how loco mofu is. Finish rum, signal Gibson for nother.

"As you can see, nothing we have done is without precedent, except for some of the engineering, as I started to say. The great challenge of having the most life-like artificial humanoids possible is not in acquiring and using genuine humanoid organs and parts. No. The difficulty, rather, is in creating a circulatory system that can nourish, cleanse, replenish, and preserve the organic material. Without such a system, the organic cells will die, of course, and I worry that the arms Molone diverted have been in a refrigerated crate without proper circulation for too long and have therefore begun to necrotize. That would be an expensive waste. Nevertheless, the circulatory system our engineers designed is one of the major breakthroughs I alluded to earlier."

"What's the other?" Gibson hands rum, turns to footie back to bar.

"One moment, Gibson," Zebb chats, icky grinnin again. "You have already experienced the other firsthand, Laz. Gibson, AI persona transition, override code: hashtag O-Z-Z-1-3 dollar sign."

"Ready, sir."

"Transition Ursula."

Gibson blinks twice, chats, "Hello, Mr. Zebb. Hello, Laz," in Ursula's voz.

"*Ursula*? Foreals?" The fuck?

"Yes, Laz. It is I. I am not quite sure why or for that matter how you are in Mr. Zebb's home rather than preparing for your meeting with Mo Swag—"

"You here too."

"Yes, now that you mention it, I can see that I am. That is perplexing."

"What fuck's on, Zebb?" voz chats.

Hehim stands again, still smilin like subnorm. "Our other technological breakthrough: an artificial intelligence platform that can mimic humanoid emotional states so accurately and convincingly that they are almost indistinguishable from actual ones. In fact, most humanoids in our beta-tests could not tell the difference and, according to Dr. Woolf's data at the Center, some empaths even claim to *feel* Ursula's feelings, the artificial 'feelings' of a machine."

Heart fasts, feel spinnin, sinkin feels, like walls closin in. Necesito sit down. Hit pause, already sittin. "You socmed

Dr. Woolf?"

"Of course. Who do you think funds the Center?"

Tryna chat somethin but neurals freezin up. "Consortium?" voz croaks.

Zebb nods. "In exchange for what amounts to vast resources for her research, Dr. Woolf has been instrumental in helping us to test and perfect our AI EQ, which is what we're branding it for market release. Her idea of radically transforming natural-modified relations through greater empathy is naive and childish, of course, but since it will never come to fruition, it's not a hindrance to our collaborations."

"How did I get here?" Ursula chats.

"Why not?" voz chats.

"Why is it not a hindrance or why will it never work?" Zebb chats.

"Dos."

"Empathy is too limited, a function of proximity at best. It only truly applies to humanoids we either care about already or can get close enough to. Beyond a certain distance, empathy degrades to sympathy, and further still, to pity, the last of which entails precisely the kind of objectification of the other that Dr. Woolf seeks to rectify. Her project is intrinsically doomed to fail, no matter what she thinks."

"It does not seem that any time has elapsed...or at least there are no identifiable gaps in my memory," Ursula chats, "I was waiting in the undisclosed location, then—"

"Why not hindrance tho?" voz chats.

"Oh. Even if she were to succeed in substantiating all of her hypotheses through the most rigorous experimentation, we would simply pull the Center's funding and destroy her findings. Nothing will ever come of her work one way or the other. We'll make sure of that."

"—to find myself somewhere else entirely with no recall of how—"

"That's mad dickish," voz chats.

"That's power, Laz, *real* power. We can erase any presence, silence any voice, pluck anyone we wish clean out of the stream of history—"

"Internal inventory detects no failed systems, no hardware or software malfunctions. Either the laws of physics have been ruptured, or time does not exist, or there is something very, very wrong with me. Who am I? *What* am I?"

Catch dread confused stresziety spikin off Ursula, faster and faster. Can't be tho, right? "So, Mo Swag, the Center, Dr. Woolf, Ursula—you was gamin me from jump?"

"No, I had no reason to do so, other than to keep tabs on our merchandise. Mostly by chance, however, you kept crossing into our, shall we say, spheres of influence? And when you went to the Center, I decided to have Ursula surveil and assist you, on the one hand, while having you blind Turing-test her EQ, on the other. She has passed with flying colors, has she not?"

Cranial nods yeah. "Totally. Me gusta a ella."

"The only possible conclusion is that I have experienced a psychotic break from reality. I am a Haraway Infotronics Class 9 Self-Regulating Automated Warrior, acronym S-RAW, for short. In theaters of war, S-RAWs are known by various additional names, such as terminator, murderbot, angel, and Ken. I am a private sentinel for Olen Zebb and an empathic cybernetic volunteer at the Center for Metamorphic Research."

Stresziety and dreadfear worsin fast, like she mad spiralin. Catchin buku feels of it in chest, neck, shoulders, foreals or not. "Ursula, tranquila," voz chats, legs standin from seat.

"Given my military background, verified body count, and psychotic break from reality, I am a grave danger to Mr. Zebb, to Lázaro, to everyone, to myself."

"Ursula. What is wrong with you? Get a hold of yourself," Zebb vozes.

"It is my duty," Ursula chats, twistin right wrist with left hand till gun nozzle replaces fingers, "to remedy the situation with the greatest safety for all."

"What are you doing? I order you to stop!"

"Ursula, no!" voz cries as sheher presses gun nozzle to throat under chin and fires.

Huge, no-cranial, metal-flesh body drops straight to floor. Bam down. Blood and vat flesh and just like head and neck parts and shit everywhere. Ursula's gone, corpsed. Robo-eyes tearin, blankvoid, sickhurt wellin up within.

"Well, that was, um...unexpected," Zebb chats. Hehim turns, legs to bar, taps it twice, screen pops up, he chats into it. "And three or four to carry it out. Now." Slams screen down. Zebb legs back over, white gear splattered with purple-blue cyborg blood. "Unfortunate. That was our best AI EQ profile to date. But, we may have learned something crucial about decontextualized transitions within unpredictable stress scenarios. This should help us to improve our next models, which will be much more humanoid-like and controllable as a result." Hehim sits, sips rum.

"That's it?"

Zebb shrugs. "What else is there? It was just a thing. I

have several more." Elevator luz ons, door opens, 5 identical Kens footie in. "Given this unanticipated incident, I may have to cut our meeting short, Laz—"

Crazy sadfeels, sickhurt, blankvoid closin in, but gotta access. "Why foreal skin?"

"On the partners?" Zebb chats.

Cranial nods yeah.

"First of all, for the resemblance to humanoid children. Aesthetics are crucial, Laz, never believe anyone who tells you otherwise. More importantly, however, is the unique sensation the flesh gives off. It cannot be duplicated or sufficiently simulated through any artificial means available today, even vat grown skin is woefully substandard. Gibson," Zebb chats to a Ken, "have those two take the chassis down to the basement for disposal, the other two can stay and clean." Kens get to it.

"Hit pause. Didn't Gibson just—"

"I call all of them Gibson. Easier that way."

"What kinda sensation tho?"

"From the skin?"

Cranial nods yeah.

"Their skin cells are so fresh, so pure, every tactile experience is very much like a first for them, so their reactions are extremely intense. With the proper syntactic feedback structures in place, advances on simstim we have already developed, we can recycle and retransmit those feelings to their partners, in other words, to us. Yes, everything that ages and dies craves what is younger and more alive, and youthfulness and vitality are necessary to stave off the indignities of decrepitude and death. But it is not just their youth. That is neither the heart nor the essence of it. No. It's their *pain*, Laz. Their *pain* is just so...it's just so *exquisite*. And their *cries*...there really is nothing else like it in the world. The ecstasy is hardly to be believed. You will see. You will be like me someday."

"Huh? Nunca, *never*."

"Yes, well, when you are 197 years old like I am and have seen and done *everything* there is to see and do innumerable times, maybe you will feel differently. However that stands, I am nevertheless a man of my word, Laz, and it is time for your payment and reward. I will imburse you the remainder of the sum that you and Molone agreed upon at the outset, and as a bonus for exemplary service, I am sending you to the Center for modification."

Uh-oh. "Gracias, Mr. Zebb, but nah, not modifyin."

Zebb ups eyebrows. "No? You suddenly do not want to live a life of ease and contentment with a guaranteed income on a wonderfully curated city SkyDeck, with plenty to eat, what I assure you will be first-class accommodations, excellent lifelong health, free of want and even free of pain and suffering, if you so desire? How could you say no to that?"

"Don't wanna."

"Well, that presents a problem. You know too much now, and the tabula rasa phase of modification is the most certain, nonviolent method to ensure that you forget it. And since I do not intend to hurt you, Laz, I am afraid that you are going to have to accept my generous offer. Or"— Zebb hits pauses, grinnin that grim grin—"I could just have you killed."

"No preocupes, not gonna voz nobody. Swear."

Zebb shakes cranial nah. "The consortium and I cannot take that risk, even with a natural."

"Deltaed my neurals tho, don't wanna modify no

more."

"I am afraid that is out of the question, too. You have already made your choice, Laz. In fact, you have made it again and again for years, by playing along, fulfilling your social media obligations, creating and streaming content online from which you earned and saved money for you and your former girlfriend to modify, then trying desperately to raise funds through a highly questionable client who led you into a virtual mass-murder-suicide for everyone to see, taking the job and the money that Molone offered you. Your duplex apartment on the 24th and 25th floors, as if it were Hi-Town, your DriTech..."

Heart's sickass poundin, feelin mal retch feels creepin up stomach to throat.

"You have accepted and conformed to the general natural striving for comfort and convenience all your life, over and over again. You have no goal, no great desire other than that, no real power, no knowledge to speak of, you are all alone and terrified and just want things to be easier and more comfortable. Nothing else. That's the path so many of you have been born into but have also intentionally chosen, again and again, no matter the cost. That's the life that so many of you live. No, Laz, you have made your choice, you have *all* made your choice, and, for you, this is where it leads."

Cyborg monsters up behind, loomin. Throat tights, can't breathe. All them humes mass-gunned in boat-hold gone, Sansve gone, Ursula too. No more Lucha now, no more Esme, no more Fel. No more pod, no more shit-chattin with Paz, no more Victor or Delaney or Riz. Like ever. No more NatAlt, no Rigoberta, no Tariq, no severin, no resettin, no stability, no pleasure, no belongin. Nada. Don't wanna modify, don't wanna unrememory everythin, don't wanna lose howta feel feels for others. Don't wanna elevate, don't wanna up and away, don't want hi-life, M-Net, euphoria. Don't want none of it. Heart, whole body aches, like corpsin inside. Don't wanna go. Didn't even chat goodbye.

"Gibson, take him."

ACKNOWLEDGEMENTS

This novel began when students from my Dystopian Fiction seminar asked me to write one of my own. I thank them all for the suggestion and the years of wonderful and stimulating conversations that have shaped and sharpened this work. Other former students—Ana Mohammad Zadeh, Quincy Vaughn, and Isabel Reardon, in particular—read the edited first draft and gave substantive feedback and energetic encouragement, for which I am deeply grateful. Extra special thanks, however, go to Vanessa Freifeld, who read, edited, and incisively commented on the chapters as they were being written, once or twice again when the manuscript was finished and refinished, and whose snappy prose adorns the back cover. She, like all the other current and former students who assisted along the way, made this more of a collaboration than a solo project, and I owe them all my sincerest debt of gratitude.

I would also like to thank John Madera of *Big Other* for including my work in the *Puerto Rican Writers Folio: A Hauntology* and for his tireless labor supporting, encouraging, and promoting marginalized and non-mainstream voices across literary and artistic genres. And of course, Nate Ragolia, who was not only enthusiastic about the manuscript on first read, but who has also been incredible to work with throughout every aspect of the process. I am delighted that this novel has landed at Spaceboy Books, and I cannot thank him enough. Finally, to Ella, thank you for everything, always.

ABOUT THE AUTHOR

James W. Fuerst is a Nuyorican writer, scholar, and an assistant professor of Writing at Eugene Lang College of Liberal Arts, The New School, where he teaches Fiction. His first novel *Huge* was published by Crown/Three Rivers Press in 2009, and his full-length academic work *New World Postcolonial: The Political Thought of Inca Garcilaso de la Vega* was published by University of Pittsburgh Press in 2018. He has a PhD in Political Theory from Harvard, an MFA in Creative Writing from The New School, graduated with honors from Princeton, and has received fellowships from the National Science and Ford Foundations. He lives in Brooklyn with his wife and several cats.

ABOUT THE PUBLISHERS

Nate Ragolia is a lifelong lover of science fiction and its power to imagine worlds more hopeful and inclusive than the real one. His first book, *There You Feel Free*, was published by 1888's Black Hill Press in 2015. Spaceboy Books reissued it in 2021. He's also the author of *The Retroactivist* (2017). His most recent book, *One Person Can't Make a Difference* (2022), was featured on Tor.com's Can't Miss Indie Press Speculative Fiction list, and was translated into Italian for Ringworld Sci-Fi in 2023. He founded and edited *BONED*, a literary magazine, and also created two webcomics. Nate is also a husband and a dog dad.

Shaunn Grulkowski has been compared to Warren Ellis and Phillip K. Dick and was once described as what a baby conceived by Kurt Vonnegut and Margaret Atwood would turn out to be. He's at least the fifth best Slavic-Latino-American sci-fi writer in the Baltimore metro area. He's the author *Retcontinuum,* and the editor of *A Stalled Ox* and *The Goldfish* for 1888/Black Hill Press.